BOOKS BY AVA MARIE SALINGER

FALLEN MESSENGERS

Fractured Souls - 1

Spellbound - 2

Edge Lines - 3

Oathbreaker - 4

Harbinger - 5

Crimson Skies - 6

Wicked - Fallen Messengers Short Story Collection

THE MAGE AND HIS BRUTE

Arcane Entanglement - 1

Stolen Magic - 2

CONTEMPORARY ROMANCE WRITTEN AS A.M. SALINGER

NIGHTS

One Night - 1

The Escort - 2

Tokyo Heat - 3

Sweet Obsession - 4

Sweet Possession - 5

TWILIGHT FALLS

AVA MARIE SALINGER

COPYRIGHT

Stolen Magic
(The Mage and His Brute #2)
Copyright © 2025 by Ava Marie Salinger
All rights reserved.
Registered with the US Copyright Office.
Paperback edition
ISBN: 978-1-912834-56-3

www.AMSalinger.com
shop.adstarrling.com

Edited by The Wallflower Editing

~

NOTE TO READERS

This book is written in British English, as befits the story and its characters.

APPENDIX

Welcome to the world of *The Mage and His Brute*. To help you navigate this complex and fascinating realm, we've compiled this appendix of key terms, concepts, and institutions.

This guide is designed to enhance your reading experience, providing quick references to the rich tapestry of magical and social elements that make up our alternate London. Feel free to consult this appendix whenever you encounter an unfamiliar term or want to delve deeper into the intricacies of this world. It's our hope that this resource will enrich your journey through the streets of magical London alongside Evander and Viggo in the fascinating, arcane world of *The Mage and His Brute*.

Magic and Magic Users

1. Mage: The most powerful and versatile of magic users, able to manipulate the fundamental elements of water, wind, earth, and fire. More rarely, there are mages who can manipulate light and dark magic. The latter two are referred to as Light Mages and Dark Mages.

2. Archmage: An extremely rare and powerful mage who can wield at least four elements and perform complex, large-scale magical feats. Some Archmages can temporarily lend their magic to other mages.

3. Charm Weaver: A specialist who creates enchanted objects and imbues items with magical properties. Artisans and crafters who spend long hours weaving intricate spells into their creations, their magic is more subtle and indirect than that of mages, but can be just as powerful in its own way.

4. Enchanter: A magic user who can influence the minds and emotions of others. Enchanters are often diplomats, negotiators, or even spies, using their magic to smooth social interactions and gather information. However, their powers can also be used for manipulation and control, making them potentially dangerous.

5. Alchemist: A specialist who deals with magical potions, elixirs, and substances. Their creations can be used for medicine, magical enhancement, or even as weapons in the right circumstances.

6. Healer: A rare magic user who can perform healing magic. The strongest ones are considered on a par with mages. They can command high fees for their services, with most attending only to nobles. There are few healers among the poor social classes and none among thralls.

7. Caster: The lowest rank of magic users, specialising in simple, formulaic spells.

8. Light Mage: A rare mage who can use light-based powers and possesses the ability to foretell the future.

9. Dark Mage: A rare mage who practices forbidden dark magic.

Important Terms

10. Thrall: The lowest class in society, consisting of magicless individuals who are often treated as property.

11. Brute: A rare breed of magicless individuals with extraordinary strength and resistance to magic.

12. Blood Magic: A forbidden form of magic that manipulates life force and vitality.

13. Sanguine Subjugation: A form of Blood Magic allowing complete domination over another person.

14. Noctis Bloom: A purple powder derived from the same named flower, it is used by dark mages in their rituals and can augment their powers. The Noctis Bloom flower only blooms at midnight during a new moon.

15. Nullification Magic: A rare form of magic that enables the user to undo all but the most powerful elemental magic.

Artefacts and Devices

16. Illusion Amulet: A magical item used to alter one's appearance.

17. Disruptor Rod: An anti-magic artefact used to interfere with spell casting.

18. Anti-Magic Marbles: Artefacts that create a thick fog that obscures vision and disrupts magical targeting.

19. Blood Siphon: A device created to absorb and store the life force of magicless individuals.

20. Midnight Obsidian: A rare substance that can absorb and amplify magical energy.

Organisations and Institutions

21. Royal Institute for the Arcane: A prestigious magical academy for training gifted magic users.

22. Mage Council: The governing body for mages.

23. Arcane Division: A department of the Metropolitan Police dealing with magical crimes.

24. Arcane Forensics Division (AFD): A specialised unit within the Arcane Division for magical crime scene investigation.

25. Nightshade: An information guild run by Viggo Stonewall.

Historical Events

26. War of Subjugation 1825-1830: A historical conflict between magic users and the magicless.

Magical Techniques & Abilities

27. Shadow Imprint: A magical technique used by Archmages to reveal where a soul recently left the world.

28. Shadow Manipulation: A dark magic ability that allows the user to control and shape shadows. It can be used for concealment, creating illusions, or even as a means of transportation.

29. Shadow Creatures: Monstrous entities created from pure darkness through potent dark magic. These beings can interact with the physical world and are

often used to attack enemies. Only the most powerful dark mages can create and control shadow creatures.

CHAPTER 1

Pale fingers teased the back of Evander Ravenwood's eyelids and warmed his skin. He stirred and blinked slowly, sleep gradually relinquishing its hold over his body.

Sunlight filtered through a gap in the heavy velvet curtains of his bedroom, the dust motes dancing in the golden stream sparkling as they moved languorously in the morning air.

For a moment, he simply lay there and listened to the sounds of Mayfair coming to life in the distance while he savoured the pleasant weight of the muscular arm draped possessively across his waist and the solid body pressed against his back beneath the plush goose-down comforter.

Having had his fill of this rare moment of peace, Evander turned carefully to face his bedmate.

Viggo Stonewall slumbered beside him, his dark lashes fanned against his cheeks and his handsome face relaxed in sleep. The usually daunting countenance that inspired respect and dread in all those who met the Brute for the first time had softened into something almost boyish as he lay defenceless in Evander's bed.

The sight made Evander's pulse flutter in a way that still surprised him, even after two weeks of waking up beside the man who had laid claim to his heart.

He reached out, unable to resist grazing the line of Viggo's jaw with his fingertips. He danced his hand down his lover's throat to his chest, tracing the dark ink of the tattoos marking his sun-kissed skin in captivating patterns.

Evander's chest grew heavy at the sight of the puckered scar beneath Viggo's left collar bone. The letter A could be made out amidst the wrinkles. He brushed it gently, his heart clenching as he recalled the horrific circumstances under which the Brute had earned the wound.

Viggo's eyes opened at the touch, dark and immediately alert. His features eased as he focused on Evander. A slow smile spread across his face.

"Good morning, your Grace," he rumbled, his voice rough with sleep.

His gravelly tone made Evander's manhood twitch.

"I've told you not to call me that in bed," he admonished without real reproach.

"And I've told you I enjoy the way you squirm when I do." Viggo's smile turned wicked as he tightened his arm around Evander's waist, drawing him closer for a kiss. "Besides, old habits are not so easily broken."

"Two weeks is hardly enough time to form a habit," Evander murmured before surrendering to his lover's lips.

What began as a gentle press of mouths quickly deepened, Viggo's hand sliding up to cradle the back of Evander's head as he rolled them over, pinning the mage beneath him. Evander sighed into the kiss, the sensuous movements of Viggo's tongue against his momentarily banishing all thoughts of the day ahead.

Though his body was a little sore still from last night's passionate lovemaking, it responded eagerly to Viggo's touch as he worked a hand down his chest to his hip, the evidence of the Brute's arousal where it dug insistently into his stomach making his own cock swell with a delicious hunger that would only be quenched by his lover's ardent possession.

A sharp knock at the door shattered the intimate moment.

"My Lord?" Jasper Hargrove called from the corridor. "I've brought your morning tea and paper, and the day's correspondence."

Viggo groaned and dropped his forehead to rest against Evander's. "Your manservant possesses an uncanny talent for interruption."

"A skill he has cultivated with remarkable dedication," Evander contributed drily. He raised his voice to address the door. "One moment, please."

Viggo shifted away, allowing Evander to slip naked from the bed. The mage was conscious of his lover's burning stare as he donned his dressing gown and secured the sash before crossing to the door.

He opened it just enough to reveal his face, blocking Hargrove's view of the rumpled bed and its occupant.

"Good morning, my Lord," Hargrove greeted, his demeanour proper save for a knowing glint in his eyes that spoke silent volumes. "Would your Lordship prefer I return with your breakfast tray at a more convenient hour?"

Heat crept up Evander's neck. His manservant knew damn well who was in the room with him.

"You may bring it in now, thank you," he said primly.

He stepped aside, allowing Hargrove to enter with the silver tray. The manservant moved with practiced efficiency as he set it on the small rosewood table by the window before crossing the floor to draw back the curtains. Sunlight flooded the bedroom, illuminating Viggo where he sat propped against the headboard, the sheets pooled around his waist and his impressive bare chest.

"Good morning, Mr. Stonewall," Hargrove intoned, as if finding a half-naked Brute in his master's bed was the most ordinary occurrence in the world. "Will you be partaking of breakfast with his Lordship this morning?"

Evander narrowed his eyes a little at the manservant's saccharine smile.

"I believe I shall," Viggo drawled, amused. "Your master was particularly vigorous last night. I am practically faint from hunger."

Heat warmed Evander's cheeks at his lover's blunt

admission. Viggo wasn't exactly wrong. He'd initiated their lovemaking the previous evening and had worked the Brute to his very limits.

Judging from Viggo's heated gaze, food wasn't the only thing he was hungry for.

"Very good, sir," Hargrove said brightly. "I shall add an additional table setting."

Viggo and Hargrove exchanged a smile.

"You two are getting along mighty well," Evander noted sharply.

"I'm not sure what you mean, my Lord." Hargrove's expression turned suspiciously innocent. "As someone in charge of your physical well-being, may I express how pleased I am that you no longer have a need for your...*toy*."

Evander drew a horrified breath at this blatant betrayal of trust.

"What toy?" Viggo's gaze swung from Evander's accusing glare to Hargrove's unrepentant grin.

The manservant glanced pointedly at the bedside table.

Viggo frowned and leaned over to open the drawer.

A violent burst of wind slammed it closed, startling the Brute.

"Silence is an underestimated virtue, Jasper," Evander fairly growled as he retracted his magic. "I'm sorry, Viggo," he added briskly, not quite meeting his lover's eyes. "There are certain matters I would prefer to keep private."

Suspicion wrinkled Viggo's brow at his evasive

behaviour. He studied the drawer as if he intended to make it his mission to find out what was inside.

Hargrove rocked back on his heels, eyes fairly twinkling.

Evander had little inclination to reveal to his lover that he'd once procured an enchanted device from the exclusive sex club he occasionally attended in Bloomsbury so as to satisfy his libido on those lonely nights when his needs could not be satisfied with his hands. He had no doubt he would forever be teased for it if he did.

"Incidentally, Mrs. Sinclair would like to know if Mr. Stonewall will be present for luncheon," Hargrove continued, as if he hadn't just thrown the cat among the pigeons. "She is finalising the menus for the week."

Evander and Viggo traded a glance, the question highlighting the still-uncertain nature of their arrangement. They had fallen into a pattern of sorts since they became lovers, Viggo spending several nights a week at the Mayfair townhouse. But neither had broached the subject of more permanent plans.

It was a topic Evander was aware they were both carefully avoiding while they navigated a burgeoning relationship neither of them could have anticipated a few weeks ago.

"I'm afraid I have matters to attend to at Nightshade this afternoon," Viggo said lightly, sparing Evander from having to answer. "Please convey my regrets to Mrs. Sinclair."

"As you wish, sir." Hargrove dipped his head graciously. He turned his attention back to Evander, his face growing serious. "There is a message from Scotland Yard among your correspondence, my Lord. The constable who relayed it pressed upon me the urgency of the matter."

Evander's brow furrowed as he lifted the sealed envelope from the tray. The familiar insignia of the Arcane Division was stamped in the wax.

"Thank you, Jasper. That will be all for now."

The manservant bowed and departed, closing the door behind him with a soft click.

Evander sat on the edge of the bed and broke the seal.

"Trouble?" Viggo inquired. He looped his arms around Evander's waist from behind and kissed the side of his neck.

Evander unfolded the message and scanned the contents. "Potentially. Commander Winterbourne wants to meet urgently." He frowned. "Something must have happened."

Viggo's fingers flexed involuntarily on his belly. "Isn't today your first rest day in over a week?"

"It is," Evander admitted guilty.

Unease swirled through him as he studied Winterbourne's missive.

It was rare for his commander to demand his presence so pressingly, especially on his long overdue day off. As one of the most formidable magical duelists in the history of the Metropolitan Police, Reginald Winterbourne was not a man who could be easily rattled.

Viggo let go of him, swung his legs over the other

side of the bed, and reached for his trousers where Evander had discarded them on the floor the night before.

"Surely you're not the only Arcane Investigator Winterbourne can call upon for grave matters?" the Brute grumbled as he slipped into the garment.

CHAPTER 2

He was conscious Viggo didn't approve of the long hours he put in at the Met. Which was ironic considering the Brute invested as much time and energy in his work as the head of *Nightshade*.

"Apparently not," Evander murmured. He set the message aside and poured them both tea from the silver pot. The fragrant steam curled upward, carrying the relaxing scent of Darjeeling.

The mage was well aware he was overdue this rest day.

Alas, the fallout from the ghastly affair with Caine Renwick, the dark mage who had threatened to blow up the southern embankment and kill thousands of thralls a few weeks ago, was still ongoing.

Following Evander's reports to the Ministry of Arcane Affairs and the War Office, the corridors of power were alive with whispers of a conspiracy that could threaten the very order of not just London society, but the British Empire at large. Whispers that had reached Parliament and were stirring just as much havoc in the House of Lords and the House of Commons.

The growing tensions in the city between magic users and thralls had only served to make matters worse.

Both Evander and Rufus Grayson, his friend and fellow inspector in the Met, had been asked to provide more detailed accounts of their investigation into what had gone on during the week that had begun with the murder of Alastair Millbrook, the Charm Weaver Renwick had tasked to build a device that could steal the life force of thralls so as to augment the magic powers of mages, and ended with an explosion that had brought down the warehouse where Evander and Viggo had confronted Renwick.

Viggo frowned as he came around the bed and accepted the cup Evander handed him. He plopped down beside him, the mattress sinking under his weight.

"Do you think it might have something to do with the letter you received and that '*T*' character?"

Evander's fingers tightened on his drink as he recalled the chilling contents of the missive that had been delivered to his Mayfair townhouse following Renwick's death.

"Maybe."

The sender had made it clear that the dead mage had been but a pawn in a much larger scheme. The letter was currently locked inside Evander's desk, in the small office adjoining his bedchamber.

"Things have been far too quiet these past few weeks," he observed in a troubled voice.

Viggo kissed his head. "Quiet is a good thing sometimes."

Evander leaned against his lover, grateful for his warmth and his strength. "It is most quiet before the storm."

A chuckle vibrated through Viggo, the sound low and rich.

"My, you are feeling very poetic this morning, your Grace."

Evander rolled his eyes at his teasing tone.

They finished their tea and freshened up in the bathroom before getting ready for the day ahead.

Evander watched as Viggo began to dress, admiring the play of muscles beneath his tattooed skin. Despite the sliver of anxiety still singing through his veins at Winterbourne's curt message, he found himself reluctant to leave the warm intimacy of their shared morning.

Viggo's gaze captured his in the mirror. His fingers slowed where he was buttoning his shirt.

"I fear we may never make it downstairs if you keep looking at me like that." A sultry smile tugged at the Brute's lips.

Evander flushed and busied himself selecting his uniform for the day, a dark blue wool coat with the silver-and-gold aiguillette that marked him as a Special Arcane Investigator.

He had yet to reveal to Viggo the significance of the blue threads weaved within it.

They enjoyed a pleasant breakfast in the dayroom before parting ways at the servants' entrance. Though Evander had insisted Viggo enter and leave his home through the front door, the Brute wished to maintain discretion for the time being, not just because of the delicate circumstances of their affair but because their enemies were still out there.

"Are we still meeting for dinner at Ginny's this evening?" Viggo asked as Hargrove handed him his coat.

"Yes," Evander murmured. "She was quite insistent."

Viggo grinned at his irritated expression. "You don't seem terribly pleased about the matter."

"She probably wants details of our torrid love affair," Evander said tartly.

"Graphic details, no doubt," Hargrove added in a devilish tone under his breath.

Evander cut his eyes to the deadpan manservant. He was distracted by Viggo leaning in towards him.

"It's a valuable talent for an informant," the Brute observed drily. "See you tonight, your Grace." His eyes twinkled as he pressed a kiss to Evander's mouth that made a passing scullery maid squeak. He turned and vanished out the door.

Evander flushed and traced his lips with his fingers, the Brute's gesture of affection making desire stir inside him all over again. He became aware of Hargrove's grin and heaved a heavy sigh.

"Jasper?"

"Yes, yes, I shall wipe my indecent smile off my face before you punch me, my Lord," Hargrove declared in a voice devoid of remorse.

It was nine o'clock on the dot when Evander's carriage deposited him outside the gates of Scotland Yard.

"I shall send a message when I have need of you," he told his coachman.

Graham nodded courteously.

Samuel beamed and bobbed his head with a shy, "Have a great day, your Grace!"

Evander bit back a dry smile. The young footman seemed absolutely delighted that his hero Viggo was romantically involved with his master. He watched the pair leave before turning to study the Metropolitan Police Headquarters.

It rose dauntingly before him, a rambling gothic fortress with a stone facade blackened by decades of London's coal smoke. He greeted the sergeant and constables manning the gates and crossed over into the main yard, the protective wards embedded into the perimeter wall brushing against his skin.

Evander's thoughts drifted once more to the events of the past month as he made for the worn steps leading to the ironclad doors of the main entrance, the voice of the drill sergeant training the new recruits in the grounds echoing against the walls around him.

The investigation into Alastair Millbrook's murder had led him and Viggo down a perilous path, none worse than the nearly disastrous outcome of their battle with Renwick in Charing Cross. His magic and

Viggo's brute strength had saved many a life that day, after Renwick and a group of mages attacked the station and attempted to send a magic-driven train crashing into a platform packed with stricken passengers. Evander still shuddered at the thought of what might have been had his lover not been at his side during that dangerous incident.

Though they had prevailed, the identity of the mysterious "I" remained elusive, as did the location of the *Blood Siphon*, the device Alastair Millbrook had made for Renwick and his master. Those two facts lurked insidiously at the edges of Evander's consciousness, setting his nerves on edge whenever he gave them a moment's thought.

The letter that had arrived after Renwick's death had made it clear their adversary was far from finished with this horrid affair.

Evander pushed his dark musings firmly aside when he entered the building. The morning bustle of Scotland Yard enveloped him in its familiar embrace as he navigated the marble floor of the impressive lobby. Constables and secretarial staff rushed about with files clutched to their chests, the scent of strong tea mingling with ink and magic as it rose through the administrative block of the Met.

The mage was acutely aware of the stares that followed his passage as he answered colleagues' greetings and made his way to the west wing of the fortress. Several officers nudged one another, their gazes locked on him with barely concealed curiosity.

Though the scandal that had accompanied

Evander's recently revealed status had all but died down, it was still the talk of the town in some circles, chief among them the taverns where coppers hung out.

It seemed the novelty of having an Archmage in their midst hadn't worn off yet.

As uncomfortable as it made him some days, he'd resigned himself to the fact that it would take time for the people around him to realise he was the same person they had known before his true identity was revealed.

Three salutes and five more "your Grace" greetings later, Evander finally reached Commander Winterbourne's office in the administrative quarters of the Arcane Division. He crossed the open area crowded with desks at which men and women already sat hunched over their paperwork and paused before the heavy oak doors.

Muffled voices came from within. Evander glanced at Winterbourne's secretary.

"Please go in, your Grace," the man said with a dip of his chin. "The commander is expecting you."

Evander knocked, announced himself, and entered.

"Ah, Ravenwood. Just the man." Winterbourne sat behind his desk, his uniform immaculate and the enchanted map on the wall behind him glowing with orange markers that indicated active crime scenes across the capital.

Rufus occupied one of the chairs in front of the commander, his expression uncharacteristically grave. A bolt of sympathy darted through Evander at the sight of the shadows beneath his friend's eyes.

The inspector looked as worn out as he felt these days.

"You wished to see me, sir?" Evander asked, closing the door behind him.

Winterbourne gestured to the empty chair beside Rufus. "Yes. I'm afraid I have worrying news. Professor Walter Whitley from the Royal Institute for the Arcane has disappeared."

The name sparked immediate recognition. Evander raised an eyebrow as he took the seat the commander indicated.

"The advanced Elemental Magic specialist?"

"The same," Winterbourne said.

Rufus took over the conversation while Evander digested this startling revelation. "His wife reported he went missing two nights ago. Apparently, he failed to attend a faculty dinner and never returned home."

Evander frowned as Winterbourne slid a file across his desk. "Why did she wait so long to report him missing?"

"Because Whitley has a habit of staying over at the Institute when he's out late," the commander grunted. "He's also renowned for shutting himself in his laboratory for days on end when he's engrossed in his research."

"Lady Whitley said her husband had been looking forward to attending the faculty dinner," Rufus continued. "She was expecting him home last night at least. When he didn't turn up, she went knocking on the doors of the Institute at first light this morning."

Evander raised an eyebrow. "And you presume foul play because…?"

Rufus's expression grew hooded. "According to Lady Whitley, they refused her access to her husband's rooms."

"We dispatched a forensic mage to examine the premises. She just sent in a preliminary report indicating Whitley's chambers showed probable signs of magical disturbance," Winterbourne said.

Tension oozed through Evander. It was clear to him now why Winterbourne had requested his presence. This was not a straightforward missing person case.

He glanced at Rufus as he took hold of the file. "Is Shaw the one at the scene?"

Rufus nodded.

Lyra Shaw was a forensic mage working for the Arcane Forensics Division and one of the best investigative minds to ever grace the halls of Scotland Yard. Everyone had high hopes for her, including Evander and Winterbourne.

Shaw was on track to become the AFD and Scotland Yard's first female inspector, a status they hoped would attract more women to the profession.

Evander opened the file and scanned the forensic mage's preliminary survey of the suspected scene of the crime. He narrowed his eyes. "She found a trace of *Noctis Bloom* on the premises?"

"So it seems," Rufus murmured. "Mr. Brown will have to confirm the nature of the evidence she discovered, but it is likely the residue is indeed *Noctis Bloom*."

CHAPTER 3

VINCENT BROWN WAS THE HEAD ALCHEMIST ANALYST AT the AFD and had been of great help to them during the investigation of Millbrook's murder. As for *Noctis Bloom*, it was a rare purple flower that only bloomed at midnight on a full moon. Drying and finely grinding its petals produced a powder that could be used in magic rituals.

More notably, dark mages were said to ingest it in some capacity or another to enhance their powers.

"I want you to lead the investigation, Ravenwood," Winterbourne declared. "Your connections to the Institute will prove invaluable. According to Whitley's wife, the faculty has proven challenging to deal with lately. They even tried to obstruct her when she attended the premises this morning. They may be more forthcoming with one of their own, especially someone of your"—he waved a vague hand—"*particular* status."

Rufus's mouth pressed to a thin line. Winterbourne

ignored the inspector's brooding look and studied Evander expectantly.

Though he didn't like it one bit, Evander understood the commander's implication. The recent revelation that he was an Archmage had sent ripples not just through London's high society and the government, but across the Empire's magical community. While many magic users regarded him with newfound awe, others—particularly within the Institute's conservative hierarchy—no doubt viewed his choice to serve in the Metropolitan Police with barely concealed disdain.

"I'll do what I can," Evander said reluctantly. "Though I must admit, my relationship with the headmaster has been somewhat strained since I declined his offer of a teaching position in favour of joining the Met."

Winterbourne waved this away too. "All the more reason. They wouldn't dare hinder an Archmage, regardless of their personal feelings on the subject of you being an officer of the law. And your familiarity with their protocols will prove invaluable. Miss Shaw will continue to assist in this investigation." He cut his eyes to Rufus. "As for Inspector Grayson, he too will work with you on this case. I already have the approval of the head of the Homicide Unit."

Rufus's expression told Evander he had been informed of this decision.

"This is not a homicide case." Evander observed to his commander steadily. "Unless there's something you're not telling us, sir."

Winterbourne's eyes grew hooded. "Let's just say certain people in the Ministry of Arcane Affairs recommended we provide you with all the necessary support," he admitted cagily. He hesitated a beat. "I've authorised full Arcane Division resources for this case."

Evander heard Rufus's sharp inhale. He kept his gaze on the commander, his shoulders knotting at the enormity of the assets that were being put at his disposal.

"Is this because of the rumours running amok in Parliament?"

Winterbourne's expression grew razor-sharp. "You're not a fool, Ravenwood. You must be aware that the two chambers are experiencing a deep...*malaise* over a possible magical conspiracy to overturn the order of our society."

"And yet there was no sign of such malaise when they were turning a blind eye to the plight of the magicless individuals they should be serving," Evander retorted sharply.

Rufus sighed and pinched the bridge of his nose.

Winterbourne lowered his brows. "Don't quip with me, Ravenwood."

"I apologise, sir." Evander rose stiffly and picked up the case file. "We'll leave immediately."

"Did you really have to rile him up?" Rufus muttered once they were outside Winterbourne's office, his stride matching Evander's brisk steps as they navigated the crowded hallway.

"I was making a point."

"He's not the one you should be making a point to," Rufus argued. "You know he's on your side."

"He should make it more obvious then!" Evander snapped. Remorse immediately stabbed through him at Rufus's hurt expression. "I apologise. That was uncalled for."

Rufus exhaled noisily and rubbed the back of his neck with an awkward movement.

"You know I'm of the same mind as you." Concern darkened the inspector's eyes. "It's just—these matters are best handled with the precision of a scalpel, not the recklessness of a sledgehammer." His face grew pinched. "Which you are usually very good at, I might add. I fear a certain recent acquaintance is rubbing off on you."

Evander pursed his lips. Though their relationship had mellowed a little, Viggo and Rufus still acted like bickering cats and dogs on the best of days.

"Do you think this might be connected to Renwick and that mysterious 'I' character?" Rufus asked uncertainly as they descended a staircase.

"It's too early to tell." Evander frowned. "But if Shaw is correct about the *Noctis Bloom* she found, then dark mages should be our first suspects."

He didn't tell Rufus that what concerned him the most was the fact that a renowned professor who was an expert in advanced Elemental Magic had gone missing. He had no doubt Whitley had been a colleague of Caine Renwick, who had also been a professor at the Royal Institute for the Arcane and had taught Elemental Magic.

It was only after Renwick's death that the latter's involvement in dark magic had come to light, as had unsavoury rumours that he had influenced a number of his students into taking up the forbidden practice. Whitley's disappearance so soon after the truth about Renwick's activities had emerged could not be seen as a mere coincidence.

"The sooner we examine the scene and speak with Whitley's colleagues, the better." Evander tucked the file under his arm as they exited the building.

A police carriage awaited them outside the gates of Scotland Yard, its black-lacquered sides emblazoned with the Met's insignia. A pair of familiar faces sat in the box seat.

"Your Grace, Inspector Grayson." Constable Freddie Fitch tipped his hat as they approached, his lanky figure bowed where he held the horses' reins.

Constable Oliver Bartley beamed at them beside Fitch. "Top o' the morning to you, your Grace, Inspector."

"Constable Fitch, Constable Bartley," Evander murmured.

"You appear quite chipper this morning, Constable Bartley," Rufus remarked.

"Every day is another day to be grateful for this wonderful life, sir," Bartley positively gushed.

"He won a game of cards last night," Fitch explained at Evander and Rufus's stares.

Rufus frowned. "Gambling is an unhealthy enterprise, Bartley."

"But a legal one, sir," the constable quipped.

Evander's mouth twitched.

Fitch sighed. "Ollie?"

"Yes, Freddie?"

"Remember how I told you there are times when you're too cheeky for your own good?"

Bartley's expression turned sheepish. "Was this one of those times, Freddie?"

"Yes, it was, Ollie."

Rufus rolled his eyes. "Royal Institute for the Arcane, if you please."

They climbed aboard. The carriage lurched into motion, wheels clattering on cobblestones as they joined the flow of traffic on Parliament Street. Evander gazed out the window and watched London pass by in a blur of grey stone and bustling humanity as they headed north, his stomach churning despite his outwardly calm appearance.

He hoped there was a simple explanation for Whitley's disappearance. Maybe he'd run into old friends, had gotten blind drunk in some downtrodden tavern in the slums, and was currently waking up from a terrible hangover. Or maybe he had a lover and had disappeared to a bolthole in the countryside with her.

Alas, he feared his suppositions would prove to be incorrect.

Because his instincts were telling him that this case involved dark mages. And if he was right, the ultimate outcome of this new investigation might turn out as bad or worse than the Millbrook and Renwick affair.

~

VIGGO FURROWED HIS BROW AS HE REVIEWED THE STACK of paperwork on his weathered walnut desk, a cup of tea cooling next to his hand. Though the concoction was nowhere near as delectable as the ones he'd gotten used to having in Evander's home, it did the job of quenching his thirst and warming his bones.

The reports he was examining had come in overnight from various *Nightshade* agents working outside London and across wider England. The ones from his men and women on the main continent were shipbound and would not arrive until tonight.

Bar a few squabbles in the north between crime gangs, there was no news of growing disputes between thralls and magic users or dark magic and dark mages being sighted. A muscle jumped in Viggo's jawline.

That's one thing to be grateful for, I guess. Although, this does feel like the calm before the storm, as Evander surmised.

There was a soft knock at the door.

Solomon Barden entered the room Viggo called his office, inside the network of limestone caves that constituted the headquarters of *Nightshade* and under an area of Stepney locked in by Limehouse and London Docks. The only way to access the guild was via a nondescript door at the back of *Ironclad Shipping*, the merchant company belonging to Viggo's uncle, Jack Stonewall, and the hidden tunnels that led to the Thames, as well as various exit points throughout central and north London.

The hum of activity filtering through from the underground chambers died down as Solomon closed the door behind him.

Viggo's right-hand man crossed the floor, his quiet footfalls barely audible on the stone. He wordlessly replaced Viggo's cold cup of tea with a mug of steaming coffee and settled in the chair opposite him.

"Thanks," Viggo murmured. He took a sip of the hot brew and met his friend's cool stare. "What's wrong?"

"Are we really doing this?" Solomon said stiffly. "Continuing to aid the Met?"

Viggo sighed and leaned back in his chair, wood creaking under his weight. "We've already had this conversation, Sly. Winterbourne wants us on board until this whole affair is over. Considering what's at stake, I don't really see a reason to refuse his offer."

"There are other ways to protect thralls," Solomon intoned bullishly.

Viggo lowered his brows. "Not against dark magic there isn't. However many anti-magic devices we get our hands on, we cannot battle hordes of dark mages."

"You can."

Solomon's quiet statement filled the fraught silence.

Viggo's face tightened as he recalled what had happened at Charing Cross and inside the warehouse where he'd almost lost Evander.

"I'm not invincible, Sly. It was a miracle I survived that explosion."

"We can rally the Brutes in England to our cause." Solomon leaned forward, elbows on knees and face growing animated. "Even the ones on the Continent would be willing to—"

"Do you really think the War Office would allow that?" Viggo scowled. "That they will look the other way while I gather a force that could bring havoc to the city?!"

He cursed softly under his breath at Solomon's hurt look.

Viggo rose, came around the desk, and dropped into the chair next to his friend.

"I know it's hard to trust Scotland Yard. To trust mages." The Brute hesitated and pressed a hand on Solomon's knee. "To trust Evander." He clenched his jaw. "God, Sly, never in a million years could I have imagined that I would be saying these words to you right now, but I am. I am *asking* you to trust Evander."

A fraught hush ensued.

"I don't dislike the man, Viggo." Solomon's shoulders drooped. "It's just..." He trailed off and shot a conflicted look at Viggo.

"It's just what?"

"He's an Archmage." Solomon ran a hand through his hair and released a sigh heavy with frustration. "And there hasn't been a single Archmage in history who's ever been on our side."

CHAPTER 4

Viggo retracted his hand and stared moodily at the floor. He could not deny the truth of his friend's words. But he also knew Evander would never abandon him. Abandon thralls.

The mage had made it his lifelong mission to bring equality and justice to his kind, after all. And Viggo was determined to help him in any capacity to achieve his nigh-impossible dream. Not just because he loved Evander, but because he trusted the man behind the name.

Solomon's words interrupted his troubled thoughts. "You should know that I'm not the only one in our guild who thinks this."

Viggo gave him a wry look. "Do I hear murmurs of a revolution?"

Solomon rolled his eyes. "Like any of us would stand a chance against you."

They shared a small smile. One borne of decades of

friendship and built upon the sweat, blood, and tears they'd shed as children trying to survive the horrors of growing up in the slums of the capital.

"Have you heard from your source at the Ministry of Arcane Affairs?" Viggo asked quietly.

"Not a squeak," Solomon confessed with a grimace. "The one at the War Office is being similarly tight-lipped."

Viggo grunted, unsurprised. In the weeks since Renwick's death, their efforts to uncover the identity of the mysterious *"I"* had yielded frustratingly little results. It was as if the puppet master who had been controlling the dark mage and his lackeys had vanished into the ether, leaving no trace for even *Nightshade's* extensive network to follow.

"What about the *Noctis Bloom* trade?"

Solomon's expression darkened. "There's been a surge in demand across the city. Local sources report several large purchases in the past fortnight, all by different buyers, but with similar descriptions—hooded figures, speaking with educated accents."

Viggo's jaw tightened. "Mages."

Solomon drummed his fingers on his knee. "Most likely those affiliated with dark magic. And they're paying well above market rate, which suggests urgency."

Viggo furrowed his brow. "Whatever they're planning, they need it soon. Are we any closer to identifying who's supplying the vendors?"

"Not yet," Solomon said in a hard voice. "He's a

crafty bastard, whoever he is. Our agents haven't been able to identify even a hint of his shadow."

Viggo clenched his jaw. It had become clear to them that someone influential was behind the sudden influx of *Noctis Bloom* in the London underground market, where illegal substances and objects traded hands after dark.

He wondered if the Met had unearthed any clues yet as to their nemesis's future scheme. Viggo frowned.

Evander would have told me if they had.

Though the mage abided by the strict rules that prevented him from sharing confidential police information with people outside the Met, he would have put Viggo and *Nightshade* on the right path if he and his colleagues had stumbled upon information concerning their common target.

The Brute's grim musings were interrupted by Finn Callaghan's arrival, the Irishman's usual swagger absent as he knocked cursorily and strode inside the room. His expression was steely, his sea-green eyes lacking their customary mischievous glint.

"Boss, we've got a visitor. Says it's urgent."

Viggo exchanged a puzzled glance with Solomon. "Who?"

"A woman from Whitechapel. A thrall. Her brother's gone missing."

Solomon lowered his brows. "We're hardly a missing person's agency, Razor."

"You'll want to hear her out." Finn's voice hardened as he met Viggo's gaze. "Her brother works for a nobleman. An alchemist by the name of Lord Fairfax."

Viggo stiffened. Lord Aldous Fairfax was Ginny Hartley's new business partner and a man known to be generous to thralls and charities supporting the magicless. Viggo had met the man for the first time when he'd attended an intimate dinner party at Ginny's home a few days ago.

He could tell from Solomon and Finn's tense expressions that the same troubling thought going through his mind had crossed theirs too. Their friend and fellow Brute Magnus Graveoak had been a recent victim of dark mages. He too had vanished under mysterious circumstances two years ago, only to reappear and attack Evander and Ginny's carriage as they'd returned from a ball.

Viggo came to a decision, rose, and took his seat behind the desk. "Bring her in."

Finn disappeared and returned moments later with a young woman whose threadbare shawl and calloused hands spoke of a life of hard labour. She clutched her worn bonnet nervously, her eyes darting around the chamber with a mixture of awe and trepidation.

"This is Emma Simmons," Finn introduced. His voice grew kind. "Emma, this is Viggo Stonewall."

The woman curtseyed awkwardly. "Thank you for seeing me, sir. I—I didn't know where else to turn." She swallowed heavily.

Viggo gestured to the empty chair next to Solomon. "Please, sit."

Emma perched on the edge of the seat, her back ramrod straight.

"Tell us about your brother," Viggo said.

She blinked and took a shaky breath.

"His name is Tom, sir. Tom Simmons," she said in a rush. "He works—worked—as a footman for Lord Fairfax, in Belgravia. Two nights ago, he didn't come home." Her voice caught. "He always comes home, sir, even when his Lordship keeps him late." She gazed pleadingly at Viggo.

Solomon frowned. "His Lordship keeps him late?"

Emma blinked. "Oh. Oh, it's not what you think, sir!" she protested, some colour returning to her cheeks. "Lord Fairfax is nothing but kind to the thralls in his service. It's just, he's a busy man and sometimes his work does not finish until the dark hours."

Viggo kept his face impassive as he observed the young woman. It reassured him that his first impression of Aldous Fairfax had been correct.

"Has your brother been in Lord Fairfax's service for a while?"

Emma nodded jerkily. "Yes, sir. It will be a year come the spring."

"Why did you not report this to the police?" Solomon asked gently.

Emma's fingers clenched on her bonnet.

"I did. I reported it to a couple of bobbies who work our neighbourhood," she said stiffly. "They wouldn't even take down his name." Her tone turned bitter. "Said he probably found himself a girl or got drunk in some tavern." Her hands twisted in her lap. "But Tom's not like that. He's steady. Responsible-like."

Viggo frowned at the mention of the coppers' reaction. Although he'd met and liked many of Evander's work colleagues, there was no denying that contempt for thralls still ran high within the halls of the Met.

"Has Lord Fairfax enquired about your brother's absence?" he pressed.

"That's the strange thing, sir. When I went to the house to ask after him this morning, the butler claimed Tom had sent them a note yesterday to give his notice. The butler was surprised by his sudden resignation. He told me Tom was a well-liked member of the staff." Emma's voice trembled as she stared wide-eyed at them, her desperation clear. "But Tom would never— He wouldn't leave without telling me, without making sure our family was provided for. I fear something terrible may have happened to him."

Viggo exchanged a guarded look with Solomon and Finn.

"You did right to come to us, Miss Simmons," he told the young woman quietly. "Rest assured, we shall look into your brother's disappearance."

Relief flooded Emma's face. She sagged in the chair. "Thank you, sir."

~

THE POLICE CARRIAGE TURNED ONTO A BROAD, TREE-lined avenue in Bloomsbury. Elegant townhouses and shops gave way to the imposing collection of buildings that housed the Royal Institute for the Arcane as they neared the end of the cul-de-sac.

Evander gazed at the familiar frontage as the carriage pulled to a stop before the impressive wrought-iron gates. Unlike the more modern University College nearby, the Institute wholly embraced its medieval origins, its gothic spires and buttresses rising as if to pierce the very sky and the stone eyes of the enchanted gargoyles perched along its rooflines and gutters following visitors and students with unsettling attentiveness.

Evander's chest tightened a little. He had fond memories of the place that had witnessed his formative years as a mage. But he also recollected many instances that had left a bitter taste in his mouth. And they'd had everything to do with the complex politics that simmered beneath the Institute's venerable facade, including the elitism that had seen too many who aspired to gain entrance to the prestigious establishment quietly leaving after getting a taste of the unfavourable treatment it bestowed to those whose only fault lay in coming from the wrong lineage.

"I should warn you," Evander told Rufus as they prepared to disembark, "the Institute can be challenging for outsiders to navigate. The faculty not only guard its secrets jealously, they are not welcoming to those they deem beneath them."

Rufus frowned. "I'm well acquainted with their arrogance, Evander. Least you forget, I visited the premises when I was investigating Renwick's origins."

"This is different," Evander insisted. "Renwick was a

dark horse who had already been proven to be a criminal. They were duty bound to assist us." He hesitated. "The Institute isn't merely a school—it's the oldest magical institution in Britain. Some of the professors trace their lineage back to the founding families. They consider themselves above the law in many respects."

Rufus's face hardened. "No one is above the law."

Evander gave him a sad smile. "I'm not disagreeing with you, old friend. Just be aware that what you see and what you hear inside these hallowed walls is often a game of smoke and mirrors that hides a much deeper truth."

"Consider me warned," Rufus grunted.

They stepped out of the carriage and instructed the two constables to wait for them. Rufus eyed the gargoyles along the roofline warily as they entered the premises. A familiar tingle washed over Evander, the Institute's ancient wards brushing against the magic that lived under his skin.

The courtyard was immaculate, the perfectly manicured lawns enclosed by hedges trimmed with arcane symbols. Students in dark blue robes hurried across the grounds, their arms laden with books and magical implements. Several paused to stare when they spotted Evander.

"It seems your reputation precedes you here as well," Rufus observed drily as they whispered urgently behind their hands.

Evander sighed. "So it would seem."

They were heading for the stone steps rising to a

portico guarded by a pair of stone statues depicting mages holding grimoires and firing off spells, when a commotion reached their ears. Evander stiffened.

A familiar figure in a Metropolitan Police-issued coat was being forcibly escorted out of the main entrance.

CHAPTER 5

Alarm rippled through him at the sight of Lyra Shaw being manhandled by a man who was doing little to mask his hostility towards the forensic mage.

"I have every right to be here, you louts!" Shaw protested, her voice carrying across the courtyard. "This is an official investigation!"

"And I've told you that the Institute does not recognise the Met's authority in this matter." The thin man with the expression of barely concealed contempt who had her by the collar sneered. "Professor Whitley's absence is a private matter."

One of the figures flanking him tossed Shaw's bag onto the steps. An outraged sound left the forensic mage at the clatter of the precious forensic tools inside.

Evander narrowed his eyes. He recognised the faculty member with his hand on Shaw.

Gordon Dearmont had once been his classmate. A nobleman who believed that bloodline was stronger than merit, he and Evander had often clashed during the social debates held regularly among the student body. Judging by the silver embroidery on his midnight-blue robes, he was now a professor at the Institute.

Evander quickened his pace, Rufus close behind. He climbed the steps and picked up Shaw's bag.

"Lord Dearmont," he called out sharply, his voice cutting through the tension like a blade. "I see your hospitality remains as warm as ever."

Dearmont turned. His eyes widened momentarily before his features settled into a mask of cool politeness. He let go of Shaw.

"Duke Ravenwood. What an unexpected pleasure. And it's Professor Dearmont."

Evander did not miss the impudence underscoring his tone.

Shaw's face brightened with relief as she joined Evander and Rufus.

"Your Grace! Inspector! Bloody hell, am I glad to see you. These pompous gits"—she gestured emphatically at Dearmont and the two robed figures flanking him—"were just explaining how a missing professor is apparently none of our damn business, despite the fact his poor wife is half out of her mind with worry."

"Is that so?" Though Evander kept his voice steady, he did not hide the steel beneath it.

"'Git' is a bit of strong word, Shaw," Rufus reprimanded without real vigour.

"I call it as I see it, inspector," Shaw grumbled as Evander passed her bag over. She inspected the contents and visibly sagged. "Nothing is broken." The mage shot a dirty look at the portly professor with the florid complexion who'd unceremoniously flung her things out of the building. "No thanks to that fat-fingered bastard," she muttered, to Rufus's growing consternation and the hidden smirks of several students.

Dearmont's gaze shifted from Evander and lingered on the inspector with undisguised scorn. "I'm afraid we've already had the pleasure of Inspector Grayson's company. I hear his enthusiasm during his last investigation left much to be desired. I sincerely hope this is not going to be repeat of that ghastly incident, Ravenwood."

Evander noted the casual drop of the honorific his station merited with an inscrutable stare.

Rufus straightened to his full height, his jaw clenching and a muscle twitching near his temple as he struggled to contain his ire. "I was merely doing my job. As we all are right now."

"Your job," scoffed the portly professor next to Dearmont, "seems to be harassing respectable magical institutions based on the flimsiest of pretexts."

"A missing person is hardly a flimsy pretext," Evander countered coldly, keeping a tight rein on the irritation causing magic to flare inside his chest. "You may believe yourselves above the common concerns of society, but that is far removed from the truth. Particularly when the person in question is a distinguished member of your faculty."

"Professor Whitley has taken leaves of absence

before," Dearmont said dismissively. "His wife is hysterical. There's no need for the Metropolitan Police to involve themselves."

"And yet, here we are," Evander replied in a deadly tone. He stepped forward until he practically stood toe to toe with Dearmont.

A tense silence fell over the group. Evander could feel the weight of dozens of stares from the students and faculty members who'd paused to watch the confrontation. The air thickened with unspoken challenge.

Dearmont curled his lip, evidently unimpressed by Evander's stance.

"With all due respect, your Grace, your current occupation does not grant you special privileges here. The Institute governs itself."

"With all due respect, *Professor*," Rufus interjected, his patience visibly wearing thin, "a man is missing and the evidence suggests foul play. We have jurisdiction."

"Evidence?" The portly professor snorted. "What evidence could your little forensic mage possibly have gathered in the short time she was allowed inside before we discovered her snooping?"

Shaw bristled. "I wasn't bloody snooping! I was conducting a lawful investigation, as is my damned right as an officer of the law, you insufferable ponce!"

Titters rose from a group of students. They cleared their throats and schooled their features into polite masks when they became the target of their professors' glare.

"That's quite enough, Miss Shaw," Evander cut in, giving her a warning look.

Dearmont narrowed his eyes. "I think it's time for you to leave. The Institute has its own methods for locating Professor Whitley, should that prove necessary."

"I'm afraid I can't do that," Evander said stonily. "Commander Winterbourne has assigned me to lead this investigation with the full backing of the Arcane Division. I would like to remind all of you that the Institute is not a sovereign territory, nor does it stand on foreign soil." He scanned the hostile faces behind Dearmont before focusing on the professor. "As such, you have to abide by the laws of this country." Evander arched an eyebrow. "I trust that won't be a problem?"

He was doing his best to hide his astonishment at the way Dearmont and some of the faculty were behaving towards them. This wasn't mere academic arrogance. Dearmont and his colleagues were acting like they were protecting a secret, which only roused his suspicions.

The hairs rose on Evander's neck with his next heartbeat, his pulse quickening at the subtle shift in the atmosphere. Shaw tensed when she sensed the magical pressure around them intensifying.

Dearmont glared at them.

"What are you doing?" Evander asked stiffly.

"It seems we need to be more persuasive." Dearmont's fingers twitched.

Evander's spine stiffened, a cold jolt of alarm racing through him as he sensed the elemental magic gathering around the man. This wasn't mere posturing anymore; it was an outright threat.

A gasp came behind him. Evander whirled around.

A thin tendril of wind magic had coiled around Rufus's throat, lifting him an inch off the ground. The inspector's eyes widened in shock, his hands flying to his neck.

"Bloody hell!" Shaw gasped.

White-hot fury surged through Evander, bringing forth his magic. The power crackling to life between his fingers caused the air to whoosh outward from his body.

The sight caused several faculty members to retreat hastily, pulling the closest students along with them.

The fear painted across their faces brought Evander to his senses. He took a deep breath and clamped down on the riotous magic roaring through his blood. When he spoke, it was with the deadly quiet before a storm.

"Gordon." His voice was dangerously soft as he addressed his old classmate by his first name. "Release him. Now."

"Or what?" Dearmont challenged, though there was a flicker of uncertainty in his eyes. "Will you arrest me, *Special Investigator?*"

Evander didn't respond to the taunt. Instead, he surrendered to the anger churning inside him at the sheer audacity of Institute members who believed they could attack a Metropolitan Police officer without suffering any repercussions.

The power that flooded his veins was cold and fierce and as familiar to him as breathing.

The temperature around them dropped several degrees in an instant as he released his ice magic. Frost crystallised on the stone steps, spreading in delicate patterns across the ground and up the pillars of the portico.

The wind magic holding Rufus started to dissipate as Dearmont's breath misted before him, glittering particles racing across the professor's body and freezing his hair and skin.

His associates fell back with abject cries.

"I said, *release him!*" Evander growled.

Loathing filled Dearmont's eyes. He retracted his wind magic.

Rufus crashed to the ground. His knees buckled under him as he gasped desperately for air, one hand clutching his throat while the other braced against the flagstones. Shaw helped him up as he dragged himself upright, the stone truncheon that had materialised in her hand steady in her grip as she wielded it like a club, ready to defend her superior if needed.

Defiance burned in Rufus's eyes as he glowered at Dearmont.

The professor ignored him and stared daggers at Evander.

"You dare use your powers against fellow mages?!" he spat.

"You cannot begin to fathom what I dare do, Gordon," Evander said silkily, the power still thrumming inside him making his skin itch as it begged for release. He looked around and met the anxious stares of the faculty as he raised his voice.

"Make no mistake. I will do what is necessary to conduct this investigation." His gaze clashed with Dearmont's once more. "Now, will you let us in or shall I carve my own path to Professor Whitley's chambers?"

Rufus and Shaw drew closer to him.

Evander was aware it wouldn't take much more provocation for him to give Dearmont and his colleagues a taste of the violence they'd just visited upon the inspector and the forensic mage.

The standoff might have escalated further had a commanding voice not cut through the tension.

"That is quite enough, Professor Dearmont."

CHAPTER 6

ALL HEADS TURNED AS AN ELDERLY MAN IN ELABORATE robes of midnight blue and silver emerged from the foyer. Though his back was slightly bowed and his skin wrinkled, he moved with the grace and authority of someone accustomed to being obeyed without question.

Evander experienced a complex surge of emotions at the sight of Cornelius Rigley. Respect mingled with wariness. Nostalgia tempered by regret.

The man had been his mentor during his student days, pushing Evander to strive for excellence while simultaneously attempting to mould him into the Institute's ideal of what a mage should be. Evander was aware Rigley had long held suspicions about his true abilities, his identity as an Archmage a secret he could not readily reveal during his years at the Institute.

Even now, over half a decade later and with his own considerable power and status, Evander couldn't quite suppress the instinctive straightening of his spine in the old man's presence.

"Headmaster Rigley." Dearmont groomed his features into an impassive mask and inclined his head respectfully. "I was just explaining to Duke Ravenwood that—"

"I heard quite clearly what you were explaining," Rigley interrupted a tad sharply. He dismissed Dearmont with a glance and addressed Evander. "Duke Ravenwood. It has been too long since you graced these halls with your presence. Though I confess, I had hoped your next visit would be under more pleasant circumstances."

"Pleasant circumstances, my sweet fanny," Shaw muttered behind Evander.

Rufus hushed her.

"Headmaster Rigley." Evander dipped his head stiffly. "I thank you in advance for your cooperation and that of your staff in our investigation."

The glint in Rigley's eyes told Evander he'd grasped and heeded his subtle warning.

"I apologise for my faculty's conduct, your Grace. The Royal Institute has always valued its relationship with the Crown and its representatives." Rigley paused. "Even when those representatives choose unconventional paths." His gaze flicked meaningfully to Evander's uniform.

Evander swallowed a sigh. He could tell Rigley still resented him for not accepting the position he'd offered him all those years ago. It had been the old man's intention to eventually cede the position of headmaster of the Institute to him.

He introduced Rufus and Shaw to Rigley.

The headmaster acknowledged them with polite courtesy.

"Now then, I believe you wish to examine Walter's chambers? Professor Harrington will show you the way." Rigley turned to a young woman with brown hair and blue eyes standing a little way behind him. "Cecillia, if you would please do me the favour of escorting our distinguished visitors to Professor Whitley's quarters?"

She bowed her head at Rigley, her face inscrutable. "Of course, Headmaster."

"I know the way, sir," Shaw protested.

Rigley flashed the forensic mage a small smile. "Still, it would be best if you had an escort."

Evander masked a frown at this, unsure if it was a hint or a threat.

A strange expression darted in Cecillia's eyes as she met his gaze fleetingly.

Rigley looked calmly at Evander. "I trust what you find will put Lady Whitley's mind at ease." He turned and addressed his faculty and the gawping students with a gentle clap of his hands. "Come now, let us all get on with our day."

Dearmont watched Evander leave while the crowd dispersed, jaw clenched and fingers curled into fists at his sides.

As they followed Cecillia inside the Institute, Evander couldn't help but note how Rigley's cooperative demeanour seemed at odds with the mild tension evident in his bearing. The old mage was being helpful, but there was a guardedness in his eyes that suggested he was measuring every word and every gesture as he'd interacted with Evander.

Shaw's voice distracted him.

"What was that tosser's problem anyway?" the forensic mage hissed.

Rufus cut his eyes to her. "How about you mind your language, Shaw?"

"This is me minding my language, sir," Shaw grumbled. "I could have referred to Professor Dearmont as a pox-ridden prick if I so wished."

Cecillia choked on a snort.

Evander sighed as Rufus and Shaw bickered in low voices.

They traversed grand hallways lined with portraits of distinguished mages from centuries past, the painted eyes seeming to follow their progress. Students pressed themselves against walls to let them pass as they headed deeper into the building, many whispering excitedly behind their hands.

Evander noted this with a wry twist of his lips. The news of his presence and his confrontation with faculty would be all over the Institute by lunchtime, the establishment's gossip network having always moved with supernatural efficiency. By nightfall, the story would no doubt feature him breathing fire and Dearmont cowering in terror.

He became aware of Cecillia's side glance as they negotiated a sweeping staircase to the first floor.

"I do not believe we've met before, Professor Harrington," Evander said curiously.

"I joined the Institute the year after you left, your Grace."

Surprise danced through him. "You must have impressed Headmaster Rigley to have made professor so quickly."

An odd smile curved Cecillia's mouth. "I did. Though many would claim I achieved the position through other means."

Evander gave her a puzzled look.

"Do not mind me, your Grace," Cecillia murmured.

Something caught her eye then. She stiffened and stopped in her tracks.

Evander followed her gaze out the window of the hallway they were navigating and across a courtyard featuring a garden with a fountain and benches where students and faculty could sit and enjoy the outer air.

A trio of figures in the dark blue robes were running along a passage on the third floor of the east wing of the Institute, their features indistinguishable behind the mullioned glass.

Cecillia began walking again, her robe swishing around her ankles as she quickened her pace. "We should hurry."

Evander exchanged a faint frown with Rufus and Shaw as they kept up with her. "May I ask why?"

Cecillia's expression hardened as she shot a glance to where she'd been staring a moment past. "Because it's clear that farce you just witnessed at the entrance was a ruse to distract your attention."

It took a moment for her meaning to sink in. Evander's shoulders knotted.

"Shaw, how long has it been since you were removed from Professor Whitley's chambers?" he asked urgently as he matched Cecillia's strides.

"It's been fifteen minutes, sir," Shaw replied, confused.

Rufus's eyes widened when he finally deciphered the meaning behind Cecillia's words. "They wouldn't dare interfere with a crime scene!"

Shaw sucked in air, outrage darkening her face.

They reached the third floor, hurried along a series of halls, and turned a corner.

A heavy door bearing a brass nameplate labelled "Professor Walter Whitley, Chair of Elemental Magic Studies" stood at the end of a short corridor.

It was ajar. Cecillia slowed alongside Evander, her face pale.

"Shaw?" Rufus asked the forensic mage tersely.

Shaw lowered her brows. "I locked up the premises, sir. Dearmont and his lackeys took the key off me before escorting me to the exit."

Evander's pulse raced as he took the lead and approached the door. He released a small burst of elemental magic when he got within five feet of it.

Nothing triggered his alarm.

Evander unfolded the enchanted cane strapped to the inside of his forearm and carefully pushed the door with the tip. It creaked fully open, revealing a spacious room lit up by the sunbeams streaming through the mullioned windows.

Shaw scowled. "It was not like this when I locked up, your Grace."

A muscle twitched in Evander's cheek. He could tell from Cecillia's expression that she too was shocked by what she was witnessing.

Whitley's office was in a state of disarray that could not be explained by the simple clutter of a busy and distracted academic. Gaps dotted the bookshelves lining the walls, the leather-bound tomes and scrolls that had seemingly occupied the spaces lying pell-mell across the floor. Cupboards were half-open, contents spilling out in a muddle.

The massive oak desk sitting under the windows also showed signs of having being hastily searched, its drawers ajar and half-melted candles and magical instruments lying on their sides between the papers strewn haphazardly across the surface.

Evander strode swiftly to a door on their left. It connected to a private suite with a small bedroom, bathroom, and dressing room. He frowned.

It was clear from their state that they too had been hastily searched.

"It appears your conjecture was correct," Rufus told Cecillia in a hard voice as Evander joined them.

Cecillia swallowed. "Trust me when I say I wish I had been wrong, Inspector."

"Do you have any idea who might have done this?" Evander asked, stopping in the middle of the floor.

He could not detect the tell signs of dark magic around them. There was no unearthly chill to the room, nor the faint stench that would have characterised the recent presence of a dark mage.

Cecillia hesitated. "No."

"It's clear Professor Dearmont and that fat-fingered fool are involved in this, your Grace," Shaw protested. "We should just question the bastards."

"We cannot go around accusing the faculty without proof, Shaw." Evander frowned. "Besides, they have an alibi. They were with you when this happened."

Shaw jutted her chin, undeterred. "What of the key they took off me?"

"The headmaster no doubt has a master key." Evander moved past a sitting area with comfortable armchairs and squatted to examine the hearth. The lack of cold ashes suggested it had been days since a fire burned there. "And it wouldn't be that hard to make a copy of the one in the charge of the caretaker."

He rose and turned to face a slightly deflated Shaw.

"Tell us exactly what the room was like when you walked in and what you found."

The forensic mage hesitated and glanced at Cecillia.

"I believe Professor Harrington will prove of help to us in this investigation," Evander reassured the forensic mage smoothly. He arched an eyebrow at Cecillia. "I take it you also suspect foul play was involved in Whitley's disappearance?"

Cecillia hesitated before nodding.

"It's not like Walter to disappear like this. He is very close to his wife. He would have told her if he intended to travel somewhere for a while."

CHAPTER 7

IT WAS ALMOST MIDDAY BY THE TIME THE HANSOM CAB Viggo had hired pulled to a stop in Belgrave Square. The Georgian townhouse belonging to Lord Fairfax dominated the corner of the quadrangle, its grandeur asserting itself even among the distinguished residences of one of London's most fashionable districts. Viggo disembarked from the cab with Solomon and looked around the square.

An elegant carriage rolled past, lacquered wood gleaming in the sunlight and wheels clacking against the cobblestones. Well-dressed ladies and gentlemen strolled along the iron-fenced central garden across the road. A nanny supervised two children playing with hoops near the corner of the green space, their laughter carrying on the late autumn breeze.

Viggo's face tightened.

Life here was as different from the slums of the East End as night was from day.

He turned to face the residence before them.

Three stories of white stucco rose against the crisp blue sky, the sunlight washing over the facade glinting off tall windows with dark ironwork. Stone steps led up to a portico flanked by classical columns and a black door with polished brass fittings.

Viggo adjusted his cravat as he and Solomon climbed the steps, still uncomfortable with the restrictive garment despite the quality of the tailoring. Before leaving *Nightshade,* he'd changed into one of the new outfits he'd recently acquired. Finn had teased him mercilessly about his appearance before he'd left the guild, causing Solomon to smack him on the back of the head.

Still, Viggo was conscious that appearing presentable would not only gain them easier access to Lord Fairfax's residence, it would be acknowledged as a sign of respect towards a nobleman who favoured thralls.

"Remember, we're here to gather information, not make accusations."

Solomon grunted in acknowledgement. "I'm aware of the delicacy required, Viggo." He'd also changed into his best shirt and jacket.

Viggo knew the outfit hid at least half a dozen weapons.

"Just ensuring we're of the same mind," he told his right-hand man. "Your temper has been rather unpredictable lately."

"My temper is perfectly predictable," Solomon protested. "It flares when I encounter injustice, is all."

Viggo sighed as they reached the door. He raised

the gleaming brass knocker and let it fall with a resonant thud that seemed to echo across the square.

The door swung open a moment later, revealing a butler wearing immaculate livery and an expression of polite inquiry. To his credit, he did not immediately ask them to go to the servants' entrance.

"Good afternoon, gentlemen. How may I assist you?"

"Mr. Viggo Stonewall and Mr. Solomon Barden to see Lord Fairfax," Viggo stated, his tone brooking no argument. "We're associates of Lady Hartley."

The mention of Ginny's name had the desired effect. The butler's demeanour shifted subtly from dismissive to attentive.

"One moment, please. If you could step inside while I determine if his Lordship is receiving visitors."

The foyer they entered was a study in understated opulence. A crystal chandelier hung from a ceiling adorned with intricate plasterwork, the pendants casting prismatic patterns across marble floors so polished they reflected the antique console tables and the tasteful arrangements of fresh flowers atop them.

Solomon's gaze swept the space, likely noting exits and potential obstacles should a hasty departure become necessary. It was a habit born of years spent navigating the treacherous waters of London's underworld and one hard to get rid of.

The butler returned promptly. "His Lordship will see you in the library. This way, gentlemen."

They followed him through corridors lined with paintings and antiquities that spoke of generations of wealth and taste. According to *Nightshade*'s sources, Lord Fairfax had recently inherited the property from a wealthy, deceased relative.

The library was a warm and inviting space despite its splendour. Floor-to-ceiling bookcases lined three walls, the shelves filled with leather-bound volumes whose spines gleamed in the light from the tall windows. A fire crackled in a marble hearth, taking the edge off the autumn chill.

Fairfax rose from behind a massive mahogany desk as they entered. He was a tall man in his fifties with silver-streaked dark hair and intelligent eyes that missed nothing. Unlike many of his station, there was a lack of condescension in his bearing as he greeted them.

"Mr. Stonewall. This is an unexpected pleasure." He shook Viggo's hand and acknowledged Solomon with a courteous nod before gesturing to the comfortable chairs arranged before the fire. "Please, be seated. May I offer you a refreshment? Tea, perhaps? Or something stronger?"

"Tea would be most welcome, my Lord," Viggo said, settling into one of the chairs. Its proportions were generous enough to accommodate his frame comfortably, a thoughtful touch that did not go unnoticed.

It was likely why Fairfax had chosen the library to greet them in rather than the sitting room.

Solomon relaxed a fraction as he took his own seat.

Fairfax nodded to his butler, who bowed and withdrew to fulfil the request for refreshments. The nobleman's expression grew more serious once the door closed.

"I suspect this isn't a social call. Lady Hartley mentioned you run an information guild the last time we met," Fairfax told Viggo steadily. "I am honoured to be hosting the owner of *Nightshade*."

"You knew?" Viggo asked, surprised.

A faint smile quirked Fairfax's mouth where he stood by a chair. "Come now. Even you must be aware the gossip rags have been full of tales of your recent heroic achievements alongside Duke Ravenwood."

Viggo's ears grew warm. He glimpsed Solomon's smirk out of the corner of his eye.

"Has something occurred that requires my attention?" Fairfax asked carefully.

"Yes," Viggo replied. "We're here about one of your footmen, Tom Simmons."

A flicker of concern crossed Fairfax's features. "Tom? What of him?"

Viggo studied the aristocrat. Fairfax was composed yet alert. Though his manner remained cordial, there was a tension in the set of his shoulders that suggested he already suspected the purpose of their visit, a fact Viggo found perplexing.

"His sister came to see us this morning," Solomon explained. "She's worried because he hasn't returned home in two days."

"I see." Fairfax furrowed his brow and crossed to the window, his hands clasped behind his back. He stood gazing outside at the square for a moment. "My butler informed me yesterday that Tom had sent a note of resignation. I thought it rather abrupt, but not entirely surprising. The young man had seemed restless as of late."

Viggo and Solomon exchanged a startled glance.

Fairfax turned back to face them, his frown deepening. "I must admit, I was rather disappointed. Tom has been an exemplary footman—punctual, diligent, and quick to learn. I had plans to promote him to valet for one of my guests next season."

"When you say he was restless, what do you mean?" Viggo asked.

"He seemed distracted. I've known him a fair while now and he has not been himself." Fairfax hesitated. "If I had to hazard a guess, he looked like he was afraid of something. I even questioned him on the matter, but he assured me all was well."

Viggo's insides knotted. A thrall had many reasons to be fearful these days.

"Did you keep the resignation note?"

Surprise briefly widened Fairfax's eyes. "I believe my butler has it. I can have it fetched if you wish."

"That would be most helpful."

Fairfax crossed the room and pulled a bell cord. The butler reappeared. Fairfax instructed him to bring the note.

"May I ask why *Nightshade* is involving itself in the matter of a missing footman?" Fairfax inquired after the butler left. "While I appreciate the concern for Tom's welfare, it seems unusual for your organisation to take an interest in such matters." He settled into a chair opposite them.

A maid arrived with a tea tray before Viggo could respond. The service was silver, the china delicate and clearly expensive. The woman set it down on a side table and began pouring their tea, occasionally stealing a glance at Viggo and Solomon from under her lashes.

Fairfax smiled kindly. "It's alright, Glenys. You can say hello to Mr. Stonewall and Mr. Barden if you wish."

Glenys flushed as she put the teapot down. She curtsied awkwardly and greeted Viggo and Solomon with a shy, "Hello, sirs."

Viggo stared after the maid as she scurried away.

"She's another thrall in my service," Fairfax explained.

"Oh." Solomon scratched the back of his head awkwardly. "Do you have many in your service?"

"Half a dozen at this property. Many more in my various business enterprises." Fairfax smiled. "I am in the process of hiring thralls for my country estate too."

Solomon didn't seem to know quite what to make of that.

"Pardon my frankness, but why?" he finally blurted.

"Sly," Viggo warned in a low voice.

"It's quite alright," Fairfax murmured. He met Solomon's gaze steadily. "I guess my answer takes the form of another question. Why not?"

Solomon frowned and opened his mouth to voice a reply.

Fairfax put his hand up and curbed his words. "I know what you intend to say, Mr. Barden. That thralls are held in contempt by magic users. But I and others like Lady Hartley and Duke Ravenwood firmly believe that the magic we possess is nothing but an accidental virtue of our birth. We did nothing to deserve it and therefore cannot and must not wield it with arrogance. It is a gift that we should use to improve the fate of all mankind, not just those born with magical abilities." His face tightened. "To keep that power in the hands of a few is not only sheer madness, it is a guaranteed path to destruction."

The nobleman's statement startled Solomon and evoked the same feelings in Viggo as the night Evander had said almost the same words to him.

Admiration. Respect. Humility.

It took a strong man or woman in a position of privilege to look at the world around them and declare that they intended to do something about its blatant social inequalities.

They sipped their tea in silence for a moment, Solomon holding his cup like it was some kind of explosive device.

"Tom's sister was quite distressed," Viggo said finally. "She insists her brother would never leave without informing her of his whereabouts. They support their younger siblings together."

Lines wrinkled Fairfax's brow. "That does sound consistent with what I know of Tom. He spoke of his family often and with great affection." He paused, swirling the amber liquid in his cup. "The timing is rather troubling, I must say."

Viggo tensed. "How so, my Lord?"

Solomon leaned forward slightly, equally alert.

Fairfax set his cup down with a soft clink, his

expression brooding. "I received word this morning about another possible disappearance. A young woman named Katherine Stoker—Katie, as she preferred to be called. A thrall of exceptional promise whom I've been sponsoring this past year."

CHAPTER 8

Viggo's pulse quickened. He exchanged a wary glance with Solomon.

"In what capacity were you sponsoring her?"

"Education, primarily. She showed remarkable aptitude for mathematics and languages—skills that are valuable in commerce regardless of one's magical abilities." Pride coloured Fairfax's voice despite his obvious concern at his protégé's fate. "I arranged for her employment with Hampton Shipping two months ago. She was making quite an impression there until—" He faltered, his fingers curling into fists in his lap.

"Until she went missing," Viggo finished softly.

"Yes. Three days ago to be exact, according to Hampton. She failed to report for work, which is entirely out of character for Katie. When someone was sent to her lodgings, they found everything in order but no sign of Katie herself." Fairfax's expression darkened. "Hampton informed me that a resignation letter was delivered to his residence the following day."

Dread churned Viggo's stomach as he stared blindly at the plush Persian carpet covering the floorboards.

Two missing thralls. Two resignation letters. It couldn't be a coincidence.

The butler returned with a folded piece of paper and handed it to Fairfax. The nobleman's shoulders knotted as he read it. He passed it to Viggo.

"Tom's note. Rather terse, wouldn't you say?"

Viggo studied the missive. The handwriting was neat but hurried, the message brief and formal. The footman expressed heartfelt gratitude for the opportunity to serve his master, but cited "personal matters" that necessitated his immediate departure.

"May I?" Solomon held out his hand.

Viggo passed him the note and watched as his friend scrutinised it. Solomon had forged many a document for *Nightshade*'s missions.

"Are we certain this is his handwriting?" Solomon said with a frown.

"Alas, I do not believe I have anything in my possession that could help determine that," Fairfax replied, chagrined.

Viggo doubted Emma Simmons would either.

"Did Katie's resignation letter follow a similar pattern?" he asked.

Fairfax nodded. "It was almost identical in tone and brevity, according to Hampton." He sighed and pinched the bridge of his nose, his frustration clear. "I should have insisted on reading Tom's note. I might have found it suspicious enough to begin making inquiries into his disappearance."

"Neither Tom nor Katie gave any indication they were unhappy or planning to leave?" Solomon pressed, unable to completely mask his suspicion.

"None whatsoever. In fact, both had recently expressed enthusiasm about their futures." Fairfax hesitated. "There is one other detail that may be relevant. Katie recently mentioned feeling watched during her walks home. I dismissed it as the natural wariness a young woman might feel in London after dark, but I now wonder if I was mistaken."

Viggo stiffened. "When did she speak of this?"

"A fortnight ago. She came to one of my weekly gatherings," Fairfax said. "I host dinners for promising thralls to network with potential employers and mentors," he added at Viggo and Solomon's puzzled expressions. His eyes clouded with regret. "I advised her to vary her route and to consider arranging an escort if she became more concerned. I should have taken her concerns more seriously."

"Did Katie and Tom know each other?" Viggo asked.

"Not to my knowledge. They moved in different circles despite my patronage of both." Fairfax shrugged. "Though I suppose they might have encountered one another at this residence at some point."

"Two thralls connected to you, both disappearing within days of each other. And both leaving suspiciously similar resignation letters." Though Solomon kept his tone neutral, his implication was clear.

Fairfax met his gaze directly, giving no sign that the

silent accusation rankled him. "I assure you, Mr. Barden, I am as troubled by these disappearances as you and Mr. Stonewall are."

"We're not suggesting otherwise, my Lord," Viggo clarified smoothly, shooting a warning glance at Solomon. "But the connection can't be ignored."

"Indeed not." Fairfax rubbed his chin thoughtfully. "An idea comes to mind. Let me contact my associates and inquire if they know of similar cases among their staff."

Viggo's stomach fluttered with surprise. "I was about to suggest the same thing."

"You would do that for us?" Solomon asked somewhat incredulously.

A tired smile curved Fairfax's mouth. "Of course. We are on the same side, are we not? I shall send you a note if I find anything. Would you like to see Katie's resignation letter?"

"Please," Viggo said with a firm nod.

"I'll draft messages this afternoon," Fairfax said briskly. "My associates share my views on thrall rights. They will assist however they can."

Viggo and Solomon thanked the nobleman and took their leave.

"The timing of these disappearances is worrying," Solomon said as they emerged from the residence and descended the steps to the pavement. "Could this be connected to the increase in the *Noctis Bloom* trade we're seeing?" He shot a worried glance at Viggo.

Viggo frowned as he flagged down a passing hansom. "I have a feeling we'll soon find out." His tone hardened. "In the meantime, we should conduct our own investigation into missing thralls through *Nightshade*'s channels."

The journey back to the guild was tense, both men lost in their own thoughts as the hansom cab navigated the crowded streets of central London towards the East End.

Viggo popped his head into *Nightshade*'s main office when they arrived at the guild and called to the young woman organising correspondence. "Harriet, I need someone sent to Emma Simmons's residence immediately. We need samples of her brother's handwriting if she has any—letters, notes, anything with his signature, if possible."

"Right away, sir," she replied, already reaching for a message slip.

"And see if there are any reports of thralls going missing in the past fortnight or so," Solomon added.

"Oh." Harriet blinked. "We already have some. Hawk came in an hour ago with news of several people disappearing under strange circumstances. He intended to mention this to you."

Viggo's blood ran cold. "Where's Hawk right now?"

They found the *Nightshade* undercover agent in the dining hall. Hawk put his soup spoon down and got up as they approached the table where he was having an early supper.

"Boss."

"We didn't mean to interrupt your meal," Viggo protested apologetically.

"I was almost done," Hawk said laconically. "I have some news to share."

Viggo exchanged a look with Solomon. "We heard. Come to my office."

Hawk had barely begun telling them about the missing thralls when Harriet knocked on the door and entered, her face flushed.

"Sir, we've had reports just come in from our agents in Whitechapel and Limehouse," she announced. "Three thralls went missing in the past week alone." She placed a stack of papers on Viggo's desk.

Viggo's stomach knotted as he leafed through the hastily compiled notes. "Any connection to Lord Fairfax or one of his businesses?"

"No. Different employers, different neighbourhoods." Harriet tucked a loose strand of hair behind her ear and hesitated. "There is one thing they have in common though."

Viggo eyed her sharply. "What is it?"

"They all worked for a noble," she said awkwardly.

Viggo instantly grasped the reason behind her evident discomfort.

The fact that he and Evander were a couple was *Nightshade*'s most well-known secret.

"It's the same for the cases I heard about, boss," Hawk said with an impassive expression. "There's something else these disappearances have in common. In every case mentioned, the thralls vanished at night."

Viggo's heartbeat quickened.

"Were they alone?" Solomon picked up a report and skimmed it, a muscle jumping in his cheek.

"Yes," Hawk replied with a nod. "All of them were last seen leaving their employers' homes or businesses. Heading home, running errands—nothing unusual as far as we know."

Tension sang though Viggo's veins. "And the locations?"

"That's the third thing that caught my attention." Hawk's eyes gleamed. "Most disappeared while passing through the wealthier districts of London. Mayfair, Belgravia, Kensington to name a few."

Viggo frowned. "Areas where nobles live and socialise."

A fraught silence ensued.

"So they vanished at night, alone, in areas frequented by the magical elite?" Solomon summarised in a hard voice.

"Precisely," Hawk said quietly. "Places where a thrall might already feel uncomfortable or out of place. Where they might be more cautious, more alert to danger—"

"And yet still disappeared without raising any alarm," Viggo finished in a hollow tone.

Hawk nodded. Harriet chewed her lip worriedly.

Heavy footsteps sounded outside. Finn burst into the office, startling them all. His red hair was dishevelled, like he'd been running his hands through it.

"You're not going to believe this!" he blurted without preamble. "I was just out on the docks. Four thralls have gone missing from the shipping companies there. All of them had the same story as Tom Simmons

—resignation letters delivered after they failed to show up for work!"

"Bloody hell," Solomon cursed.

Dread formed a leaden pit in Viggo's stomach. "How many does that make now?"

"Including Tom and Katie, and these new reports…" Harriet counted. "Thirteen that we know of in the past three weeks."

"Thirteen," Viggo repeated, the word hanging heavy in the air. "And not a single one being investigated by the Met?"

Harriet shook her head regretfully, as did Hawk.

Solomon ran a hand through his hair, his face tight with annoyance. "To them, it probably looks like thralls moving on and seeking better employment opportunities elsewhere. Even if they've been reported as missing persons, no one's going to be interested enough to connect these cases."

"Or maybe no one cares," Finn added bitterly.

Viggo did not bother correcting him. His mind raced as he rose from behind his desk.

"This has to be the work of a group of individuals or an organisation. We need to compile everything we have on these missing thralls. Names, dates, locations, employers." He scowled. "There has to be a pattern to these disappearances." He crossed the room to the map of London on the wall. For a moment, he wished he had a magical one, like Evander and Commander Winterbourne possessed. An idea came to him then. "Let's mark out the locations of *Noctis Bloom* transactions and the last known positions of the missing thralls."

Solomon narrowed his eyes. "So you think there might be a connection after all?"

Viggo dipped his head. "We should assume there is for now."

"Shouldn't we warn the thrall communities?" Finn asked, his tone flinty.

"The last thing we need is panic in the streets." Viggo sighed and rubbed the back of his neck. "But you're right," he said reluctantly. He looked at Harriet. "Tell our agents to spread the news. Carefully, mind. Any thrall with connections to a noble should be wary of being outside on their own at night from now on."

"And Evander?" Solomon said, his tone carefully neutral. "The Met should know about this, if they aren't already aware."

Viggo hesitated, briefly torn between his instinct to protect his own kind and his trust in Evander.

"Yes," he said at last. "But I need to tell him in person. This isn't something to be conveyed in a note."

He glanced at the weathered clock on the wall. It was nearly four—he was supposed to meet Evander at Ginny's for dinner in two hours. He came to a decision.

"Harriet, I will draft messages to Lady Hartley and Duke Ravenwood giving them my apologies and informing them I won't be able to join them this evening. Can you please see to it that they get delivered immediately?"

Harriet nodded jerkily.

"Good." Viggo's voice hardened with resolve as he observed the room's occupants. "We have work to do."

CHAPTER 9

EVANDER'S FRUSTRATION MOUNTED AS THE AFTERNOON wore on. Interviewing the faculty of the Royal Institute was proving to be an exercise in futility. Each professor they'd spoken to so far had been the picture of politeness and had offered vague platitudes about Professor Whitley's character that revealed nothing of substance to aid the investigation into his disappearance.

"I'm afraid I cannot recall when I last saw Walter," Professor Abbingdon Musgrave said affably. The specialist in magical artefacts and enhancements who shared an office on the same floor as Whitley adjusted his spectacles and pursed his lips thoughtfully. "Perhaps at the faculty meeting a week ago? He keeps to himself these days."

"And what was his demeanour at this meeting?" Rufus pressed, his patience visibly fraying.

"Quite normal, I should think," Musgrave replied

with a shrug. "Walter has always been unhealthily preoccupied with his research."

This pattern repeated itself with maddening consistency. Professor Whitley was described variously as "brilliant but distant," "dedicated to his research," and "not one for social engagements." When pressed about the nature of his current work, his colleagues either claimed ignorance or cited academic confidentiality.

"It's almost as if they've all been coached on what to say, your Grace," Shaw muttered in disgust as they left yet another office. "Or rather, what not to say."

Evander couldn't disagree with her. The uniformity of the responses suggested coordination, though whether born of genuine concern for a colleague's privacy or something more sinister remained unclear.

By late afternoon, they had interviewed eight professors and made precisely zero progress. Evander's temples throbbed with the beginnings of a headache as they returned to Whitley's chambers for a final examination before departing.

Luckily, Shaw had secured the sample of *Noctis Bloom* she had found in the room and had dispatched it to the AFD for analysis along with her preliminary report before she'd been escorted out of the premises.

Surprise shot through Evander when they entered the missing professor's office.

Cecillia Harrington was waiting for them, shoulders stiff and figure silhouetted against the window as she gazed out at the courtyard below. She turned at their entrance, her expression troubled.

"I take it your interviews proved fruitless?" she asked, her tone suggesting she already knew the answer.

"Remarkably so," Evander replied curtly. "One might almost think there was a concerted effort to hinder our investigation."

Cecillia's mouth twisted into a wry smile. "The Institute protects its own. Even from those who once belonged to it."

"You seem less inclined to such behaviour, Professor Harrington," Rufus observed, his eyes narrowing slightly. "May I ask why?"

She hesitated and glanced towards the open door. She closed it with a flick of wind magic, the subtlety of the gesture demonstrating her absolute control over her ability.

"Because I'm concerned," Cecillia confessed anxiously. "Walter has been different these past few weeks. Ever since the news about Caine Renwick broke."

Evander exchanged a cautious look with Rufus. "Different how?"

"Paranoid," Cecillia said bluntly. "Jumpy. He began locking his chambers even when stepping out for a moment. He'd fall silent when others entered the faculty lounge. And he was researching something that clearly troubled him deeply."

Shaw leaned forward eagerly. "Do you know what he was studying?"

"Rare magical abilities," Cecillia replied reluctantly.

"Particularly those that manifest in only a handful of individuals in every generation."

A chill skittered down Evander's spine. "Such as?"

Cecillia looked nervously towards the door again, as if half-expecting someone to burst in. When she spoke, her voice had dropped to barely above a whisper.

Still, her words sent a jolt of ice though Evander's veins that confirmed his worst fears.

"Shadow manipulation," she began, each word seeming to cost her considerable effort. "Blood Magic. And something called *Midnight Obsidian*. A rare mineral from Siberia that can absorb or augment magic." She crossed her arms across her body as if she were experiencing a chill, her fingers fidgeting with her sleeve. "Walter was particularly interested in—" She faltered, clearly struggling with how to continue.

The room seemed to grow colder. Dread roiled Evander's stomach.

He prompted her gently nonetheless. "Professor Harrington?"

Her eyes finally met Evander's, something like resignation reflected in their depths. "The powers of Archmages," she finished, the words hanging heavily in the air between them. "Especially the more obscure manifestations of such power."

Rufus and Shaw exchanged a startled glance.

Evander kept his expression carefully neutral despite the alarm bells ringing in his mind, conscious Cecillia was watching him closely. Perhaps looking for some reaction to confirm whatever suspicions had driven her to share this information.

"That's quite a range of subjects for someone whose specialty is advanced Elemental Magic," he said evenly. "Did he share why he was interested in these particular powers?"

"Not explicitly. But he intended to make some sort of announcement at the faculty dinner two nights ago. The dinner he never attended." Cecillia wrung her hands, a gesture at odds with her otherwise composed voice. "He told me it was important—that it could change everything."

"Change everything how?" Rufus pressed.

"He wouldn't say." Cecillia's expression grew pinched. "But he was frightened. Genuinely frightened." Her voice dropped even lower as she met Evander's gaze. "And Walter Whitley was not a man who frightened easily."

Evander frowned, the implication behind her words not lost on him. "Did he mention any names? Anyone he was wary of?"

"No." Cecillia hesitated. "But there is one thing you might want to look into. Walter was collaborating with a French professor." She furrowed her brow. "He was quite secretive about it. He never told me his name. But I gathered it was someone from the Paris Institute for the Arcane."

Evander's pulse raced. He took a sharp step forward. "When did their collaboration begin?!"

Cecillia blinked at the urgency of the question. "Two months ago, I believe."

Evander could tell Rufus was thinking the same thing from his darkening face. Caine Renwick had commissioned Alastair Millbrook to create the *Blood Siphon* over three months ago.

Is there a connection?

"I think Walter's consultations with his French counterpart had become more frequent in recent weeks," Cecillia continued. "Walter seemed increasingly agitated every time he received his correspondence."

"Did Whitley mention any plans to travel?" Evander asked stiffly.

"He did request leave for next month," Cecillia confirmed. "He told the headmaster he needed to consult archives in Paris, though he was uncharacteristically vague about the specific purpose."

Evander digested this with growing unease. "Is there anything else, Professor Harrington?" he pressed. "Anything at all that struck you as unusual?"

Cecillia faltered, her fingers worrying at the cameo brooch at her throat.

"The night before he disappeared, I saw him burning papers in his fireplace," she finally admitted. "When he noticed me at the door, he seemed startled. Almost guilty, in fact. He claimed they were failed drafts of a new paper, but Walter never disposed of his work that way. He was meticulous about keeping his archives."

Shaw's eyes lit up. "That's why the hearth was so clean when I examined it." She glanced at Evander and

Rufus. "He must have thoroughly cleared away the evidence."

"And you believe these papers were related to his current research?" Evander pressed Cecillia.

"I can't be certain, but I cannot see what else they would have been about." She frowned and glanced at Whitley's desk. "He'd been making notes in a small, leather-bound journal for weeks. He always kept it with his papers. I noticed it was missing when I came to check on him the morning after the dinner."

CHAPTER 10

EVERY INSTINCT EVANDER POSSESSED SCREAMED AT HIM that the missing journal was a key lead in their investigation.

"Could it be what they were searching his chambers for this morning?" Shaw pondered.

"The same thought crossed my mind," Rufus muttered.

Evander's gaze swept the room once more, taking in the disarray with fresh eyes. The missing journal, the burned papers—all of it pointed to a man desperately trying to conceal something of great importance.

It seemed his instincts on the ride here had been correct, after all.

He turned to Cecillia. "Thank you, Professor Harrington. You've been more helpful than the rest of the faculty combined."

A shadow crossed her face. "I hope I haven't betrayed Walter's trust. But if he's in danger…" She faltered and bit her lip.

"If he is, we're his best chance," Rufus assured her. "And we'll do everything in our power to find him."

"I do have one final question for you," Evander told Cecillia.

She gave him a puzzled look.

"How was Walter Whitley's relationship with Caine Renwick?"

Cecillia's expression grew shuttered, but not before Evander glimpsed a spark of dread in the depths of her eyes.

"It wasn't the most amicable of work relations," she confessed in a strained voice. "Though many in the faculty considered Professor Renwick to have a brilliant mind, Walter once privately told me he thought Renwick was dangerous. He was civil to the man, but he did not engage with him beyond what was strictly necessary."

"Thank you for being candid with your answer," Evander said quietly. "It's a breath of fresh air compared to what we've endured today."

Cecillia smiled weakly. She handed Evander a small card as they prepared to leave.

"My address, should you need to reach me. I'm not staying in my Institute quarters at present. I don't feel safe here, what with Walter's disappearance."

Evander pocketed the card with a nod of thanks. The sun was starting to sink as they departed the Royal Institute. He felt dozens of eyes follow their progress to the gates as they crossed the long shadows in the courtyard.

Bartley was snoring softly beside Fitch. He awoke

with a startled "Gnnhh!" when his colleague jabbed an elbow sharply in his ribs.

"Glad to see one of you stayed alert," Rufus remarked acerbically.

"I was just resting my eyes, Inspector," Bartley protested. His jaw-splitting yawn did little to support this blatant lie.

"Ollie?"

"Yes, Freddie?"

"Now would be a good time to shut up."

"Well, that was illuminating," Shaw said once they were safely inside the carriage. "Rare magical abilities, secret French collaborators, burned papers—why, it's like something out of a penny dreadful."

Evander could tell from the gleam in her eyes that she was relishing the challenge of their investigation.

"And yet entirely too real," Rufus contributed grimly. "The question is, what did Whitley discover that frightened him so badly?"

"And how does it connect to his disappearance?" Evander murmured.

The journey back to Scotland Yard was spent in thoughtful silence. Shaw departed to file her report with the AFD once they arrived, while Rufus accompanied Evander to his office.

"I'll speak with Winterbourne about reaching out to the French authorities," Rufus said as they entered the west wing. "They might be able to find out who Whitley was collaborating with."

"Agreed," Evander replied with a frown.

Rufus's suggestion proved unnecessary in the end.

A sealed message marked urgent was waiting on Evander's desk when he entered his office. He broke the wax seal and scanned the contents rapidly.

What he read had his stomach plummeting.

"What is it?" Rufus asked tensely at his expression.

"It seems the French magical authorities are already involved." Evander handed over the message. "They're sending one of their Arcane Investigators to London. Apparently, a specialist in advanced Elemental Magic by the name of Professor Henri Chevalier has gone missing. He worked at the Paris Institute for the Arcane." He frowned. "He must be the French professor Whitley was collaborating with."

Rufus cursed softly as he read the missive. "Two elemental specialists from two different countries, both connected by their research, and both vanishing within days of each other? This is no accident."

"No," Evander agreed grimly.

He looked at his pocket watch. The French investigator was due to arrive the following morning and would be meeting them at Scotland Yard.

"Why don't we stop here for today? We should ask Shaw to send a forensic team to Walter Whitley's home tomorrow."

Rufus nodded.

Evander began gathering his things. "Will you be at Ginny's tonight?"

Rufus's ears turned red. "Yes. She's invited Ophelia for dinner."

The daughter of Baron Miller, a representative of the House of Lords, Ophelia Miller was not only the current belle of the social season but also a rare light mage. Though her power was a secret she and her family had kept all their lives, she had stepped in briefly to assist Evander during the Renwick affair. He was now part of the inner circle who knew about her wondrous abilities and had sworn to protect her confidentiality, along with Ginny, Viggo, and Rufus.

Evander's chest lightened as he observed the inspector.

No one had been more surprised than he and Ginny when Ophelia and Rufus had developed an instant attraction for one another upon their very first meeting a few weeks ago.

"How goes the courting?"

"It's going well, thank you," Rufus murmured.

Evander arched an eyebrow. "Are you ready to talk to the baron yet?"

Rufus's eyes widened with alarm. "Should I? I've been wondering about that. I mean, Ophelia insisted we court in secret for now and I am ever so grateful Ginny has chaperoned our meetings, but—" he babbled.

"Relax, Rufus." Evander crossed the floor and pressed a hand on the inspector's shoulder. "I was only jesting. Besides, I doubt the baron will be able to resist his daughter's demands if she insists on marrying you."

Rufus blanched. "Oh God. Should I propose? Isn't it too early? I was thinking of the spring, so we could plan a summer wedding. What if Ophelia is expecting a marriage demand and I end up disappointing her—" He stopped, his chest heaving with panic.

A hurt look washed across his face at Evander's muffled snort.

Evander swallowed and did his best to keep a straight face. "You're going to be a mess at the altar."

"That is not helpful, Evander," Rufus groaned. "Keep teasing and I'll choose another groomsman."

By the time Evander's carriage delivered him to his Mayfair townhouse, night had fallen and he was looking forward to the prospect of dinner with Viggo and his friends.

Hargrove greeted him at the door with his usual efficiency.

"Good evening, my Lord." The manservant took Evander's coat. "I trust your day was productive?"

"More frustrating than productive," Evander replied with a weary sigh. "I shall have a bath and get ready."

"Of course, my Lord. I'll have it prepared immediately." Hargrove hesitated. "There's a message for you from Mr. Stonewall. It arrived an hour ago."

Evander's spirits lifted at the mention of Viggo. "Where is it?"

"In the study, my Lord. Along with your other correspondence."

Evander swiftly made his way to his office, where the evening post had been neatly arranged on a silver tray. Viggo's note was on top, the paper folded and sealed with plain wax.

Evander broke the seal and unfolded the message. His heart sank.

Evander,

Regretfully, I must cancel our dinner engagement with

Lady Hartley this evening. Urgent matters at Nightshade require my immediate attention. I shall explain when we meet next.

Yours with affection,

V

Evander frowned. The note was short, even for Viggo. He'd given no indication of when they might next see each other.

"Is everything alright, my Lord?" Hargrove asked from the doorway. The manservant had followed at a discreet distance.

"It seems Mr. Stonewall has been detained by business matters and won't be able to attend tonight's dinner function at Lady Hartley's," he murmured.

Though the peculiar timing of Viggo's cancellation nagged at Evander, he pushed the concern aside as he headed upstairs to freshen up. At least he would have pleasant company this evening.

CHAPTER 11

Gas lamps cast feeble pools of light across the narrow streets of Whitechapel, their glow barely penetrating the thick fog that had rolled in from the river. Viggo pulled his coat tighter around his broad frame as he navigated the labyrinthine alleyways of the East End, Solomon and Finn flanking him like shadows.

The stench of the slums, a noxious blend of sewage, coal smoke, and human misery, hung heavy in the damp air. It was a smell that Viggo had grown accustomed to over the years, though he never quite managed to ignore it entirely. Tonight, it seemed particularly oppressive, as if warning them of danger.

"Thirteen thralls," Solomon muttered, his breath misting before him. "I can't believe thirteen people vanished without a trace and not a single copper appears to give a damn."

"That's hardly news," Finn said, his usual levity

absent from his voice. "When have they ever concerned themselves with the plights of our kind?"

Viggo shot them a glance. "Evander cares."

"One mage doesn't change the system, Viggo," Solomon countered, though without his usual bite.

Viggo frowned. His thoughts had been circling back to Evander all evening. He would have to make amends for failing to make their dinner plans. For now, the missing thralls demanded his full attention.

They turned into a cramped courtyard off Brick Lane. A collection of dilapidated tenements loomed over them, dark rooflines dotted with chimneys spitting out thin trails of smoke. The building they sought was marginally better maintained than its neighbours—a lodging house known to accommodate thralls who worked for the more respectable establishments in the city.

"This is it," Solomon confirmed, checking the scrap of paper in his hand. "Third floor, room twelve."

They'd spent the better part of the afternoon talking to the relatives of some of the missing thralls and interrogating other magicless folks in half a dozen taverns and boarding houses. It was Hawk who'd come up with Daniel Fletcher's name as they attempted to piece together information about those who'd vanished.

Apparently, the man used to work as a servant for the Carmichael family and had recently left his position in a panic. He'd confessed to someone while drinking a couple of nights ago that something unnatural had happened to him, but had refused to go into details. Though many might have considered the claim an absurd flight of fancy, Hawk had not.

There was a good chance Fletcher had somehow escaped the fate that had befallen the thirteen thralls from the East End. Whatever he knew might be their only lead to finding out the fate of the missing and stop the next disappearance.

The staircase creaked ominously beneath Viggo's weight as they ascended, the worn wood protesting with each step. The hallway on the third floor was lit by a single guttering candle that cast their shadows eerily across peeling wallpaper.

Solomon rapped sharply on the door marked with a faded *12*. There was a moment of silence followed by the sound of shuffling footsteps.

"Who's there?" a nervous voice said from within.

"*Nightshade*," Viggo answered, keeping his own voice low. "We heard you had a close call recently. We'd like to talk to you about it."

The door opened a crack, revealing a thin face with hollow cheeks and wary eyes. Though the man couldn't have been more than twenty-five, fear had etched lines around his mouth that aged him considerably. His eyes rounded.

"You're him, aren't you?" Fletcher whispered, his gaze locked on Viggo. "The Ironfist Brute."

Viggo nodded once. "May we come in?"

Fletcher glanced nervously up and down the hallway before stepping back to let them inside. The room beyond was small but meticulously clean, with a narrow bed, a rickety table, and a single chair. A washbasin stood next to the open hearth where embers glowed. The trunk at the foot of the bed likely contained all of Fletcher's worldly possessions.

Finn took up position by the door. Solomon crossed the room to the window and pulled the curtains closed, leaving a tiny gap though which he could keep watch on the courtyard below.

Fletcher swallowed nervously, his gaze darting between them.

Viggo leaned against the wall and indicated the chair. "Please, have a seat."

Fletcher hesitated before perching stiffly on the edge.

"I didn't think anyone would believe me," he mumbled. "The constables I reported the incident to certainly didn't."

"Can you tell us what happened?" Viggo prompted.

Fletcher's knuckles whitened on his lap. "It was five nights ago," he quavered. "I was walking back from the Carmichaels' townhouse in Kensington. It was late—past midnight. Lord Carmichael had guests and they stayed longer than expected."

"You were alone?" Solomon asked.

Fletcher nodded. "Yes." He paused, his fingers unconsciously moving to touch something in his waistcoat pocket. "I was cutting through Hyde Park when I felt it—like the air had gone cold and thick. It became hard to breathe all of a sudden."

Viggo exchanged a guarded glance with Solomon and Finn.

The description the man had just given sent a chill

down his spine and brought to mind his recent clashes with dark mages. Fletcher's next words made his belly knot, memories of his final confrontation with Caine Renwick flooding back in waves.

"The shadows started moving." Fletcher faltered, his gaze pleading as he looked at them. "I don't know any other way to describe it. The night came alive around me, along with the most awful smell. There were shapes—figures and faces the likes—the likes of which I've never seen before!" He shuddered and hugged himself. "They were clawing the air and reaching for me."

Finn had gone pale. A muscle twitched in Solomon's cheek.

"These shadows," Viggo said stiffly, "did they have a consistency to them? Like smoke that could somehow grip?!"

Fletcher startled. "Yes. How did you know?!"

Viggo fisted his hands. He would never forget the shadows Renwick had manifested when he and Evander had fought the dark mage in the warehouse on the south embankment. They had moved with that same unnatural purpose.

"I've encountered them before," he said grimly. "They're shadow creatures—manifestations of darkness created by magic, but with a will imposed upon them by their creator. Not many have lived to bear witness to their existence."

Fletcher's already pale face turned ashen.

"How did you manage to escape?" Solomon asked curiously.

Fletcher's fingers trembled as he withdrew a small metal object from his waistcoat pocket. "My father gave me this before he died. I've carried it ever since. The moment I grabbed it, those shadows recoiled as if burned. I ran away as fast as I could."

Viggo studied the crude but effective anti-magic disruptor. Unlike the more sophisticated versions *Nightshade* agents carried, this was a simple copper and iron disc etched with arcane symbols.

"That saved your life," he told Fletcher. "Keep it close."

It seemed thralls who'd gained employment with nobles still didn't trust their employers fully. Viggo's jaw tightened at that thought.

And who can blame them?

"Did you notice anything else that night?" he urged. "Mages close by? Or something that might help us identify where those shadows came from?"

Fletcher shook his head. "There wasn't anyone else with me in that section of the park." He closed his eyes, clearly forcing himself to relive the terrifying moment. "There was a whispering though. Not words exactly." Lines wrinkled his brow. "More like many voices murmuring just below hearing." He opened his eyes, his expression miserable. "I'm sorry, that's all I recall."

"There's no need to be sorry," Viggo grunted. "Your account will hopefully help us track down the thralls who have recently gone missing."

A grateful look brightened Fletcher's tired eyes.

CHAPTER 12

THEY LEFT THE YOUNG MAN'S LODGINGS AND HEADED back into the alleyways of the slums.

"Viggo, these shadow creatures—how powerful would a mage need to be to control them?" Solomon frowned. "Could any dark practitioner summon such things?"

"No," Viggo said firmly. "Shadow manipulation at this level requires significant power and knowledge. Even Renwick needed his corrupt device to manifest the ones that attacked us when we fought him. For someone to deploy them across London, hunting specific targets..." He trailed off, the unpleasant truth sinking in reflected in Solomon and Finn's eyes. "We're dealing with a dark mage of considerable power. Someone who's found a way to extend their reach beyond normal limitations."

"What happened to those thralls?" Finn asked sourly. "Since no bodies were found, we can presume those shadows took them somewhere, correct?"

Viggo dipped his chin reluctantly. "Solomon and I saw what shadow manipulation could do in that church where we fought those dark mages. Evander believes shadow creatures are used for transportation as much as attack. They can envelop a person, then move through darkness to deposit them elsewhere."

"So they could still be alive?" Finn pressed.

"Possibly." Viggo frowned. "We need to move quickly regardless."

The fog had thickened considerably, shrouding the streets in an impenetrable veil that distorted the glow of the gas lamps into eerie halos. They walked in silence for a few blocks until they came in sight of the *Broken Lantern*.

The tavern was half empty, the usual raucous atmosphere subdued by the late hour and the fear spreading through the thrall community. Hawk was waiting for them at a corner table.

"Well?" he asked when they joined him, his grip tightening imperceptibly on his pint of dark ale.

"Fletcher's story confirms our suspicions." Viggo signalled to the barkeep for drinks. "He's one of the lucky ones. It seems he was ambushed by shadow creatures."

Hawk frowned faintly as Viggo briefed him on the ghastly manifestations and what Fletcher had revealed. "They don't sound like the kind of things I want to meet in an alleyway somewhere on a dark night."

"You and me both," Finn muttered.

The barkeep, a weathered woman with shrewd eyes,

brought over three pints of ale. She lingered a moment longer than necessary, her gaze on Viggo.

"Word's going around," she said quietly. "People are frightened, Viggo." She paused. "Two regulars of mine have gone missing this past fortnight alone."

"We're working on it, Vera," Viggo assured her grimly.

"See that you do. After all, *Nightshade* is the only one us thralls can rely on." She returned to her post behind the bar, her words leaving a bitter taste in Viggo's mouth that could not be washed down by the ale he drank.

"So what's our next move?" Finn asked after a short silence. "We can't simply wait for more thralls to vanish."

Viggo lowered his brows and finally voiced the idea that had been brewing at the back of his mind. "We need to catch the culprits in the act. They may take us to where the missing thralls are."

Solomon sat back, his expression growing calculating. "You want to set a trap."

"Precisely."

Solomon rubbed his chin thoughtfully. "Then we should plant a thrall in the employ of a noble household and have them walk alone at night through the areas where the disappearances have occurred."

"That's madness," Finn protested, his gaze swinging around the table. "Even with our anti-magic devices, whoever plays that role would be in serious danger."

"I'll do it," Solomon volunteered calmly.

Unease coiled through Viggo. "Are you sure?"

"I'm the most logical choice," Solomon replied with a shrug. "I can move silently, I know how to defend myself, and I've got the best chance of anyone here at surviving if things go wrong." He cut his eyes to Finn. "Besides, someone like Finn wouldn't last five minutes in a noble household without insulting someone important."

"Hey!" Finn protested.

Hawk hid a smile behind his pint.

Viggo studied Solomon's resolute expression. "It's not a decision to be made lightly, Sly."

"I know the risks involved, Viggo," Solomon said quietly. "But we need answers and this is the fastest way to get them."

A heavy silence fell over the table as Viggo weighed the proposal. The thought of putting Solomon in harm's way made his stomach churn, but the alternative—waiting helplessly as more thralls disappeared—was equally unthinkable.

"You need to be employed by someone of sufficient standing to make you a target, but also a person we can trust completely," he said reluctantly.

"How about Lady Hartley?" Finn suggested. "She's already involved in this business with the dark mages and she has the social standing."

They stared at him.

"What?" the Irishman asked defensively.

"That's a terrific idea, for a change," Viggo grunted.

Finn looked pleased for about five seconds before he grasped the insult behind the Brute's words.

"Ginny will be happy to help us," Viggo observed

while the Irishman groused under his breath. "Her reputation for employing thralls is well-established." He hesitated. "We should coordinate with Evander as well. The Met must be informed about this, in case we need backup."

Though Solomon's expression remained carefully neutral, Viggo could sense his friend's reservations.

"Are you certain that's wise?"

"Yes," Viggo replied firmly. "Evander has resources we don't." He clenched his jaw. "And there's no way in hell I'd put you or any other thrall in a dangerous situation without having everything at my disposal to ensure you make it out alive."

The fog had thickened to a soupy miasma by the time Viggo left the *Broken Lantern*, his mind heavy with the plans they'd set in motion. Solomon and Finn had returned to *Nightshade* to coordinate with their agents, while Hawk had departed to gather more intelligence from his network of informants.

Viggo pulled his collar higher against the damp chill as he navigated the warren of narrow streets on his way to the modest home he shared with his uncle Jack, in Stepney. The gaslights struggled to pierce the murk around him, their halos diffused into ghostly spheres that barely illuminated the path ahead.

He shivered. It was the kind of inclement weather criminals loved.

The back of his neck prickled after he passed a dark alleyway off Old Bethnal Green. Years of surviving in London's underbelly had honed his senses to a razor's edge. And they were telling him he was being followed.

Tension oozed through Viggo as he maintained a steady pace. The footfalls behind him were too measured and too careful to be a random passerby.

Someone was making a deliberate effort to remain undetected.

He turned down a side passage, one that would lead him past the abandoned cooperage where barrels had once been made for the nearby breweries. The dilapidated building offered multiple points of concealment and was perfect for what he had in mind.

As he passed the sagging doorway of the cooperage, Viggo abruptly ducked inside and pressed himself against the wall in the darkness. The footsteps trailing him hesitated, before continuing forward more slowly. Whoever was following him had lost visual contact and was proceeding with caution.

Viggo waited, breathing controlled and silent, his muscles coiled like springs.

A cloaked figure paused at the entrance, slender form silhouetted against the meagre light from the street. There was something distinctly unnatural about its movements.

Viggo narrowed his eyes.

They were too graceful to belong to a thrall.

He lunged forward in a single explosive motion, hand reaching for his pursuer's throat. His fingers closed on fabric.

The figure twisted with impossible speed.

The sudden chill in the air made Viggo's skin crawl and his breath mist before his face. His shoulders knotted when he recognised the sensation.

His instincts had been right. His pursuer was a dark mage.

The figure's outline blurred and wavered, as if the very substance of the man was dissolving into the surrounding shadows. Though Viggo tightened his grip, it was like trying to hold on to smoke. A low, sibilant whisper reached his ears then—not words, but a sound reminiscent of what Fletcher had described: many voices murmuring just below the threshold of comprehension.

"Who sent you?" Viggo demanded, his voice a threatening growl in the gloom.

The figure gave no answer save for a soft, mocking laugh. There was a sudden surge of foul power. Viggo stiffened as the shadows in the cooperage coalesced around them both, the darkness icy cold against his skin. He was reaching for the pouch of anti-magic devices inside his coat when he realised he was alone.

His quarry had vanished.

Viggo stood motionless, senses straining against the silence. Nothing remained of his pursuer but a lingering chill in the air and the acrid scent he now recognised as the telltale marker of shadow manipulation.

"Damn it all to hell!" he cursed under his breath.

Their investigation into the missing thralls had clearly stirred the hornet's nest and quickly at that. It seemed whoever was behind the disappearances had eyes and ears throughout London.

A troubling thought brought a heavy frown to his face.

The enemy may even have infiltrated *Nightshade*.

Viggo exited the cooperage, his eyes scanning the fog-shrouded street with renewed vigilance. Their plan to use Solomon as bait had just become considerably more dangerous. If their enemies were already watching *Nightshade*'s movements, they would need to be exceptionally careful.

One thing was certain. They were on the right track.

And someone was very concerned about what they might discover.

CHAPTER 13

THE MORNING SUNLIGHT STREAMING THROUGH THE
windows of Scotland Yard cast pale beams across the
polished floors of the west wing. Evander stood in the
busy reception area of the Arcane Division, his fingers
drumming an impatient rhythm against his thigh as he
awaited the arrival of the French investigator.

Viggo had not come to the townhouse last night.

He was distracted from his restless thoughts by the
sight of Rufus checking his pocket watch for the third
time in as many minutes.

"The eight o'clock train from Dover should have
arrived by now," the inspector said with a frown.

"Perhaps there was a delay," Evander murmured, his
mind still preoccupied with the events of the previous
evening.

Dinner at Ginny's had been a subdued affair
without Viggo's presence. Though Ophelia and Rufus
had provided pleasant company, Evander had found
himself unable to shake the feeling that something

significant was brewing beneath the surface of their investigation. Ginny had noticed his preoccupation and attempted to draw him out, but even her considerable social skills had failed to fully engage him.

I should apologise to her when we next meet.

"Your Grace." Shaw's voice echoed along the corridor leading to the reception, her coat flapping behind her as she hurried towards them. "The French investigator is here. He just finished signing in at the gates."

Evander nodded. "Thank you, Miss Shaw."

Shaw hesitated and pursed her lips.

"Why do you look like you've bitten into a lemon?" Rufus grunted.

Shaw didn't take offence at his words, too absorbed it seemed by what was eating at her. "About this French investigator. I should warn you, he's rather— well, you'll see soon enough."

Before Evander could question her cryptic statement, footsteps came from the passage Shaw had just emerged from. An eerie premonition raised the hairs on the back of his neck as he listened to their familiar cadence.

No. It cannot be, surely?!

A tall figure turned the corner and strode into the room with the confidence of one who knew precisely the effect his entrance would create.

Evander would have cursed out loud had his breath not caught in his throat.

Hell and damnation!

The crowded reception grew quiet as everyone

stopped what they were doing and stared at the flamboyant newcomer.

"Who the devil is this peacock?!" Rufus hissed to Shaw out of the corner of his mouth.

"I tried to warn you, sir," Shaw said laconically.

The stranger had eyes only for Evander.

"Mon dieu! Evander Ravenwood, as I live and breathe."

The man standing across from them was striking in every sense of the word. Tall and lithe, with wavy blond hair that caught the light like spun gold and sparkling grey eyes that danced with mischief, his tailored royal blue-and-purple suit was cut in the latest Parisian fashion and accentuated his athletic build, the silver aiguillette on his shoulder that marked him as the French equivalent of a Special Arcane Investigator matching his many accessories.

"Leon," Evander managed, his voice sounding strangely tight even to his own ears.

He glimpsed Rufus and Shaw's startled glances.

Leon Beaulieu's handsome face split into a dazzling smile as he closed the distance between them in three long strides. Before Evander could react, the Frenchman clasped his shoulders and pressed a warm kiss to each of his cheeks in the Continental manner.

There were gasps all around the reception, though none louder than Shaw's delightfully shocked one and Rufus's outraged inhale. Sergeant Griffiths looked like he was about to pop a clog behind the main desk.

Evander bit back a groan. This was going to make the Met's infamous grapevine by lunchtime.

"Mon cher ami, it has been far too long," Leon declared, his English perfect but for the musical lilt of his French accent. He held Evander at arm's length, his gaze sweeping appreciatively over him. "The years have been most kind to you, I see. Though perhaps you work too hard, non? There are shadows beneath those magnificent eyes of yours."

Evander felt heat creep up his neck. "It's good to see you too, Leon," he said stiffly, acutely aware of Rufus and Shaw watching this exchange with undisguised disgust and fascination respectively.

Leon turned his attention to his companions, his smile full of charm. "Ah. You must be Inspector Grayson," he said, extending his hand to Rufus. "I have heard much about your excellent work."

Rufus shook his proffered hand like it might be contagious, his expression a mixture of disapproval and wariness. "A pleasure to meet you…?"

"Please, you can call me Leon. My official title is Comte Beaulieu, but we shall be working closely together, after all." The Frenchman's gaze shifted to Shaw, his eyes twinkling. "And who is this enchanting creature?"

To Evander's astonishment and Rufus's displeasure, Shaw actually blushed.

"Lyra Shaw, Forensic Mage, Arcane Forensics Division, my Lord," she simpered with a short curtsey, her usual brisk manner melting in the face of the Frenchman's charms.

"Enchanté, Mademoiselle Shaw." Leon took her

hand and brushed his lips across her knuckles. "I look forward to witnessing your expertise firsthand."

The colour in Shaw's cheeks deepened until they resembled apples.

Evander clamped down on his growing irritation and cleared his throat. "Perhaps we should continue this discussion in my office," he said coolly.

"Of course." Leon released Shaw's hand. "Lead the way, mon cher duc."

The familiar endearment had Evander narrowing his eyes fractionally.

His former lover seemed intent on ignoring the fact that their breakup had been less than amicable when they'd parted ways over half a decade ago. Still, Evander felt the weight of Leon's presence behind him like a physical force as they navigated the corridors of Scotland Yard to his office.

Memories he'd long since buried threatened to surface—of whispered conversations and stolen kisses in the library of the Royal Institute, of moonlit walks along the Seine, and of more intimate moments he dared not recall in present company.

He and the Frenchman had been a perfect fit in the bedroom, a fact that had long chagrined him considering their relationship had been less than perfect out of it.

"Your headquarters is most impressive," Leon remarked as they entered Evander's office. "Much grander than our humble facilities in Paris."

"The Met spares no expense when it comes to magical law enforcement," Rufus said, his tone suggesting he still found the Frenchman's effusive manner disagreeable.

Evander gestured for Leon to take a seat. Shaw perched a hip on the edge of his desk, while Rufus positioned himself by the window, arms crossed and expression mildly belligerent.

Leon settled into the chair opposite Evander with the easy grace of a cat. He crossed one leg over the other and regarded Evander with undisguised interest.

"I must say, I was surprised to hear you had joined the Metropolitan Police," his former lover murmured. "The last time we spoke, you were considering a teaching position at the Royal Institute."

"Plans change," Evander said curtly. He leaned his elbows on his desk. "Let's discuss why you're here, shall we? The message we received from the French magical authorities mentioned the disappearance of a Professor Henri Chevalier."

Leon's expression sobered. "Ah. Straight to business, as always." He sighed dramatically. "Very well. Professor Chevalier vanished four days ago. Like your Professor Whitley, he was last seen at his place of work, the Paris Institute for the Arcane. He never returned to his residence. His manservant reported his disappearance to the authorities the next morning."

Evander digested this with a frown. "How did you figure out this was connected to our own missing elemental specialist?"

"Because Chevalier was a clever man and seemingly made plans in case something happened to him." Leon reached inside his coat. "He left a key and a notarised note with his manservant. It allowed us to gain access to a deposit box at his bank, in which we found this." He placed a small, leather-bound journal on Evander's desk.

Evander's pulse quickened at the sight of it. "May I?"

"Bien sur," Leon murmured.

Evander reached for the journal. Rufus and Shaw gathered around him as he carefully undid the leather straps holding it closed.

He opened it and began leafing through the pages.

"What the—?!" Rufus exclaimed.

Shaw lowered her brows. "It's written in code."

"Precisely." Leon sighed. "That thing is currently as useful to us as a lead brick. We were about to call on a cryptology expert when news of Whitley's disappearance reached our ears. We discovered correspondence from him at Chevalier's home. It was clear they were in regular communication."

Evander stared at Chevalier's secret writings, his mind racing. He raised his head and finally met Leon's gaze.

"Did the Paris Institute reveal to you what Chevalier was working on?"

Leon's eyes narrowed slightly. "You believe the subject matter of his work is the reason for his disappearance?"

Evander glanced guardedly at Rufus. The inspector dipped his chin, clearly of the same mind.

"How much do you know about the recent dark magic incident in London?" Evander asked Leon quietly.

CHAPTER 14

LEON FROWNED. "YOU MEAN THE CHARING CROSS disaster? Only a little. It made the newspapers in Paris."

Evander spent the next ten minutes bringing the Frenchman up to speed on the growing tension between thralls and magic users in London, the escalating presence of dark mages in the capital, and the sinister plot the Met had recently foiled.

Leon stared.

"A dark mage commissioned a Charm Weaver to invent a device that can absorb the life force of magicless individuals so that it can be used to fuel magic?" he asked, his tone underscored with disbelief.

"It's the truth, Leon," Evander said calmly. "I recovered a crucial component of the *Blood Siphon* from Alastair Millbrook's murder scene. It's currently in the possession of the Ministry of Arcane Affairs."

The Frenchman frowned. He hesitated for a moment.

"Chevalier was researching rare magical abilities," he finally admitted.

Evander traded a sharp glance with Rufus and Shaw before fixing Leon with a focused stare.

"Did Chevalier's chambers show any signs of dark magic having been recently used?"

"None," Leon replied. "But there was something unusual found at the scene." He reached into his breast pocket and withdrew a small glass vial filled with a small amount of a familiar purple powder. "This was hidden beneath a floorboard in Chevalier's office. Our alchemists identified it as *Noctis Bloom*."

Shaw sucked in air. "Just like in Whitley's chambers."

"Shaw found a trace of the same substance next to Whitley's desk," Evander explained at Leon's confused look.

"Does this mean the *Noctis Bloom* Shaw discovered in Whitley's office was not left there by whoever attacked him, but was part of what he and Chevalier were researching?" Rufus said with a frown.

"It would seem so," Evander said grimly. "We should ask the Met's cryptology expert to take a look at Professor Chevalier's journal." He glanced at Rufus and Shaw. "And we should check in with Viggo and *Nightshade*. They may have fresh information for us."

Leon tensed. "*Nightshade*? You mean the infamous information guild run by the Ironfist Brute?"

Evander nodded. "Viggo Stonewall and *Nightshade* are currently assisting the Met in our investigation of the trade of *Noctis Bloom* in the capital. We are certain it is linked to dark mages and whatever Renwick and his mysterious master are attempting to achieve."

Leon's jaw tightened. "I am well aware of your sentiments concerning thralls, mon cher, but Viggo Stonewall is a dangerous man. His reputation precedes him even on our side of the channel."

Heat flushed through Evander. "Viggo helped me bring down Caine Renwick," he said in a hard voice. "I would have died had he not been there."

A fraught silence descended around the office.

"Somehow, I doubt that." Leon arched an eyebrow. "I'm surprised your commissioner has agreed to work with thralls."

"Times are changing, Leon." Evander furrowed his brow. "Lord Watson and I share the same views about expanding the rights of the magicless. I, for one, believed you did too." He couldn't help the tinge of accusation his words contained.

"I still do." The undercurrent of steel creeping into Leon's voice made Evander all too aware that the charming facade the Frenchman projected was a ruse to mask his intelligence and his commitment to his work. "But I would prefer not to associate with suspected criminals to achieve that goal."

"Uh-oh," Shaw mumbled as Evander fisted his hands.

Rufus hushed her, his expression wary.

"Then I am as much of a criminal as Viggo Stonewall," Evander snapped, not even bothering to hide his fury. "At least wait until you meet the man before you pass judgement!"

Leon blinked at his enraged voice. A chagrined light dawned in his eyes when he realised he'd crossed a line.

"I apologise. I should not have said that."

Evander unclenched his fists and swallowed. "And I apologise for my rudeness."

A sad smile curved Leon's lips. "You always were loyal to a fault."

A sharp knock at the door broke the awkward moment.

"Come in," Evander called out briskly, his emotions under control once more.

A constable entered. "Sorry to interrupt, your Grace. An urgent message just arrived for you and Inspector Grayson." He handed Evander the missive and left.

Evander stiffened when he recognised the seal of the Royal Institute. He broke it and unfolded the paper.

The note was from Cecillia.

His blood ran cold as he read her message, the slight tremor of the letters in her otherwise elegant handwriting betraying her distress.

Concern clouded Leon's eyes at Evander's expression. "What is it?"

"There's been another disappearance," Evander said grimly, passing the note to Rufus. He rose and came around his desk. "A student from the Royal Institute. James Thornfield, a promising young mage being privately tutored by Professor Whitley."

Shaw cursed under her breath. "When?!"

"Last night," Evander replied, already reaching for his coat. "His roommate reported him missing this morning when he failed to return to their quarters. We need to return to the Institute immediately."

Leon stood and smoothed down his suit. "I shall accompany you."

Evander hesitated. The thought of navigating the Institute's politics with Leon at his side was less than appealing, particularly given their history. The Frenchman's expertise might, however, prove invaluable, especially if this incident was connected to Chevalier's disappearance.

"I'm not certain that's wise," he began. "You know—"

"On the contrary, mon cher," Leon interjected smoothly, "as the French representative in this investigation, I have a diplomatic obligation to observe all aspects of this case." His grey eyes glinted with determination. "Besides, I speak the language of academia as fluently as you do. Perhaps between us, we might extract more information than either could alone."

Rufus cleared his throat. "He has a point, Evander."

Evander mulled this over a moment before sighing. "Very well. But I must ask that you follow my lead. You know how difficult the Institute can be."

"Mais oui," Leon replied with a slight bow. "I shall be the very soul of discretion."

Evander narrowed his eyes. "The last time you said that, we ended up in Rigley's office and had to stand there and endure a twenty-minute lecture on why mages shouldn't duel in the dining hall."

Leon shrugged. "You must admit, that imbecile deserved it."

Evander's mouth twitched. The idiot who had insulted the Frenchman had been built like a brick house and had a nasty reputation for bullying those he deemed weaker than him. Being repeatedly slammed face first into the ceiling of the dining hall with wind magic had fast remedied that unpleasant situation. Even the prospect of having to foot the bill for the repair hadn't deterred Leon's enthusiasm during the incident.

The journey back to the Royal Institute was tense, the carriage filled with a hush broken only by Leon's occasional observations about the London scenery where he sat next to Evander.

"You're thinking very loudly, mon cher," Leon murmured after some time, his voice low enough that only Evander could hear. "Your brow always furrows in that particular way when you're piecing together a puzzle."

Evander met his gaze briefly. "Some habits never change, I suppose."

"Indeed," Leon replied, a wistful smile playing on his lips. "Though many things do."

The carriage pulled up to the Institute's gates before Evander could respond to his enigmatic words. The atmosphere had changed markedly since their earlier visit. Students huddled in small groups across the courtyard, their expressions anxious as they whispered among themselves. Faculty members moved with purpose amidst them, robes billowing as they hurried between buildings.

Cecillia was waiting at the entrance, her face drawn with worry.

"Thank you for coming so quickly, your Grace."

Evander made the introductions. "Professor, this is Leon Beaulieu. He's a Special Arcane Investigator from Paris who will be working with us on this case. Leon, this is Professor Cecillia Harrington, a close colleague of Professor Whitley."

Leon nodded politely to a surprised Cecillia. "Enchanté, Professor Harrington."

She murmured a greeting and worried her lip for a moment, clearly eager to ask questions but conscious their surroundings were not suited to sharing confidential information. She ignored the curious stares of students and faculty alike and led them swiftly through the courtyard.

"Headmaster Rigley has granted you access to Thornfield's quarters and Professor Whitley's laboratory," she explained in hushed tones. "Though I suspect it's only because he fears the scandal should another disappearance become public knowledge."

"Has Headmaster Rigley ordered a full accounting of all students and staff?" Evander asked as they climbed the grand staircase.

"Yes. The entire Institute is in an uproar about it."

"And so it should be," Rufus muttered. "It will be a miracle if this doesn't make the gossip rags."

"Has anything been disturbed?" Shaw asked sharply.

Cecillia shook her head. "Not to my knowledge. I insisted the rooms be sealed until your arrival."

She led them through a maze of corridors and up several flights of stairs to one of the male student dormitories. Unlike the grand public spaces of the Institute, these quarters were more austere, though still far more luxurious than most university accommodations.

The corridor where Thornfield's quarters were located was eerily silent, with only a prefect standing guard outside the door.

Cecillia thanked him and dismissed him with a nod.

"James Thornfield shared his rooms with another student, Geoffrey Hunniford," she explained as she unlocked the door. "Hunniford is currently being questioned by Professor Dearmont."

"I'm sure that's going splendidly," Rufus remarked dryly.

Evander turned to Shaw. "I'd like you to speak with the housemaster and the students on this floor. Find out if anyone heard or saw anything unusual not just last night, but in the past week."

"Yes, your Grace."

"I'll help Shaw," Rufus volunteered.

Evander nodded. "Very well. Leon and I will examine the rooms."

Thornfield's quarters consisted of a modest sitting room with two desks, bookshelves, a sitting area with a fireplace, and doors leading to separate bedchambers. The chamber was neat but looked lived-in, papers and books stacked on both desks and a half-played game of chess abandoned on a small table between two armchairs.

Evander released a faint pulse of magic. It failed to pick up anything untoward.

"Which side belongs to Thornfield?" he asked, scanning the room.

"The desk by the window and the bedchamber on the left," Cecillia replied.

CHAPTER 15

Evander moved to the desk first.

The surface was meticulously organised. The notebooks were arranged by subject, the quills were lined up by size, and the reference texts were stacked in neat piles. It spoke of a methodical mind.

Evander opened the topmost notebook. He frowned as he skimmed the contents.

"What is it?" Leon joined him.

"Thornfield was writing a thesis on elemental transmutation theory." Evander flipped through several pages of precise diagrams and equations. "Quite advanced work for a student, even one under Whitley's tutelage."

"Walter said he was the most brilliant student he'd had in years," Cecillia commented.

Leon began examining the reference texts, his fingers trailing along the spines of the tomes before he opened them.

"It seems he was looking into rare magical

phenomena," he observed with a frown. "Many of these texts are restricted at the Paris Institute."

A chill settled in Evander's stomach as Leon passed him one of the books.

"Thornfield was researching the same subject Whitley and Chevalier were investigating?" He glanced at Cecillia.

"Who's Chevalier?" she asked, her confused gaze swinging between Leon and him.

Evander checked the door was closed before answering.

"Please keep this a secret for now," he said steadily. "Professor Henri Chevalier is an advanced Elemental Magic specialist at the Paris Institute for the Arcane. He was Whitley's French collaborator. He went missing four days ago."

Cecillia gasped, the blood draining from her face as she brought a hand to her mouth.

"Could Thornfield have been aware of Whitley's collaboration with Chevalier?" Leon pressed her.

Cecillia hesitated before shaking her head. "I—I'm not sure." She swallowed nervously. "But they've been working very closely, so it's possible Walter told him in confidence." Her eyes widened as she recalled something. "In fact, I think that's likely. James often assisted the professor with his correspondence."

Evander's misgivings deepened. It was becoming clear that Whitley, Chevalier, and probably even Thornfield had been watched for some time by whoever had kidnapped them.

Leon wandered into Thornfield's bedchamber

while Evander continued examining the rest of the sitting room. The Frenchman emerged moments later, his expression thoughtful.

"Nothing seems disturbed in there either. The bed is made and his clothes are hung properly. If he was abducted, it wasn't from his rooms."

"Let us examine Whitley's laboratory," Evander suggested. "If Thornfield was assisting with his research, we could find some answers there."

Shaw and Rufus joined them just as they exited the room.

Evander slowed to a halt and arched an eyebrow. "That was quick."

Shaw grimaced. "Yes, well, pretty much everyone we interviewed claimed they saw and heard nothing."

Rufus lowered his brows. "Bar one person. A first-year student. He said he heard glass breaking outside just after midnight last night. It woke him up. He got up to have some water and looked out of the window. He thought he saw two women wearing cloaks running across the quadrangle, although he cannot be certain."

Evander addressed Shaw. "Do you mind checking the quadrangle before you join us in Whitley's lab?"

"Not at all, your Grace."

Cecillia gave the forensic mage directions before escorting the rest of them into the south wing of the Institute, where some of the advanced research laboratories were housed. Few students were visible as they navigated the corridors, the atmosphere there more subdued than in the main building.

Unlike the standard classrooms and lecture halls

they passed, Whitley's laboratory was located in a secluded annex accessible through a heavy oak door reinforced with iron bands and bolts.

"Professor Whitley valued his privacy," Cecillia explained at their expressions as she produced a key and a magic-enchanted seal. "Only he and a select few students were permitted entry into this lab."

She used the seal to undo the wards on the bolts and turned the key in the lock.

The chamber they entered was a feat of magical engineering. Tall windows lined one wall, flooding the space with natural light that illuminated workbenches covered with apparatus both familiar and esoteric. Glass tubes and alembics connected by copper pipes formed intricate networks across one table, while another held crystalline structures suspended in various stages of formation. Bookshelves crammed with texts and journals interspersed with cabinets containing specimens and magical ingredients covered the remaining walls.

"Impressive," Leon murmured, his eyes bright with professional admiration.

Evander felt a similar appreciation as he examined the chamber. It was clear Whitley's laboratory represented decades of dedicated research.

"This is where James spent most of his time?" Rufus asked.

Cecillia nodded. "According to Hunniford, he was here late the past few nights, before his disappearance."

Rufus moved to inspect a large slate board covered with complex equations and diagrams while Leon drifted towards a collection of enchanted instruments near the windows.

Evander walked to the centre of the room. He stopped, closed his eyes, and released a pulse of elemental power as he focused all his senses on his surroundings. The familiar scents of alchemical reagents, parchment, and the magical residue of the experiments Whitley and Thornfield had carried out in the laboratory filled his nostrils.

He stiffened after a moment.

Beneath the expected smells he'd detected lurked something else—a faint, oily trace that made his skin crawl.

"Dark magic was performed here." Evander opened his eyes and frowned. "Recently."

Leon turned. "Are you certain?" he asked sharply.

"Yes." Evander followed the unpleasant remnant to the far corner of the laboratory.

The ambient magic in the room rippled against his skin as he approached, like water after a stone has been cast into it. The disturbance led him to a dark stain on the floorboards in front of a bookcase.

The others joined him as he knelt beside the residue.

"What is that?" Cecillia asked nervously.

The substance was viscous and black, with an iridescent sheen that gleamed when light struck it at certain angles.

Evander was reminded of what they'd discovered inside Millbrook's body a few weeks ago. According to Ambrose Mortimer, the chief medical examiner of the

AFD, it was most likely the breakdown product of dark magic.

He removed a small glass vial from his coat pocket.

"Be careful," Rufus warned.

"I will."

Evander collected a sample of the residue before bringing it to his nose so he could take a sniff. He clenched his jaw.

Though faded, there was no mistaking the foul stench of dark magic it emitted.

He put away the vial and straightened before examining the bookcase more closely. It appeared as unremarkable as the others in the room, its shelves filled with leather-bound volumes on elemental theory.

"Something happened here," Evander said with a frown. "Something that meant someone had to use dark magic."

Rufus reached for one of the books. He jerked and recoiled when magic crackled against his fingers an inch from the shelf.

"This bookcase is warded!"

Evander's pulse quickened. "Allow me."

He extended his hand cautiously, not quite touching the surface. The air around his fingertips grew warm when he encountered the wards. Heat licked his veins, bringing forth a faint aura of fire magic.

Cecillia drew a sharp breath as sparks came to life in front of Evander. They formed a shimmer that rippled as he carefully probed the ward. He narrowed his eyes.

The magic within it was complex. He could sense

layers of defensive spells designed to repel casual handling. Something dark lurked beneath them.

"Ingenious," Evander murmured. "The outer wards are standard protection, but there is some kind of trigger mechanism underlying them."

Rufus scowled. "A trigger? For what?"

"My best guess is anyone attempting to force their way through these spells would activate something quite unpleasant."

Leon moved to his side and cast his own magic, his hand mirroring Evander's movements with elegant precision.

"A nested ward with a shadow trap." The Frenchman arched an eyebrow at him. "Shall I?"

Evander couldn't help but smile faintly. "Be my guest."

"What is he doing?" Cecillia asked with a confused frown while Leon shrugged out of his coat and carefully folded it before placing it on the back of a chair.

Rufus looked similarly puzzled.

"He is going to remove the ward," Evander said quietly. "Let's give him some space."

CHAPTER 16

THEY RETREATED A FEW STEPS WHILE LEON ROLLED UP his sleeves and took up position in front of the bookcase. He cracked his neck, widened his stance, and shook his fingers loose at his side.

Evander felt the charge of magic build as the Frenchman called upon his powers. Static erupted around Leon, causing his golden hair to glow and spark. He raised his hands and skimmed the air with his fingers.

Rufus startled and Cecillia gasped when the wards became visible to the naked eye, runes coming to life in a pale haze.

Leon began unravelling the complex magical protections one by one.

"Is that—" Cecillia stopped and swallowed convulsively as she met Evander's gaze, her own stunned. "*Nullification Magic?!*"

Evander nodded curtly and watched his former

lover work. "Leon is a tri-elemental mage, with power over wind, water, and the rarer *Nullification Magic*."

Leon flashed him a cocky grin over his shoulder. "You mean, so rare I am one of a handful people on the Continent to possess the skill?"

Evander sighed. Humility had never been the Frenchman's forte.

"There," Leon said with grim satisfaction as the final layer of the ward dissolved with a faint sizzle a moment later. "Now we can see what it is Whitley was hiding back—"

The words died in his throat when the chamber suddenly darkened.

Evander's head snapped to the windows. The sky was blue and the sun was shining outside the Institute.

The temperature plummeted, frost crystallising on the nearby glassware.

A strangled sound escaped Cecillia.

"This is dark magic!" Leon barked.

Evander's chest tightened with dread. The shadows were coalescing, forming writhing tendrils that reached out with malevolent intent. Ice magic flooded his veins, his instincts driving him to summon a thick dome of ice that gleamed like a mirror around them in the rapidly dimming light.

"Evander?" Rufus asked in a strained voice. The phenomena on the other side of the crystalline wall were twisting and bulging, forming vaguely humanoid shapes with elongated limbs and featureless faces. His hand tightened on his enchanted truncheon, the defensive runes etched into the wood glowing dully as darkness encroached around them. "Are those—?!"

"Shadow creatures," Evander confirmed in a hard voice.

The apparitions moved with unnatural fluidity, slithering across the floor and ceiling as they sought a path to reach them.

Evander's heart thumped against his ribs. The defensive ice wall he'd erected was ten times thicker than the one he'd raised in his and Viggo's last battle with these monsters. Still, their stench reached him, bringing unwanted memories of their final confrontation with Caine Renwick.

The door to the laboratory opened behind them.

Evander's stomach plummeted when he whirled around and saw Shaw entering the chamber.

"Your Grace, I've finished my investigation of the quadrangle. You won't believe— *What in the unholy blazes are those?!*" Shaw stumbled back, eyes bulging.

The shadows creatures twisted sharply, a sibilant hiss escaping them as they focused on their new prey. They lunged for the forensic mage even as earth magic bloomed around her fingertips.

"*WALL!*" Evander barked, hastily creating a doorway in the ice dome.

Shaw responded instantly to his command. She raised a barricade of earth in front of her just before the first shadow creature smashed into it.

Evander bolted out of the protective dome and began closing the opening behind him.

"I'm coming with you!" Leon snarled, forcing his way through.

Evander hesitated a fraction of a second. It was enough time for Leon to emerge from the ice barrier.

Evander's gaze found Rufus and a frightened Cecillia as he sealed the doorway. "Stay in there!"

Shaw cursed near the door.

Rufus swallowed and nodded. "Go!"

Fire balls exploded into life around Evander as he marched across the laboratory, fury tightening his body. It wasn't clear to him if they'd accidentally triggered a dark magic trap in the lab or whether this was the work of the people behind Whitley's disappearance.

One thing he was certain of. No one attacked his friends and got away with it.

The shadow creatures shrieked and recoiled as he blasted them with his fire magic, Leon unravelling their ghastly forms with lassoes of biting wind and water at his side.

The monsters retreated near the ceiling before coming at them on a tidal wave of darkness, Shaw forgotten for a moment.

Evander shielded the forensic mage with a barrier of ice before grounding his and Leon's legs with earth magic. They faced the horde of creatures from inside a storm of elemental power, their combined abilities rattling the windows and glassware.

One of the monsters lunged directly at the Frenchman, its form stretching impossibly as it reached for him with clawed appendages. Leon reacted fast, his hands outlining a swift arc that summoned a wall of water between himself and the attacker. The shadow creature hissed as it slipped through the insubstantial barrier, only to vanish to wisps as Leon carved through it with an ice spear.

Whips of fire unravelled from Evander's hands, making the water in the air steam. He spun the elemental weapons above his head until they formed a ring of fire around him and Leon.

"Use your *Nullification Magic!*" Evander yelled as the shadow creatures shrieked and jerked back.

Leon glanced at him even as he sent a volley of ice spears through a couple of the creatures, pinning them momentarily to the wall before they dissolved and reformed.

"Are you certain that will work?!"

"Anything is worth a try right now," Evander said grimly.

Leon nodded sharply. "Watch my back."

Evander took up a defensive position behind his former lover.

The hairs rose on his nape when he sensed the Frenchman's magic building around them. Movement ahead had his eyes widening. He cursed.

The shadow creatures were merging into a single towering, humanoid form that nearly brushed the ceiling.

"Bloody hell!" Rufus shouted.

"*Run, your Grace!*" Shaw yelled.

Bile rose in Evander's throat as he gazed up at the monstrous apparition. A maw formed where its mouth should be, the gaping hole expanding as it dropped towards him and Leon, as if it meant to devour them whole.

"Now would be a good time!" Evander barked.

The Frenchman tsked, the sound amused. "As impatient as ever, I see."

Evander's ears popped when Leon released a powerful blast of *Nullification Magic*. The void of deadly magical energy spread outward from where they stood, snuffing out every shadow creature it touched. The giant monster descending upon them like a wall of judgement roiled violently before vanishing into wisps that faded to nothingness.

The room brightened, the silence around them so sudden and deep it made Evander's ears ring. He startled when Shaw whooped behind her ice wall.

The forensic mage froze mid-fist pumping at the sight of the figure standing framed in the open doorway of the laboratory. Sweat beaded Rigley's brow as he stood there, chest heaving and face pale, his robes and hair in disarray. His alarmed gaze found Cecillia.

"Cecillia!"

Evander dropped the ice barriers he'd erected while Rigley rushed past Shaw and hurried across the laboratory.

Cecillia fell into Rigley's arms and shuddered with relief as he hugged her tightly to his chest.

"Uncle!" she mumbled hoarsely.

CHAPTER 17

SHATTERED GLASSWARE CRUNCHED UNDER EVANDER'S boots as he approached Rigley and Cecillia, the headmaster's arms still curled protectively around his niece's shoulders.

"Uncle?" Rufus echoed. The inspector exchanged a frown with Evander and Leon.

Though his complexion remained ashen, Rigley recovered his composure. "I suppose explanations are in order."

"Indeed," Evander said coolly. "Starting with why you concealed your familial relationship with Professor Harrington."

Guilt clouded Cecillia's eyes. Evander now understood the meaning of the words she'd spoken when they'd first met.

"Quite frankly, I didn't think it relevant to your investigation," Rigley admitted.

"You didn't think—!" Rufus began hotly. He fell

silent when Evander raised a hand, the annoyance tightening his features reflected in Leon's expression.

Evander noted the defiance in Rigley's voice with a faint frown. It was clear he was being difficult for the sake of protecting his niece.

"Any connection to Professor Whitley and his research is relevant," he said, his tone measured despite the elemental magic still humming through his blood. He suppressed a grimace at the familiar tingle of ice in his fingertips and retracted his powers.

The shadow creatures had unsettled him more than he cared to admit. They reminded him of the terror he'd felt for Viggo's safety when they'd confronted Renwick. The thought of his absent lover caused a pang in his chest that had nothing to do with the recent exertion of magic.

He needed to talk to Viggo. And the sooner the better.

Cecillia broke the fraught silence.

"Headmaster," she faltered and bit her lip, her pleading gaze on Rigley. "Uncle, I think we should tell them the truth."

For a moment, Evander thought the headmaster would not budge. Rigley finally nodded.

"Perhaps we should relocate for this discussion?" Leon suggested smoothly. The Frenchman looked remarkably unruffled as he retrieved his coat and shrugged into it.

Only Evander could tell he was tense from the faint lines around his mouth.

"My office would be more appropriate," Rigley said reluctantly. "And private."

"We should have Fitch guard the laboratory while Bartley fetches more officers," Evander told Shaw and Rufus briskly. "We need someone to watch the premises until we finish our investigation."

Rigley watched as the forensic mage nodded and disappeared, his expression indicating he was uncomfortable with this arrangement. They waited until Shaw returned with Fitch before following the headmaster.

Leon fell into step beside Evander as they made their way through the corridors of the Institute.

"That was impressive work, mon cher," he murmured, his voice pitched for Evander's ears alone. His fingers brushed Evander's knuckles. "We always did work well together."

Evander carefully shifted away from his touch, an unwelcome warmth rising in his cheeks. "What are you doing?" he said under his breath.

Leon's eyes crinkled at the corners, an arresting smile curving his mouth that would have made Evander's heart skip a beat in the past. "Trying to win you over, of course."

Evander lowered his brows. "You can shelve that notion right now. I have a lover. One I am wholeheartedly committed to."

Surprise widened Leon's eyes.

Luckily for Evander, Shaw intervened before the Frenchman could question him.

"Your Grace, I found something in the quadrangle."

She produced a small cloth bundle from her pocket and carefully unfolded it to reveal several shards of clear glass. "I believe these may be fragments of a vial."

Evander frowned. A trace of purple coated the lining of the glass.

"Is that *Noctis Bloom?*"

"It's hard to tell," Shaw replied reluctantly. "It doesn't have any noticeable scent."

"Have Brown examine it."

Shaw nodded and put away the evidence.

Rigley's office on the uppermost floor of the Institute befitted the headmaster of the prestigious establishment. Dark oak panelling covered the walls and floor-to-ceiling bookshelves lined with ancient tomes gave the room a solemn, scholarly air. A large desk dominated the space beneath the tall windows overlooking the Institute grounds.

Evander fixed the headmaster with a penetrating stare once they were all seated, Rigley in his chair and Cecillia to his right.

"Now, I believe we're owed that explanation."

Rigley passed a hand over his face, suddenly looking every one of his sixty-odd years. "Cecillia is my late sister's daughter. When her parents died in the cholera outbreak fifteen years ago, I took her in and raised her. It didn't take long for me to realise she was a talented mage." He shot a kind glance at his niece.

"And her appointment to the faculty?" Rufus asked pointedly.

"Was based entirely on merit," Rigley insisted, his voice hardening. "Cecillia graduated top of her class and has published more scholarly works on hydromancy than anyone her age in the Institute's history."

"That may be true," Evander said quietly, "but your failure to disclose this relationship may have compromised our investigation."

Cecillia's knuckles whitened on her lap. "Please, your Grace, don't blame my uncle." Her voice trembled a little as she gazed pleadingly at him. "I asked him not to reveal our connection when I first applied for a position here. I wanted to make my own way through the Institute, free from whispers and accusations of nepotism."

"Yet, from what you revealed when we first met, it seems others already know your secret," Evander observed.

Alarm widened Rigley's eyes. "Is that true?!" He stared at his niece, stricken.

Cecillia hesitated before nodding miserably. "I didn't want to burden you." She reached over and clasped her uncle's hand. "You have already done so much for me."

Rigley swallowed and placed his fingers atop hers.

Evander's expression softened slightly. He understood all too well the desire to forge one's own path, independent of family connections. And it was clear to all in the room that uncle and niece cherished each other deeply.

"What is your connection to Professor Whitley's research?" he finally asked Cecillia.

She took a tremulous breath, as if to steel herself.

"I possess an unusual magical ability." Her jaw tightened as she met their stares. "I am what some call a hybrid mage."

Evander's pulse quickened. He masked his surprise behind a steady stare.

"Hybrid?" Rufus asked, confused.

Cecillia nodded reluctantly. "My primary element is water, but I also have affinity for light magic built into it."

"Cor blimey," Shaw mumbled.

Evander traded a tense look with a pale-faced Rufus.

As far as they knew, Ophelia was the only light mage in London.

"That's exceedingly rare," Leon said gravely.

"Yes," Cecillia confirmed. "Walter became interested in my abilities several years ago. He believed that studying magical hybridity might lead to breakthroughs in our understanding of how magical gifts are inherited and develop with age."

Evander wrinkled his brow. "Professor Chevalier evidently shared the same interest."

Rigley visibly startled.

"Professor Chevalier? Do you mean Henri Chevalier, the Elemental Magic specialist working at the Paris Institute for the Arcane?" the headmaster asked sharply.

Evander realised belatedly that Rigley knew nothing about the French scientist's disappearance. He briefed him about the reason for Leon's presence in London.

"My God." Rigley leaned back heavily in his chair, his expression ashen. "This is unfathomable." He stared blindly at his desk for a moment. "I recently approved Walter's leave. Though he didn't specify the reason he was going to Paris, I gathered it had to do with his research."

Something about Rigley's troubled expression had Evander's scalp prickling.

Intuition blasted through him, causing him to straighten in his chair.

"You know why they were researching rare magical abilities, don't you?"

"What do you mean?" Cecillia shot a bewildered glance at Rigley. "Whitley never told anyone why—"

Rigley stayed her words with a gentle touch upon her wrist.

"Magical transference," he confessed quietly, his gaze meeting Evander's unflinchingly. "Whitley was researching the theory that magical abilities might be transferable under certain conditions."

Evander's chest tightened painfully in the heavy silence, to the point he feared he would struggle to catch his next breath. He could tell from the way Leon had grasped the armrests of his chair in a white-knuckled grip that the same fear coursing through him was chilling the Frenchman's blood.

If Rigley was correct, then the implications of Whitley and Chevalier's research were beyond staggering. Were such knowledge to fall into the wrong hands, the consequences would be catastrophic. The power to steal magical abilities would upset the very foundations of not just their society, but the world as they knew it.

Evander's nails dug into his palms.

And it could very well spark a war between magic users and thralls the likes of which we have never seen before.

"Are you suggesting," he finally said, his voice deceptively calm despite the knots in his stomach, "that Whitley and Chevalier were attempting to find a way to transfer magical abilities from one person to another?"

"It was theoretical research only," Rigley hastened to add. "Walter was a man of science, not a dark magician. He was interested in understanding the fundamental nature of magic, not in creating some—some abomination."

"And yet," Leon observed coldly, "someone has likely employed dark magic to abduct both him and his student. Not to mention Chevalier."

Something in the Frenchman's voice had Evander shooting a glance at him.

"Which means someone felt their theoretical research could actually be put into practice," Rufus concluded softly.

Hearing the words made the ghastly possibility all the more real to everyone in the room.

Shaw cleared her throat. "Your Grace, I should take these glass fragments back to the AFD for analysis. There is still the laboratory to investigate too."

Evander nodded, his mind racing. "Please do." He studied Rigley and Cecillia with a faint frown. "We will arrange protection for Professor Harrington. If someone is targeting those involved in this research, she may be in danger too."

"That won't be necessary—" Rigley began.

"With all due respect, Headmaster, it absolutely is necessary," Evander cut in coolly. "Two professors and a student have vanished and we've just been attacked by shadow creatures in this very building. I strongly recommend you close down the Institute to external visitors for now and send the students home. The Met will carry out a thorough review of everyone involved even the slightest with Professor Whitley."

Rigley's mouth thinned to a line. "I'm afraid I cannot agree to either of those demands without consulting the Institute's board members."

"Then may I suggest you do so posthaste?" Evander snapped. His tone softened at his old mentor's mutinous expression. "Please, work with me, Headmaster. After all, we both want the same thing, do we not? To keep the Institute safe for students and staff alike?"

A heavy sigh finally left Rigley. He pinched the bridge of his nose.

"You always were stubborn to a fault, Ravenwood. I shall do my best to get them to agree to your requests."

CHAPTER 18

Evander's mind was a whirlwind as they left Rigley's office. The revelation that Whitley and Chevalier had been researching magical transference was deeply unsettling. Judging from his companions' reactions, they shared his concerns.

"I shall arrange for a forensics team to examine Professor Whitley's lab this afternoon, your Grace," Shaw said, her tone somewhat subdued.

Evander clocked her pale expression and came to a decision. "Let us delay until tomorrow morning. I believe we could all do with some reprieve after what we've just been through. Besides, I would like to have Mrs. Scarborough inspect the place for traps before we let any more officers loose in there."

Philippa Scarborough was a curse-breaker working for the AFD. She had helped free one of Viggo's closest friends from the control of dark mages during the Renwick affair.

Rufus cut his eyes to Evander while Shaw released a small sigh of relief.

"You believe those shadow creatures reacted to something we set off in Whitley's lab?"

"Either that or whoever sent them is watching this place," Evander murmured, conscious of Leon's guarded glance.

Shaw shuddered. "Anyone else feel like someone just walked over their grave?"

"You've got years left in you yet, Shaw," Rufus grunted.

"I am well aware of that, sir." Shaw glanced at the inspector. "Of course, the same cannot be said of you."

An outraged gasp left Rufus.

"I am only seven years older than you!" the inspector spluttered once he could speak again.

"Aye," Shaw responded wisely. "And that's seven years closer to the last roll call, sir."

Evander pursed his lips when the pair began arguing in low voices.

Leon raised an eyebrow. "Are they always like this?"

"Alas, yes."

The Frenchman fell silent.

"You're brooding again," Leon remarked as they descended the steps of the Institute. "I can practically hear the gears turning in that brilliant mind of yours."

Evander gave him a sidelong glance. "This is hardly the time for levity, Leon."

"Au contraire, mon cher," the Frenchman countered with a wry smile, "it is precisely when matters are most grave that we need moments of lightness."

"I'll report back to Scotland Yard and brief Commander Winterbourne," Rufus said as they approached the police carriage. His gaze flicked uneasily between Evander and Leon. "Will you be joining us, your Grace?"

"Not immediately," Evander replied. "I need to speak with Viggo about these developments. *Nightshade* might know something we don't."

Leon's expression sobered, something that looked like displeasure clouding his eyes momentarily. "Before you dash off, might I suggest we discuss our next steps over an early dinner? I've gathered some intelligence from Paris that may be relevant to our investigation."

The invitation hung in the air between them, laden with unspoken history. Evander hesitated, torn between professional necessity and personal unease as he considered his options.

The last thing he wanted was to spend an evening alone with Leon, especially when he wished to talk to Viggo. But if the Frenchman had intelligence that could help them locate Whitley and Thornfield, he couldn't afford to refuse either.

Besides, something about Leon's behaviour in Rigley's office and his current tone told Evander he needed to hear what his former lover had to say.

"Very well," he conceded reluctantly. "Where and when?"

Leon's face brightened a little. "There's a French restaurant near Covent Garden, not far from the hotel where I'm staying. It's called *Le Petit Château*. The chef is from Lyon and his coq au vin is magnifique. Say six o'clock?"

Evander had heard of the place. He dipped his head. "I shall meet you there."

They parted ways outside the Institute, Evander summoning a hansom cab to take him home. He needed to change. More importantly, he intended to send a message to Viggo to come to his place tonight.

Hargrove greeted Evander at the door when he reached his Mayfair townhouse.

"Welcome home, my Lord," the manservant said, taking his coat. He observed him shrewdly. "You appear rather fatigued. Shall I prepare a bath?"

"Thank you, Jasper. That would be most welcome." Evander removed his gloves and handed them over. "I'll be dining out this evening. *Le Petit Château*, the French restaurant in Covent Garden."

Though Hargrove's expression remained impassive, Evander detected a flicker of surprise in his eyes.

"Very good, my Lord. With Mr. Stonewall, I presume?"

"You presume wrong," Evander replied tartly. A hint of tension entered his voice. "If you must know, I am having dinner with Comte Beaulieu."

Hargrove's eyes bulged, surprise turning to full-blown shock. "Not that French dunderhead, my Lord?!"

"Mr. Hargrove!" Mrs. Sinclair warned sharply as she entered the foyer and caught the tail end of their conversation. "Please mind your language."

Evander greeted his housekeeper with a warm look. Cordelia Sinclair had been his nanny since he was an infant and had practically raised him. She was the only Ravenwood employee who knew all his secrets, including the one he had yet to reveal to Viggo.

"Has anyone ever told you that you move with the stealth of a ninja, Mrs. S?" Hargrove grunted.

Mrs. Sinclair's eyes shrank to slits. "Is that an insult, Mr. Hargrove?"

Hargrove made a face. "It's a compliment, Mrs. S. Ninjas are esteemed warriors on the other side of the world. I guess you missed what our Lord just said. The French chump he shall be dining with tonight is none other than Comte Beaulieu."

Mrs. Sinclair blinked, nonplussed.

"The count is in London?" she asked Evander warily, ignoring Hargrove the repeat offender.

"Yes." Evander sighed at the manservant and the housekeeper's uncomfortable expressions. "Leon is an Arcane Investigator working for the French authorities. He arrived in England this morning and will be participating in a joint investigation with the Met. I have no say in the matter."

"Well, this is going to put the cat among the pigeons," Hargrove muttered darkly. "You best not let Mr. Stonewall see you two together."

Evander bristled at the warning. "It's not as if Leon and I are intending to resume our former relationship."

"Your *intimate* relationship," Hargrove corrected.

"Mr. Hargrove!" Mrs. Sinclair gasped.

"What?" Hargrove said with a shrug. "It's not exactly

a lie." He narrowed his eyes. "I must admit though, there's no way that Frenchman could keep up with the Ironfist Brute when it comes to satisfying his Grace." He paused deliberately. "*Sexually*, I mean."

Heat suffused Evander's face.

Mrs. Sinclair looked like she was contemplating walloping Hargrove over the head with the closest blunt object.

"If you've quite finished talking about my personal affairs, I would like you to send a message to *Nightshade* requesting Mr. Stonewall visit me tonight," Evander instructed the manservant coolly.

A salacious twinkle appeared in Hargrove's eyes.

"Don't," Evander warned, his ears hot as he realised belatedly how the command might come across.

He climbed the stairs to his chambers while Hargrove departed to make the arrangements, his thoughts churning. Not just about the case, but about Leon himself.

Seeing his former lover again after six years had stirred memories better left undisturbed. Their parting had been less than friendly—bitter words had been exchanged, promises broken, and hearts irrevocably wounded.

Evander could not deny that he had once loved the Frenchman. But he was over him. Had been for years. Yet Leon seemed intent on acting as though those final painful weeks of their relationship had never happened.

Evander swallowed a sigh as he entered his bedchamber. Tonight's dinner would be a delicate balancing act. He would have to extract valuable information from Leon while maintaining an appropriate distance. It was a challenge he wasn't particularly looking forward to facing. And it made him feel guilty towards Viggo even though he knew he wasn't doing anything wrong.

CHAPTER 19

Viggo and Solomon studied the two handwritten notes on the weathered oak desk in his office in *Nightshade*. One was the resignation letter Tom Simmons had supposedly sent to Lord Fairfax. The other was a shopping list Emma Simmons had brought in that day, a mundane document that now held potentially vital clues. According to her, her brother had written it a week before his disappearance.

"The slant of some of the letters is wrong," Solomon finally murmured, his brow furrowed. He pointed out the difference between the two notes. "Look at how he formed his S's and T's." He straightened. "I doubt this resignation letter was written by Tom Simmons."

"So you do think it's a forgery?" Viggo asked grimly.

"Yes," Solomon replied.

Viggo frowned heavily. This confirmed what they had already suspected.

Tom Simmons had not willingly left Lord Fairfax's employ.

He became conscious of Solomon fidgeting beside him. "What is it?"

Solomon scratched his cheek awkwardly. "Although I'm certain it's a fake, it wouldn't hurt to get it confirmed by the Met. Especially after what happened to you last night."

Viggo hid his surprise at that. Still, he was pleased his friend was coming around to the idea that they should involve the authorities. After all, there were more important things at stake here than their pride.

Besides, these dark mages are watching our every move. Which means whatever their mission is, it's far from over.

"I shall inform Evander straightaway about these disappearances and our findings so far." Viggo rose to his feet.

Solomon nodded reluctantly.

A sharp knock interrupted them. Finn burst into the room, his face flushed and his breathing rapid. He held up a folded paper sealed with a crest.

"Urgent message from Lord Fairfax." He crossed the office and handed it to Viggo. "Just arrived."

Tension oozed through Viggo as he hastily broke the seal and unfolded the letter. His stomach twisted when he began reading its contents.

"What does it say?" Solomon asked stiffly.

"Fairfax heard back from his associates," Viggo replied, his tone flat. "Two in Belgravia, one in Kensington, and one in Bloomsbury. Between them, they've had five more thrall employees disappear in the past fortnight. All left similar resignation letters."

"Bloody hell," Finn muttered. "That makes—"

"Eighteen that we know of," Viggo finished, the number hanging in the air like a death knell. His knuckles whitened around the paper as he continued reading. He cursed out loud. "There's worse. The body of a man named James Harker was found washed up on the banks of the Thames early this morning. According to Fairfax, his remains have been taken to the Met. They've identified him as a thrall who worked as an assistant to a bookbinder in Mayfair."

A fraught silence fell over the room, the hush broken only by the distant sounds of *Nightshade*'s members going about their business inside the guild.

Solomon fisted his hands, his expression growing dark. "Whoever these bastards are, they're organised."

Viggo folded the letter and tucked it inside his coat, his mind still reeling from what they'd just learned. "I'm going to find Evander. He needs to hear about this. Now." He strode across the room and paused abruptly on the threshold. "Don't forget you need to visit Lady Hartley this evening," he told Solomon. "She said to come early so she could have your uniform fitted and have her butler show you the ropes."

Solomon grimaced. "She's going to make me wear a cravat, isn't she?"

Finn snorted, breaking the tension. Viggo managed to keep a straight face by a sheer act of will despite the grim tidings they'd just received.

They'd dropped by Ginny's that morning to ask for her help with their plans. Though she'd been intensely curious to find out why *Nightshade* needed the favour, she'd readily provided her assistance. The gleam in her eyes when she'd realised Solomon was the one involved in said favour told Viggo his friend had better watch himself around the courtesan.

Another messenger arrived just as Viggo was about to leave *Nightshade*, this one bearing a note with the Ravenwood crest. He took it with a sense of foreboding.

It was from Hargrove. Evander already had a prior engagement this evening but wished to see him later tonight. Viggo hesitated and looked at his pocket watch. He decided he might as well make his way over to Mayfair now and await his lover's return.

A delicious tension filled his groin as he flagged down a hansom cab on Commercial Road minutes later. One night away from Evander had been one night too many. He didn't intend to let the mage sleep tonight. Viggo frowned faintly.

We're going to have to discuss our living arrangements.

Irongate Prison loomed in the distance to his left when he looked outside.

Viggo's scar throbbed as he stared at the foreboding outline of the dark fortress etched starkly against the orange sky.

It was the main holding facility for magical criminals in London and the place where the Archmage who had destroyed his village and orchestrated the murder of thousands of innocent thralls had met his final end.

Viggo shook off his bleak mood as the hansom cab left the East End. Now was not the time to dwell on the past.

It was gone six when he reached Evander's Mayfair townhouse. Hargrove's chagrined expression when he opened the door immediately alerted him that something wasn't quite right.

"What's the matter?" Viggo said stiffly as he entered the foyer.

Hargrove recovered his composure. "Good evening, Mr. Stonewall," the manservant said smoothly. "I wasn't expecting your company so soon. Would you like to have supper while you wait for his Grace to return?"

Viggo wasn't fooled by the former Navy man's attempt to change the subject. He crossed his arms and scowled.

"Spit it out, Hargrove."

~

EVANDER'S CARRIAGE PULLED UP OUTSIDE *LE PETIT Château* at precisely six o'clock.

The restaurant occupied a handsome Georgian building with a facade of cream-coloured stone and tall, arched windows that glowed amber against the gathering dusk. Gold lettering adorned the midnight-blue awning and ornate magic lanterns flanked the entrance, the glowing orbs casting pools of warm light onto the cobblestones and the liveried footmen standing to attention beside the gleaming oak doors.

Evander stepped out of the carriage just as the evening fog began rolling into Covent Garden and requested Graham and Samuel to wait for him. He suspected Leon would otherwise make an excuse to arrange for them to spend the entire evening together.

The interior of *Le Petit Château* was the epitome of French elegance transported to London soil. Crystal chandeliers cast a warm glow over the dining room, their light reflecting off polished silverware and fine bone china. The soft murmur of conversation mingled with the gentle strains of a string quartet playing in the corner.

Evander was conscious of the curious glances he received from the restaurant's well-heeled patrons as the maître d'hôtel led him through the dining room. Word of his status as an Archmage had added a new layer of fascination to the already substantial interest in his reputation as the Ice Mage.

Leon was already seated at a table in a secluded alcove, the section half partitioned from the main dining area by an ornate lattice screen. He rose as Evander approached, a warm smile playing on his lips.

"Ponctuel comme toujours," he remarked, gesturing to the chair opposite his own. "You always were admirably on time even when we were together."

Evander noted Leon had already ordered champagne as he took his seat. A bottle rested in a silver ice bucket beside their table, beads of condensation rolling down its elegant neck.

"I hope you don't mind." Leon nodded to the waiter who stepped forward to pour their drinks. "I thought the occasion warranted a celebration of sorts."

"What exactly are we celebrating?" Evander asked, his tone carefully neutral.

Leon raised his glass, his grey eyes sparkling in the candlelight. "Our reunion, of course. It's been far too long, mon cher."

Evander suppressed a sigh and lifted his own glass.

"To finding Whitley, Chevalier, and Thornfield," he countered pointedly.

Leon inclined his head in acknowledgement before taking a sip. "Of course. Though I maintain that life's small pleasures should not be neglected, even in dire circumstances."

As they perused the menu, Leon deftly steered the conversation towards lighter topics—mutual acquaintances in Paris, developments in Elemental Magic theory, the inferior quality of English coffee compared to French. It was a familiar pattern, a dance of words Leon had always excelled at.

Evander found it almost soothing in its familiarity. Still, he guarded himself against being lulled into a false sense of contentment. Leon could be most disarming when he turned on his full charm, a trick Evander had fallen for far too easily in the past.

He waited until they'd ordered before fixing the Frenchman with a sharp stare.

"You said you had some intelligence to share."

An irritated light flashed in Leon's eyes. "We should eat first."

Evander lowered his brows. "I consider this dinner a work engagement, Leon. Nothing more, nothing less."

Leon's face tightened. He looked like he wanted to argue for a moment. He took a sip of champagne and finally released a dramatic sigh. "You have grown more dour with age, mon cher."

"It's called life experience," Evander retorted.

Leon rolled his eyes. His expression sobered.

"What I'm about to tell you is not widely known, even within French magical circles," he said, his voice dropping to ensure privacy.

Evander leaned forward slightly, his attention sharpening.

"Chevalier was once part of a secretive research group within the French Ministry of Arcane Affairs," Leon continued. "They called themselves *Les Prophètes Illuminés*—the Enlightened Prophets. Their focus was pushing the boundaries of what was magically possible." He faltered and took a measured sip of his champagne, as if to steel himself. "This included the theoretical possibility of transferring magical abilities between individuals."

CHAPTER 20

EVANDER'S BLOOD RAN COLD AT THESE WORDS.

"Is that why you acted the way you did in Rigley's office this afternoon?" he asked after a protracted pause.

"Yes."

Dread churned Evander's stomach. "So Whitley's research might not be purely theoretical, as Rigley claimed."

"Not entirely, no," Leon confirmed grimly. "The group Chevalier belonged to was disbanded nearly a decade ago when their methods became...ethically questionable. Most of their findings were sealed away."

"But Chevalier continued the work," Evander surmised.

Leon nodded. "Privately and with a more academic approach. When he met Whitley at an international symposium three years ago, they discovered their shared interest."

The waiter arrived with their first course—a

delicate arrangement of smoked salmon and capers for Evander, escargot for Leon. Neither man seemed particularly interested in the food before them.

"If someone learned of their research and believed it could be put into practice—" Evander began.

"They would need both professors' expertise," Leon finished, his expression grave. "Which means they may still be alive."

"And Thornfield?"

"Perhaps he stumbled upon something he shouldn't have," Leon proposed.

Evander absorbed this information in silence, his mind racing. If dark mages had discovered a way to transfer magical abilities, it would explain their recent boldness.

"Leon," he said at last, "why didn't you share this information earlier? At Scotland Yard or at the Institute?"

A flicker of discomfort crossed the Frenchman's handsome features. "The walls have ears, mon cher. And this information is sensitive. To the point where I technically shouldn't be sharing it with you."

Evander stiffened and narrowed his eyes. "Please tell me you did not just disclose a state secret to me?"

Leon's thin smile almost had him groaning.

"There are those in our Ministry who would prefer Chevalier's past remain buried," the Frenchman said evasively.

"And yet you're telling me about it anyway."

Leon's gaze softened. "Because I trust you, Evander. I

always have." He reached across the table, his fingers brushing against Evander's knuckles. "Despite everything that happened between us, that never changed."

Evander withdrew his hand. "That was a long time ago, Leon."

"Was it?" Leon's voice was gentle. "Six years is nothing in the span of a lifetime. And now fate has brought us together again." He smiled, a hint of his old mischief returning. "You must admit, we still work well together. The way we handled those shadow creatures was rather impressive, was it not?"

Before Evander could formulate a response that would discourage Leon's evident desire to rekindle what they had once shared, he caught sight of a familiar broad-shouldered figure being escorted through the dining room by the maître d'hôtel past the screen protecting the alcove. His eyes widened, his pulse skipping a beat as he stared at the man crossing the restaurant.

Leon followed his gaze.

Viggo struck a magnificent sight in formal evening attire as he strode across the restaurant. His dark suit emphasised his powerful build, his crisp white shirt showcased the wide expanse of his chest, and his silk cravat highlighted his tanned skin. Evander recognised the outfit as one he'd chosen himself from Blackthorne & Sons.

Despite the elegant clothing, there was something untamed about the Brute. A raw, elemental power that seemed at odds with the refined setting. It drew the rapt stares of fellow diners and made Evander's breath catch.

Viggo's dark eyes scanned the room and settled on him with an intensity that was almost physical. Evander noted the tension in his lover's jaw and immediately knew something was wrong.

"Who is that man?" Leon asked curiously.

Evander swallowed. "That's Viggo Stonewall."

"Ah." Leon's expression cooled perceptibly. "The infamous Ironfist Brute."

Viggo reached their table. He waited until the maître d'hôtel excused himself before addressing Evander.

"Your Grace." His deep voice betrayed little emotion. His gaze shifted to Leon, assessing the Frenchman with a single sweep of his dark eyes.

Evander rose from his seat, his heart racing a little at this unexpected meeting. "How did you know we were here? I sent a message—"

"Hargrove told me where to find you," Viggo explained, his tone clipped. "We need to talk. It's urgent." He glanced dismissively at Leon.

The Frenchman stood and extended his hand with a polite smile that didn't quite reach his eyes. "Comte Leon Beaulieu. Special Arcane Investigator for the Paris authorities. A pleasure to meet you, Monsieur Stonewall. I've heard so much about you."

Viggo regarded the offered hand for a moment before taking it. Evander could see the barely restrained strength in his lover's grip.

Leon's composed expression never faltered.

"Have you?" Viggo's voice was neutral. "Funny, I've heard almost nothing about you."

Leon's eyes narrowed imperceptibly.

The tension between the two men crackled in the air, like static before a storm.

Evander cleared his throat. "Would you care to join us?"

Viggo's face tightened. He was about to voice what Evander suspected would be a blunt refusal when Leon spoke.

"That's a splendid idea." The Frenchman's smile was edged with steel. "I would like to get to know Monsieur Stonewall better."

The challenge filled the space between the two men.

Evander couldn't think of anything worse and was about to suggest they leave when Viggo spoke.

"Why not?" the Brute said, arching a haughty eyebrow.

Evander stifled a groan. Having his former lover and his current lover sitting at the same table was his definition of Hell. Neither of the two obtuse men in his life appeared to notice his discomfort as Leon signalled to a waiter to bring a third chair.

"I'll have what he's having," Viggo said when the waiter presented him the menu. He indicated Evander with a tilt of his head.

A muscle twitched in Leon's cheek at the familiarity of Viggo's movement and words.

The waiter poured Viggo a glass of champagne and left hastily.

A fraught hush fell over them.

Leon broke the silence, his French charm on display in his relaxed manner as he leaned back in his chair. "Evander tells me you and your guild are assisting the Met in their investigations."

"We are," Viggo confirmed curtly. He took a sip of his drink. Surprise flashed across his face. He glanced at the bottle in the silver bucket. "This is nice," he said grudgingly.

Leon smiled. "Merci. Call it the excellent taste of a Frenchman." He glanced pointedly at Evander.

Viggo did not miss his look. He lowered his brows.

"What's a French Special Arcane Investigator doing in London?"

Evander attempted to smooth things over. "I intended to talk to you about that tonight. Something happened at the—"

"Do you really think it wise to share the details of our current investigation with this man?" Leon interrupted.

The Frenchman's tone had grown so cold Evander wouldn't have been surprised to see their breaths mist in front of their faces. Irritation prickled his skin.

"I already made it clear that I intended to inform Viggo and *Nightshade* about this case," Evander said tersely. "It is relevant to our mutual interest in dark mages."

Surprise flared on Viggo's face. "Wait. So the reason Winterbourne sent you that missive yesterday morning was because something happened that involved dark mages?"

His words hung starkly over them, the intimate

meaning behind them instantly clear to Leon judging by the way he stiffened.

The Frenchman fixed Evander with a loaded stare. "So your new lover is the Ironfist Brute?" His voice was full of accusation.

It was Viggo's turn to grow deathly still. His eyes shrank to slits.

"*New* lover? That somehow implies that you two were intimate in the past."

His suspicious gaze swung between Leon and Evander.

Evander clenched his jaw, now equally annoyed with both men. "This is not the place to be having this conversation."

He might as well have been speaking Mandarin for all the difference this made.

"We were indeed," Leon ascertained silkily. "Evander and I used to be in a relationship." He raised an arrogant eyebrow. "For several years, at that. And it is one I very much wish to rekindle."

Evander drew a sharp breath at the sheer audacity of the Frenchman. He threw his napkin on the table. "Who the devil do you think you are to presume that I would agree to—?!"

A thunk froze his words.

Evander and Leon's gazes found the dining fork Viggo had stabbed into the table.

"Over my dead body!" the Brute growled.

The possessiveness in his voice and expression sent an illicit thrill through Evander, briefly dampening his vexation.

"That can be arranged," Leon parried smoothly.

The maître d'hôtel approached, evidently sensing the discord chilling the air.

"Is everything to your satisfaction, gentlemen?" he inquired delicately.

"The meal is positively lovely," Leon replied with a pleasant smile that did not reach his eyes. "The company less so." His gaze found Viggo.

Viggo pushed his chair back and rose, his body vibrating with anger. "How about you and I take this outside?!"

Leon stood up, magic charging the air around him.

"What a wonderful idea," he ground out.

Evander's voice cracked the air. "Both of you, *stop this right now!*"

The temperature in the restaurant dropped under the pulse of ice magic he involuntarily released. Frost crawled across the windows and chandeliers, dimming the light. Shocked murmurs rose across the dining room.

Leon and Viggo studied Evander with contrite expressions.

The maître d'hôtel looked like he was contemplating turning in his resignation.

"Sirs, I must ask you to calm down," he pleaded.

Evander took a deep breath and dampened the magic bubbling through his veins. He climbed stiffly to his feet. "I apologise on behalf of myself and my companions," he told the man with a curt dip of his head. "If you could please prepare the bill, we will leave immediately."

"Evander—" Leon protested, his grey eyes dark with guilt and regret.

"Not now, Leon," Evander said coldly. "We shall speak tomorrow, at Scotland Yard."

He felt his former lover's forlorn gaze on his back as he left the restaurant with Viggo. Though the Brute remained silent as Graham brought the carriage round, Evander could feel the tension radiating off him.

It wasn't until they were safely ensconced inside that Evander finally spoke.

CHAPTER 21

"Look, I understand you're upset—" Evander began.

"Do you?" Viggo's voice was deceptively quiet. "Because I'm not entirely convinced you do."

The carriage wheels clattered across the cobblestones as they departed Covent Garden, the silence between them thick enough to cut with a knife. Evander's chest tightened with remorse when he studied Viggo's stony profile in the dim light of the passing streetlamps. The Brute's jaw was clenched so tight it looked painful.

"Leon is here on official business, Viggo. I had no idea he would be in London until this morning." Evander ran a hand through his hair. "And had I known he would behave so atrociously this evening, I would have declined his invitation."

"Why *were* you having dinner with him?"

A tendril of irritation coiled through Evander at Viggo's accusing tone.

"Because he told me he had important information to impart about our case."

Viggo crossed his arms, his face set in mutinous lines. "So this information was so important you had to drink champagne while discussing it?"

Evander lowered his brows at the Brute's mocking voice.

"The champagne was Leon's idea." He blew out a frustrated sigh. "Why are you acting like this? You know I am committed to our relationship."

Viggo's dark eyes flashed in the dim carriage. "It's clear your former lover has designs on you."

"That doesn't mean I intend to respond to his advances!" Evander snapped.

A hurt look flashed in Viggo's eyes. He turned his face to the window, a muscle twitching in his cheek. "When were you planning to tell me about him?"

"Tonight. When you arrived at my townhouse as requested in my message." Evander fought to keep his voice level. "We haven't seen each other since yesterday morning, if you recall."

A loaded silence fell between them once more.

They didn't speak again until they reached Evander's townhouse. Hargrove opened the door with an expression that was far too innocent for Evander's liking.

"My Lord," he said, bowing slightly. His gaze drifted to Viggo. "Mr. Stonewall, I'm pleased to see you found his Grace."

"He did indeed," Evander said coolly. "I trust you've enjoyed *your* evening?"

The manservant's face remained impressively impassive. "I have, my Lord."

Evander's mouth pressed to a thin line. "Please ensure we're not disturbed."

"Of course, my Lord." Hargrove bowed again, a glimmer of amusement in his eyes as he retreated.

Evander led Viggo to his study and closed the door firmly behind them. The lamps were already lit, their radiance casting a warm glow over the leather-bound books lining the walls and the polished oak desk in the centre of the room.

Evander moved to the sideboard where crystal decanters glinted in the lamplight. He was in need of some fortification after this evening's debacle.

"Would you care for a drink?"

"No," Viggo said shortly. He stood with his back to the fireplace, his broad shoulders tense beneath his formal evening attire. "I'd prefer you tell me about this case of yours."

Evander frowned as he poured himself a measure of whisky. He took a sip before speaking.

"A professor from the Royal Institute went missing three nights ago. His name is Walter Whitley. He is a specialist in advanced Elemental Magic." He swirled the amber liquid in his glass. "Leon came to London because Henri Chevalier, a French professor who is also a specialist in the same field and who was working with Whitley on a mutual research project, vanished five days ago."

Viggo stared. "The Met believes dark mages are involved in their disappearances?"

"Yes," Evander confirmed grimly. "That's only half the story. Today we discovered that James Thornfield, one of Whitley's most promising students, has also gone missing." He met Viggo's gaze steadily. "We were attacked by shadow creatures when we examined Whitley's laboratory this afternoon."

Viggo startled. He crossed the room and grabbed Evander's shoulders, his eyes dark with concern and his anger about Leon all but gone.

"Are you alright? Did they hurt you?!"

Evander's belly twisted at the fear drenching the Brute's voice and the strength in his anxious grip. He put his glass down and clasped Viggo's hand. "I'm alright. Leon and I managed to defeat them."

Viggo heaved a sigh of relief and drew Evander close so he could hug him. "Thank God!"

The tightness in Evander's chest loosened. He sank into the Brute's embrace, his lover's presence providing a rare moment of peace in what had been a tumultuous two days.

Evander hesitated, reluctant to voice the most disturbing revelation yet. "Whitley and Chevalier were researching magical transference."

"Magical transference?" Viggo pulled back, his brow furrowing. "What does that mean exactly?"

"They were investigating the theoretical possibility of transferring magical abilities from one person to another."

Viggo went deadly still. "You mean taking magic from mages and giving it to others?" he said in a dangerous voice.

"Or perhaps the reverse," Evander said quietly. "Robbing others of their magic and giving it to dark mages."

He could tell they were both thinking about the *Blood Siphon* and what it had been intended for. Viggo's next words made his blood run cold.

"Thralls are disappearing across London. That's why I came to find you tonight." The Brute's face hardened. "And now I'm beginning to wonder if this is somehow connected to your missing professors."

"What?" Evander's heart raced as he stared at his lover. "How many thralls?!"

"At least eighteen that we know of so far," Viggo replied grimly. "All were in the employ of a noble. And all left suspicious resignation letters that turned up after their disappearance. There's worse. A body was found in the Thames this morning—a thrall named James Harker. He worked for a bookbinder in Mayfair. Lord Fairfax informed us about it."

Surprise jolted Evander. "Lord Fairfax? You mean Lord *Aldous* Fairfax?!"

Viggo nodded. "The very one."

Evander's mind reeled. "How on earth is he involved in this?"

"The first thrall whose disappearance we became aware of was his footman, Tom Simmons. Tom's sister came to *Nightshade* yesterday and requested our help. When Solomon and I visited Lord Fairfax, not only did he tell us Tom's resignation letter had come as a bolt from the blue, he also informed us about another thrall who had just gone missing. A protégé of his by the name of Katherine Stoker. She started working at Hampton Shipping two months ago, a job Fairfax introduced her to."

Evander's stomach knotted. "What about the Met? Why has no one informed the authorities about these disappearances?"

Viggo's expression grew shuttered. "Their families did, Evander. But they were ignored by the officers they talked to."

Evander stiffened. "Surely you are jesting?! This is too grave a matter to be so summarily ignored!"

"Their reports never made their way up the chain of command, so no one made the connection between the disappearances." Viggo clenched his jaw. "This shouldn't come as a surprise to you. You know full well how deeply ingrained the prejudice against thralls remains, not just in the Met but in every organisation that holds authority in our society. I believe Lord Fairfax and his associates intend to visit Scotland Yard and make a case for these disappearances to be taken seriously."

Evander opened his mouth to protest and was forced to swallow his words. He could not deny the veracity of Viggo's words. He grabbed his drink and gulped the remainder of his whisky in one swallow, the alcohol burning a path down his throat.

He set the glass down with a sharp clink and finally regained his composure. "Is that why you didn't come to Ginny's dinner yesterday?"

An uncomfortable look crossed Viggo's face. "Yes. We were still in the midst of interviewing the relatives of the thralls and other persons of interest." He faltered.

Evander lowered his brows. "What is it?"

"We talked to a witness yesterday," Viggo confessed quietly. "A thrall who would have become another victim if not for the fact that he was carrying a crude anti-magic object on his person. He described apparitions that sounded like shadow creatures attempting to attack him before he managed to run away. Not long after we interviewed him, a dark mage tailed me in Bethnal Green. He used shadow manipulation to make his escape."

Evander's pulse spiked. "What?!" He scanned the Brute from head to toe. "Did he—?!"

Viggo shook his head. "I'm alright."

Evander's nails dug into his palms as he fisted his hands, his mind racing. "You believe dark mages are behind the thralls' disappearances too?"

"I'm convinced they are," Viggo said sourly. "The shadow creatures are proof of that. And for some reason, they are going after thralls with some sort of connection to the nobility. We've decided to set a trap for them."

Evander didn't like the sound of that one bit. "What kind of trap?"

"I requested Ginny's assistance in the matter. Solomon is going to pretend to be one of her employees."

Evander stared, confused.

"All the thralls who went missing disappeared at night in parts of London that are the exclusive remit of the nobility," Viggo explained. "Belgravia, Kensington, and Mayfair are among them. Solomon will visit the areas where the thralls are known to have vanished and act as bait."

Evander clenched his jaw. "Why didn't you tell me this last night?"

"It was only today that we confirmed Tom Simmons's resignation letter was likely forged, and Lord Fairfax informed us about the dead man and five more disappearances," Viggo retorted. "That's why I came to find you tonight."

Evander's temper flared. "You could have sent a note, Viggo."

"I was gathering evidence first," Viggo shot back. "I wanted to be certain before I brought it to your attention. And I wanted to do so in person."

Evander scowled. "That's rich coming from the man who just castigated me for not immediately sharing information about Leon!"

CHAPTER 22

VIGGO'S FACE DARKENED. "THAT'S DIFFERENT."

"Is it?" Evander crossed his arms. "You criticise me for not mentioning a former lover who arrived in London this morning, yet you've been investigating multiple disappearances for almost two days without a word to me."

"Perhaps I would have been more forthcoming if I'd been certain I would have your full attention," Viggo said, his voice dangerously low. "Or is your focus divided nowadays?"

Evander's magic flared with his anger, sending a chill across the room. "If you're suggesting I have any interest in rekindling things with Leon—"

"You seemed quite cozy at dinner." Viggo stepped closer, looming over him.

"Like I already told you, we were discussing the case!" Evander hissed, refusing to back away despite the intimidating wall of muscle before him. "Besides, I made it abundantly clear to him that I am already in a relationship."

Something shifted in Viggo's expression. "You did?"

"Yes, you stubborn ox!" Evander threw up his hands. "I explicitly told him I have a lover I am wholeheartedly committed to."

Viggo studied his face intently.

"I am not interested in Leon, Viggo," Evander continued, his voice softening. "What we had ended years ago and not amicably at that."

Viggo blinked. His face grew stormy. "Don't tell me that French bastard cheated on you?!"

Evander shook his head. "He didn't. In a way, it would have been better if he had. He just…wasn't there for me when I needed him most." He reached up and cradled Viggo's face between his palms, his thumbs tracing the sharp lines of his cheekbones. "My heart is spoken for, Viggo," he murmured. "Surely you know that by now."

Viggo's expression loosened marginally, his large hands coming to rest on Evander's waist. "I don't like the way he looks at you."

"That makes two of us," Evander admitted. "But Leon's feelings are irrelevant. What matters is that we have multiple disappearances that appear to be connected to dark magic, including two professors who were researching magical transference."

Viggo released a heavy breath. "You're right." His fingers tightened on Evander's waist. "But I still don't appreciate being kept in the dark."

"Nor do I," Evander countered. "We're supposed to

be partners in this, Viggo. Not just in bed, but in our work as well."

Viggo was silent for a long moment, his dark eyes searching Evander's face. He pulled Evander against his chest without warning and cradled the back of his head with one hand.

"I apologise," he said gruffly, the words muffled against Evander's hair. "I should have told you about the disappearances yesterday."

Evander melted into the Brute's solid embrace, the tension draining from his body. "And I should have mentioned Leon immediately." He pulled back slightly and looked up into Viggo's face, a soft smile curving his lips. "No more secrets between us, agreed?"

Viggo's eyes darkened. "Agreed."

He lowered his head and captured Evander's mouth in a kiss that started gentle but rapidly blazed into something fierce and possessive. Evander gasped against his lips, his body responding instantly to the familiar heat of Viggo's touch.

Viggo growled low in his throat, his hands sliding down to Evander's buttocks. He lifted him effortlessly against his chest. Evander wrapped his legs around Viggo's hips, his fingers tangling in the Brute's dark hair as the kiss deepened.

"Bed," Evander gasped when they broke apart for air, his manhood aching where it dug insistently into Viggo's belly. "Upstairs."

A wicked gleam entered Viggo's eyes. He shifted his grip and hoisted Evander over his shoulder like a conquering warrior with his spoils.

"Viggo!" Evander spluttered, half laughing, half outraged at the undignified position. "Put me down this instant!"

"I don't think so, your Grace," Viggo rumbled, his large hand firmly planted on Evander's backside as he exited the study and headed for the staircase. "I believe I'm about to demonstrate exactly how committed I am to our partnership."

Evander caught a glimpse of Hargrove's amused face as they passed through the foyer. The maid he'd been talking to gasped, let out a squeal, and blushed.

Evander groaned.

"Is—is his Lordship going to be alright, Mr. Hargrove?!" the maid whispered as Viggo took the stairs two at a time while carrying his burden with effortless strength.

"I'm sure he will be more than alright," the manservant drawled.

"I'm never going to live this down," Evander grumbled against Viggo's back.

The Brute chuckled. "I'm sure you'll survive." He squeezed the mage's backside, causing him to gasp.

By the time they reached Evander's bedchamber, the mage's mortified indignation had transformed into molten desire. Viggo kicked the door shut behind them and deposited Evander on the bed with surprising gentleness, his dark eyes smouldering as he loosened his cravat.

"Now," he said, his voice a low rumble that sent shivers down Evander's spine and made his cock twitch in anticipation, "I believe we have some unfinished business to attend to."

Evander lifted his chin in a challenging gesture as he began unfastening the buttons of his Viggo's waistcoat. "Indeed we do," he murmured. "Though I hope you don't intend to carry me like a sack of potatoes again."

Viggo's lips quirked in a smile that was pure sin as he shrugged out of his jacket. "I can think of far less dignified positions I'd like to see you in, your Grace."

Heat rushed to Evander's cheeks as he recalled all the salacious postures he'd adopted and been made to adopt during their love making, including riding the Brute like a wild horse and being bent over his desk and masterfully claimed from behind.

"Is that so?" he asked breathlessly.

"Indeed." Viggo reached into his pocket and withdrew an object before tossing it onto the bed beside Evander. "How about starting with this delightful gem?"

Evander's eyes widened when he recognised the enchanted Victorian toy he'd hidden in his bedside drawer. He looked up at Viggo, his mouth suddenly dry.

"I decided to see exactly what it was you were hiding from me yesterday," Viggo said, his voice rough with desire as he began unbuttoning his shirt. "Hargrove was kind enough to explain what this item does. I'd like to see you use it. On yourself. While I watch."

Evander swallowed hard, the illicit suggestion

bringing forth a barrage of torrid images that made all his nerve endings tingle and his hole contract on a rush of pure need.

"I can't believe you've had that in your pocket all evening!"

His pulse raced as Viggo's shirt fell open, revealing the powerful expanse of his hard chest and the dark ink decorating his skin.

"Have you used this toy since we began sleeping together?"

The question jolted Evander out of his lustful daze.

His hesitation was all the answer Viggo needed.

The Brute swore, crossed the floor, and carried one of the chairs by the window to the end of the bed. He settled into it, propped his elbows on his thighs, and steepled his hands under his chin.

"Now, your Grace. Why don't you strip and show me how you pleasure yourself with that toy?" Viggo commanded roughly. He arched an arrogant eyebrow.

Evander's heart slammed a maddening tempo against his ribs. He hesitated before reaching for the lapels of his jacket, his hands trembling.

CHAPTER 23

Viggo's blood roared in his ears as Evander began undressing with maddening slowness.

The mage's fingers shook slightly as he unfastened the buttons of his waistcoat, desire painting pink flags across his cheekbones. The silk rustled as he shrugged it off. The waistcoat was followed by his cravat and shirt. Moonlight filtered through the tall windows of the bedroom, bathing his skin in silver.

Viggo swallowed a curse at the sight of the love bites he'd left on Evander's body the last time they'd shared a bed. The marks were just beginning to fade.

"You're staring." A flush crept up Evander's neck.

"I did say I intended to watch you," Viggo countered, his voice husky with lust. "And why wouldn't I? You're magnificent."

Evander dropped his gaze shyly. The dichotomy that was the powerful and bewitchingly handsome Duke of Ravenwood, an Archmage as fearsome as he was an outstanding Special Arcane Investigator, blushing under Viggo's attention sent a rush of tenderness through him that only heightened his arousal.

He had not planned this particular scenario when he'd pocketed the enchanted sex toy earlier that evening. But discovering the Duke's secret had awakened something primitive in him. Something possessive and wholeheartedly carnal.

"Continue," Viggo instructed, struggling to remain composed. "Take off everything, your Grace."

Evander's chest shuddered as he rose to remove his trousers, every seductive move exposing his beautiful, toned flesh. Viggo's hands clenched on the armrests as more of the mage's body was revealed, including the delectably stiff manhood nestled amidst his dark curls and the shadowy space underneath his balls.

The Brute's cock strained painfully against his own trousers as Evander sat back on the bed, completely exposed.

"The oil is in the drawer." Viggo nodded towards the toy. "Now, show me how you use it when I'm not here."

The enchanted device gleamed in the low light, the crystal and brass phallus-shaped construction elegant despite its purpose, the magical enhancements it contained apparently making it more than a mere pleasure object.

Evander swallowed and retrieved the vial of oil before settling back against the pillows, his cock rising proudly against his quivering belly. Viggo's heart pounded as he uncorked the bottle, the musky scent filling the space between them. Evander coated his fingers generously and hesitated.

"Do you really want to watch this?" he asked, uncertainty flickering across his features.

"More than anything," Viggo confirmed, his voice barely above a whisper.

Evander licked his lips, his expression telling Viggo he liked his answer.

To the Brute's surprise, the mage started with his nipples first. He pinched and twisted and pulled the hard nubs until his manhood leaked and twitched uncontrollably, his breathing ragged and his eyes bright as he held Viggo's gaze. He worked his hands down his body and lavished his cock with attention next, his fingers working his flesh with achingly slow caresses that inflamed his nerve endings.

Evander's eyelids fluttered closed when he reached down between his spread legs. He bent his knees, giving Viggo an unobstructed view of his taint and hole.

Viggo's mouth went dry at the sight of the mage's slender fingers circling his twitching entrance.

Evander dropped his head back and moaned as he teased himself with feather-light touches, rubbing and circling the tight folds guarding his passage until they softened.

A soft gasp escaped his lips when he pressed one finger inside.

Viggo fought against the urge to join him on the bed immediately, to replace that elegant finger with his own cock. Instead, he remained seated, committing every detail to memory—the way Evander's chest rose and fell with his quickening breaths, the flush spreading across his skin, the way he bit his lip as he added a second finger.

"Is this how you pleasure yourself when you're alone?" Viggo could barely recognise his own voice. It was so guttural with need he was fairly certain he would soon embarrass himself.

Evander opened eyes that were dark with desire. "Sometimes," he admitted on a low moan, fingers working his entrance with slick motions that sent his hips dancing sensuously off the bed. "When I'm thinking of you."

The confession sent heat rushing through Viggo's veins. He watched as Evander worked himself open with practiced movements, his cock hard against his stomach, the moisture glistening at the tip oozing down his trembling shaft and pooling at the base.

Viggo swallowed convulsively and sat back in the chair. He spread his legs, reached down, and unfastened his trousers, his movements uncontrolled in his fevered state. He groaned when he finally freed his throbbing cock.

"The toy, your Grace," Viggo ordered gruffly as he started rubbing himself briskly. "Put in inside you. Now."

Evander licked his lips and dragged his gaze from Viggo's manhood, his mouth open with shallow pants and his pupils round with carnal passion. He reached for the enchanted device and coated it liberally with the love oil.

Viggo's breath caught as the mage positioned it against his entrance. The crystal at the base began glowing faintly when it touched Evander's skin.

"It responds to body heat." The mage hissed as he teased himself with the bulbous head of the device. "And desire."

He pushed the toy inside slowly, his back arching off the bed as it began filling him. Viggo's own arousal throbbed painfully in his grip as he watched Evander slowly take the full length of the device.

The mage groaned, belly contracting hungrily when the toy was fully seated inside him. He touched the base and cursed as the crystal pulsed brighter. The mechanical components within began to move, mimicking the thrusts of the male sex.

Evander cried out as the device impaled him over and over. He let go and fisted his hands in the sheets, the toy varying its enchanted rhythm, depth, and angle of penetration to match his needs as magic kept it inside his body.

Sweat beaded the mage's flushed face and his eyes grew glazed as he gave in to pleasure.

The sight of his lover coming undone before him was almost more than Viggo could bear. He gripped his leaking cock tightly, barely hanging on to his self-control.

"Tell me what it feels like," he commanded.

"It—it feels good!" Evander's breath stuttered as the toy's movements intensified. "It's thick and hard and hot. But it's not—" His eyes found Viggo's. "It's not you!" he confessed with a shudder.

Something inside Viggo snapped then. He rose from the chair and shed his remaining clothes with desperate movements. Evander's gaze raked over him hungrily and lingered on his erection.

"Take it out," Viggo growled.

Evander complied immediately, removing the toy with a trembling hand. The crystal dimmed as it lost contact with his skin. He set it aside, his chest heaving with rapid breaths and his body rosy with lust.

The mattress dipped beneath Viggo's weight as he joined him on the bed. He captured Evander's mouth in a bruising kiss, pouring all his jealousy, fear, and desire into the connection. Evander responded with equal fervour, his hands gripping Viggo's shoulders hard enough to leave marks.

"No more toys," Viggo murmured against Evander's lips. "No more Frenchmen. Just me."

"Just you," Evander agreed breathlessly.

Viggo's hands roamed over Evander's body, mapping every inch of him as if to claim his territory. He trailed hot kisses down Evander's neck and nipped at the sensitive spot where it met his shoulder. Evander arched beneath him, his hands tangling in Viggo's hair as he strained to get even closer.

"Please," Evander whispered, his voice breaking with need. "I want you inside me. Now, Viggo!"

Viggo reached for the oil and coated his trembling member generously. He positioned himself between Evander's thighs, the head of his cock pressing against his twitching entrance. He paused then, his gaze searching Evander's face in that carnal moment of possession.

"You are mine, Evander," the Brute growled as he pushed forward. "Never forget that!"

"Yes!" Evander cried out, his eyes dark pools of desire and his heels finding the small of Viggo's back as he hungrily welcomed the penetration.

Viggo entered Evander in one slow, relentless thrust that saw him seated to the hilt. They groaned as their bodies joined fully, the sensation overwhelming after the tension of the past two days.

Viggo held still and fought for control as Evander's body embraced him with exquisite heat.

"Move," Evander commanded, his voice raw.

Viggo obeyed, withdrawing almost completely before driving back in. He established a powerful rhythm, each thrust claiming Evander more thoroughly than the last. Evander's strong thighs squeezed his waist, urging him deeper. The mage clawed at Viggo's back and his gasps and moans grew louder as heat pulsed fiercely through their connection.

"I will never let you go," Viggo vowed, his words punctuated by the snap of his hips, the bed fairly groaning beneath them. "Never!"

Evander's response was lost in a cry of pleasure as Viggo changed the angle of his penetration, the head of his shaft striking the spot inside that made the mage see stars. The mage trembled on the edge of release, his cock throbbing where it was trapped between their bodies.

"Look at me," Viggo demanded. He slowed his pace to a torturous rhythm that made his lover sob out a moan. "I want to see your eyes when you come apart in my arms."

Evander's glazed gaze locked with his, his ice-blue eyes vulnerable and trusting in a way that made Viggo's chest tighten as he clung desperately to his back. He reached between them and wrapped his hand around Evander's quivering length, stroking him in time with his thrusts.

"Viggo!" Evander gasped and arched, his body tensing. "I'm—"

"Yes," Viggo encouraged, increasing the pace of his hips and his fingers. "Give yourself to me, Evander. All of you."

Evander shattered with a hoarse cry, his release spilling over Viggo's hand as his body clenched around him. The sight of Evander in the throes of pleasure, the feel of him pulsing and spasming fitfully around his cock, sent Viggo hurtling towards his own climax. He buried himself to the hilt with a final, deep thrust and claimed Evander from the inside with a guttural shout, his seed filling him to the brim.

It was a while before they both stopped moving. They remained locked together for a long moment, trembling in the aftermath of their devastating lovemaking. Viggo rested his forehead against Evander's, their breath mingling in the scant space between them, their torrid gazes locked onto each other.

Evander made a low sound when Viggo carefully

withdrew from his body. The Brute climbed off the bed and went into the bathroom. He returned with a pair of warm, damp towels and carefully cleaned Evander before wiping himself down. He lowered himself to the mage's side and gathered him against his chest.

A comfortable silence settled over them as their breathing gradually returned to normal. Viggo traced idle patterns on Evander's back, unwilling to break the fragile peace they'd found.

"Next time," Evander murmured, his voice drowsy with satisfaction, "I'd like to see you use that toy on me." He snuggled closer.

Viggo's eyebrows shot up in surprise. A chuckle rumbled in his chest as he pressed a kiss to Evander's temple.

"I would love to do that." He tightened his arms around the mage. "But for now, we both need to sleep."

Evander nodded, his eyes already closing. His breathing deepened within moments as sleep claimed him.

Viggo remained awake a while longer. He watched the rise and fall of Evander's chest and his captivating face until he finally drifted off, his heart brimming with a multitude of emotions for the man in his arms.

CHAPTER 24

IT WAS RAINING WHEN THEY ARRIVED AT SCOTLAND YARD the next morning.

Viggo had accompanied Evander in his official capacity as *Nightshade*'s representative and leader. They planned to talk to Winterbourne about the thralls who had quietly vanished from the city and make the case for the Brute's information guild and the Met to combine their efforts to find the culprits behind the disappeared magicless and the missing professors.

Tension knotted Evander's shoulders as they crossed the courtyard under his umbrella, his wind magic protecting them from the worst of the late autumnal shower. Time was now of the essence, especially with Viggo and *Nightshade* having already set a trap in motion that involved Solomon. He frowned.

There was also the matter of James Harker, the dead thrall whose autopsy had now become a matter of utmost priority.

Evander cast a sidelong glance at Viggo when they

entered the imposing edifice of the Met. He was impeccably dressed in a dark, tailored suit that complemented his powerful frame. To the mage's complete lack of surprise, the Brute's figure drew countless gazes as they crossed the busy foyer.

Although many had gotten used to seeing Viggo in the hallowed halls of the Met during the Renwick affair, the physical impact of his presence had not waned, especially after tales of his incredible feat in Charing Cross, witnessed by many a police officer, had gotten around.

Evander had convinced Viggo to wear the suit while they lay in bed two hours ago, still breathless from their passionate, morning lovemaking session.

"Winterbourne is a stickler for presentation," he'd told the Brute when the latter had protested. "Consider it armour for the battle to come."

Viggo had reluctantly acquiesced to his demand.

Despite the polished exterior the Brute presented as they navigated the corridors of Scotland Yard, there was no mistaking the tension radiating from him.

"It will be alright," Evander said quietly. He brushed his knuckles against the back of Viggo's hand. "I'll be by your side."

Viggo glanced at him, his face softening a little. "I know. Still, I hope he does not refuse my request."

"He won't." Evander glanced at the rain pounding the windows they passed and lowered his brows. "Not if he knows what's good for this city."

A low chuckle had him giving the Brute a startled look.

"I hope you don't intend to tell him to put it where the sun does not shine if we get into an argument." Viggo's dark eyes twinkled despite the gravity of the situation.

Evander flushed as he recalled saying exactly those words to Winterbourne a few weeks ago.

"I hardly think now is the time to be teasing me about that," he chided.

Viggo leaned closer. "On the contrary."

Evander shivered at the feel of the Brute's hot breath on his ear.

"I'm sure you will admit that I did, in fact, put it pretty magnificently where the sun does not—" Viggo whispered in an amused tone.

Evander stamped on his foot. "Will you please behave?!" he hissed, scowling.

"You two should stop flirting in public," someone said sharply behind them.

They stopped and turned.

Leon was coming down the passageway, his hair and his coat drenched. Judging from the faint circles under his eyes, he had not had a restful night.

"Look what the weather dragged in," Viggo said darkly.

Leon's jaw tightened as he ran his fingers through his wet locks.

Evander swallowed a sigh. He'd expected some tension between the two men today. He just hoped the situation didn't deteriorate like it had last night.

Leon ignored the Brute and addressed him.

"You ought to be more careful, mon cher duc. The walls have eyes and ears, even in this place."

"Why are you soaked to the bone?"

"I forgot to bring an umbrella," came the sullen reply.

"You could have used your wind magic to deflect the rain," Evander observed.

"I was distracted," Leon retorted. His gaze swung between Evander and Viggo, his expression piqued. "It appears you two kissed and made up."

Viggo drew himself to his full height.

Evander frowned at the Frenchman. "I don't see how that is any of your concern." He glimpsed Viggo's surprised glance.

A hurt look danced in Leon's eyes. He recovered his composure.

"We are to visit the Institute this morning," he said coldly. "Why is he here?"

Viggo's face darkened. "*He* has a name."

Evander pinched the bridge of his nose and prayed for patience. He was saved from the awkward situation by Rufus's and Shaw's arrivals.

"Good morning, your Grace. Leon." Rufus acknowledged Viggo with a friendly nod. "Viggo."

The veiled animosity he used to harbour for the Brute had dissipated after they'd attended several dinner parties together at Ginny's. The fact that Viggo knew Ophelia's secret and had sworn to protect it had also put him squarely in the inspector's good books.

"Whatcha doing here, Mr. Stonewall?" Shaw said cheerfully.

"I'm pretty sure I told you to call me Viggo, Miss Shaw," the Brute drawled.

Shaw rocked back on her heels and sucked air between her teeth. "It feels wrong to address a hero by his first name."

Leon curled a lip.

Viggo grimaced. "I think the citizens of London would be shocked if they heard you."

Rufus wrinkled his brow slightly, his gaze swinging from Leon to Evander and Viggo. "Are you here on business?" he asked the Brute.

"Yes."

Rufus tensed. "Do you bring news of the *Noctis Bloom* trade?"

"Not quite," Viggo murmured.

Evander glanced around. The corridor had gotten busier.

"Some new developments have come to light regarding our investigation," he explained guardedly. "We are on our way to talk to Commander Winterbourne about them. The three of you should come along."

Leon, Rufus, and Shaw exchanged a puzzled look.

Sergeant Griffiths, who was manning the Arcane Division reception, greeted Viggo with a respectful nod.

"It's good to see you, Mr. Stonewall."

"Likewise, Griffiths."

They took the stairs to the fifth floor and headed for Winterbourne's office. The men and women seated at their desks in the main administrative quarters cast curious glances at their group as they crossed the open floor space.

Winterbourne's secretary's eyes widened when he saw them.

Evander stopped in front of his desk. "Please inform Commander Winterbourne that we request an immediate meeting," he said briskly.

The secretary recovered his composure. "Yes, your Grace." He stood up and disappeared inside Winterbourne's office. He reappeared after a moment. "He will see you now."

Evander nodded curtly and knocked on the door.

Winterbourne rose from behind his desk when they entered. If he was surprised by their unexpected visit, he masked it well.

"Mr. Stonewall, it is good to see you again."

"Commander," Viggo replied with a courteous nod.

"It seems something serious has happened." Winterbourne indicated the chairs arranged before his desk. "Please, take a seat."

Leon took the chair farthest from Viggo, a sign Rufus seemed to note with a faint frown.

Evander knew the inspector would have questions for him later.

"Let's hear it," Winterbourne ordered once they were seated.

"Recent developments have led me to believe that the disappearances of Professor Whitley, his student James Thornfield, and Professor Chevalier are connected to something much larger." Evander gestured to Viggo. "Mr. Stonewall brings information that could be crucial to our investigation."

Winterbourne turned his sharp gaze on Viggo. "I'm listening."

A muscle jumped in the Brute's cheek as he spoke. "*Nightshade* has been tracking a disturbing pattern of disappearances among the thrall population. At least eighteen individuals have vanished from their places of employment over the past three weeks."

"Eighteen?" Rufus interjected, his eyes widening.

"Cor blimey!" Shaw mumbled.

Leon lowered his brows, his attention focused wholeheartedly on Viggo.

"Yesterday morning, the body of one such individual—James Harker, a thrall who worked for a bookbinder in Mayfair—was found in the Thames," Viggo continued. "We tracked down and interviewed one survivor two nights ago. A man who was nearly kidnapped under the same circumstances the other thralls went missing. He described monstrous apparitions that matched the description of the shadow creatures Duke Ravenwood and I fought in that warehouse where we faced Renwick."

His words hung heavily in the air.

Though Winterbourne's expression remained neutral, the way he tapped a finger against his desk relayed his irritation. "And why hasn't this been reported to the authorities?"

A shadow crossed Viggo's face. "It was. Multiple times, by multiple families. They were all dismissed."

An uncomfortable silence fell over the room. Rufus

fidgeted in his chair. Winterbourne's mouth tightened into a grim line.

"The thralls who disappeared all worked for nobles or in establishments frequented by the magical elite," Evander said quietly.

Shaw narrowed her eyes. "Just like the bookbinder in Mayfair."

Evander nodded.

Leon, who had been uncharacteristically silent, leaned forward. "And you believe these disappearances are connected to our missing professors?"

"I do," Evander confirmed.

Winterbourne frowned. "Why so?"

"Yesterday, we learned that Whitley and Chevalier were researching magical transference—specifically, the theoretical possibility of transferring magical abilities from one person to another."

Evander saw Leon stiffen out of the corner of his eye. The Frenchman was no doubt wary he would reveal the secret he had imparted to him the previous evening about Chevalier's work with *Les Prophètes Illuminés*.

Winterbourne's composure finally cracked, shock evident on his face. "Such a thing is impossible!"

CHAPTER 25

"It is not as implausible as it sounds," Evander countered. "We've already seen the device Renwick's master had Alastair Millbrook make to extract the life force of thralls. James Thornfield was writing a thesis on elemental transmutation theory, an essential component of magical transference. And we have established dark mages are involved in the disappearances that have taken place at the Institute and among the thrall population." He paused. "Although we do not yet know the details of how all these incidents are connected, there is no doubt in my mind that they are."

A stark hush befell them.

"I have to concur," Leon said reluctantly. "It is too much of a coincidence."

Rufus and Shaw nodded in agreement.

Something that looked like relief flitted across Viggo's face then. Evander resisted the urge to reach over and take his hand.

Winterbourne stood abruptly and strode to the window that overlooked the Thames. He stared out at the river for a long time, his back ramrod straight. He finally turned, his expression resolute.

"I want a full report on this James Harker. Expedite the necropsy and get me results by this evening." Winterbourne's gaze shifted to Viggo. "Mr. Stonewall, I'll need a complete list of the missing thralls, along with all the information *Nightshade* has gathered on their disappearances."

The tension in Viggo's shoulders eased. "You'll have it by lunchtime. I have a couple of requests of my own."

Winterbourne raised an eyebrow. "Go on."

"*Nightshade* is planning to set a trap to try and lure the ones behind the thralls' disappearances. We have already asked Lady Hartley for her assistance in the matter. I would be grateful if the Met could provide officers for this operation." The Brute paused. "We would also like one of your handwriting experts to examine the resignation notes many of the missing thralls supposedly submitted to their places of work. We believe they are forgeries."

"That shouldn't be a problem," Winterbourne said with a brisk nod. "I've already authorised full Arcane Division resources for this case. Duke Ravenwood and Inspector Grayson will see to it that we have men dispatched for the operation."

"Thank you, Commander," Viggo said solemnly.

Winterbourne hesitated. "Please be so kind as to offer my heartfelt apologies to the families of the missing," he said quietly. "I shall ensure that the officers involved are reprimanded for their actions."

Viggo blinked, his surprise evident. "I will convey your message."

Evander suppressed a smile.

Winterbourne frowned at him. "Are you planning to return to the Institute today?"

"Yes. I've requested for Mrs. Scarborough to examine Whitley's laboratory for any unexpected surprises in view of yesterday's incident."

Winterbourne bobbed his head. "Good." He stilled, his frown deepening. "Incidentally, how goes the project you entrusted to Mrs. Scarborough and Mr. McAndrew?"

A buzz of excitement shot through Evander. "I believe they might be able to complete the prototype in the next month."

"What prototype?" Viggo asked, his puzzled gaze swinging between them.

"I requested that Mrs. Scarborough and Elias McAndrew work on something that could disrupt the magic used to create shadow creatures," Evander told him. "We could all do with such a device, now more than ever."

Viggo's eyes flared. "Is that even possible?!"

"We won't know until we try," Evander said, resolute.

Viggo swallowed and nodded. He looked at Winterbourne. "I would like to accompany them to the Institute." He met Evander's startled stare. "As the representative of the missing thralls, I believe it is my duty to do so."

Evander hesitated before dipping his chin. Though they hadn't discussed the matter that morning, he could not find a reason to refuse the Brute's request.

Judging from Leon's frown and Rufus's uneasy expression, the two men harboured some reservations about this arrangement.

"Very well. I'll expect a full account by this evening." Winterbourne addressed Evander as they rose. "Ravenwood, a word in private before you leave?"

The others filed out, Leon casting a final glance at Evander that did not go unnoticed by Viggo. Winterbourne's formal demeanour relaxed slightly when the door closed behind them.

"Evander," he said, using his first name as he did only in private, "are you certain about involving Stonewall so deeply in this? The man has a complicated history with magical authorities."

Evander grasped the commander's unease on the matter.

"Viggo's network has already provided information we would never have obtained through official channels," he said quietly. "And his insight into the thrall community is invaluable." He paused, a faint smile curving his lips. "Less you forget, he was also the one who identified *Noctis Bloom* as the ingredient the dark mages were using in their rituals."

Winterbourne studied him, his expression unreadable. "There's more to your relationship with him than professional collaboration, isn't there?"

Surprise jolted Evander at the frank question. It was unlike Winterbourne to delve into his private life. A heavy feeling settled in his stomach as he met his commander's steady stare.

The fact that he and Viggo had a close association that went beyond their mutual interest in enacting justice for thralls was a secret he knew he could not keep forever. And neither did he wish to, despite London society's views on the subject of two men entering an amorous relationship. He was not ashamed of who he was and neither was Viggo.

It was a moment before he spoke.

"My personal affairs are my own concern, Commander."

Winterbourne's expression grew shuttered as he grasped the answer hidden in his words.

"Normally, I would agree. But these are not normal circumstances. If your judgment is compromised—"

"It isn't," Evander cut in. "And it never will be."

Winterbourne held his gaze for a long moment before sighing. "Very well. But tread carefully. This case has implications that reach far beyond Scotland Yard."

Queen Victoria's face swam in front of Evander's eyes.

"I'm well aware. And Reginald?"

"Yes?"

"Thank you for your concern. I know you mean well."

Winterbourne's expression softened.

Evander found Viggo and Rufus waiting in the

corridor outside the administrative offices, their postures tense.

"Did you send a message to *Nightshade?*" he asked the Brute.

Viggo nodded stiffly. "I've asked Solomon and Finn to put the information we gathered in a report for Winterbourne."

Evander frowned at his expression. He looked at Rufus. "Where are Leon and Shaw?"

"Shaw went to talk to Dr. Mortimer about James Harker's necropsy," Rufus replied awkwardly. "Leon said he wanted to get some fresh air." He glanced at Viggo.

Evander's heart sank. From the Brute's mutinous mien, it appeared words had been exchanged in his absence.

He looked out the window. The rain had abated.

"Let us leave," he said curtly. "The sooner we start investigating Whitley's lab, the better."

"Is everything alright?" Viggo asked in a low voice as they made their way back to the main entrance.

"Yes," Evander replied, though the lie tasted bitter on his tongue. "Just some administrative details."

"By the way," Rufus said to Viggo uneasily as they negotiated the stairs. "Did something happen between you and Leon that I'm unaware of? He seemed very hostile towards you just now."

Surprise flared across Viggo's face. He stared at Evander.

"He doesn't know?"

"No," Evander replied irritably. "I don't make it a

habit of shouting my past affairs from the rooftop of every building in London."

Confusion clouded Rufus's face for a moment. He stiffened when understanding finally dawned. "Oh." His expression fell. "*Oh...*"

"Yes," Viggo confirmed darkly. "And it seems that French bastard wants to rekindle their past relationship." He shot a guilty look at Evander. "Not that you have any intention of agreeing, of course. I completely trust you. You know that, right?"

Evander sighed. "How about we focus on the case?"

They were halfway across the foyer when Shaw appeared.

"I've spoken with Dr. Mortimer," she said breathlessly as she joined them, her usual brisk stride even more hurried than normal. "He's agreed to expedite the necropsy on James Harker personally, per your request."

"Good," Evander said. "Let's not waste any more time." He paused as a thought came to him. "By the way, did the forensic team find anything of note at Walter Whitley's home?"

"No, your Grace," Shaw said, chagrined. "Lady Whitley was most helpful, but there were no clues on the premises to aid our investigation."

The forensic mage fell into step beside Viggo as they departed Scotland Yard, an air of curiosity evident in her sidelong glances.

"Something on your mind, Miss Shaw?" Viggo asked eventually, his tone surprisingly patient.

"I sense some tension between you and the French

investigator," Shaw said innocently. "So, what's the beef between you two?"

Viggo blinked. Rufus groaned.

"How about you save your investigative spirit for Whitley's laboratory, Shaw?" Evander suggested coolly.

The forensic mage wrinkled her button nose, her eyes gleaming with undiminished curiosity. "But my investigative spirit senses a scandalous story, your Grace," she declared, unabashed. She grinned at Viggo. "And judging from Mr. Stonewall's expression, it's a humdinger."

"I didn't say anything," Viggo protested at Evander's frown.

Leon was waiting for them outside Scotland Yard, next to a police carriage.

The ride to the Royal Institute was swift, the tension between the Frenchman and Viggo eclipsed by that of their forthcoming task.

Evander could feel Viggo's discomfort intensify when they passed through the iron gates of the Institute. For a man who had spent his life avoiding the magical elite, entering this bastion of arcane privilege must have been like walking into the lion's den.

The courtyard was strangely quiet. To Evander's relief, they did not cross paths with any meddlesome faculty members on their way to the south wing.

Fitch and Bartley stood to attention outside Whitley's lab. They greeted Evander with a salute, their gazes settling on Viggo with undisguised curiosity.

Fitch's eyes widened with recognition. "Oh." He

recovered his composure. "It's a pleasure to meet you, sir." He bobbed his head courteously.

Viggo appeared surprised for a moment. "I appreciate the sentiment, Constable, but I am hardly a noble," he grunted.

"You are a hero of the people, sir," Fitch stated quietly. "And I believe in giving credit where it is due, regardless of status."

Evander couldn't hide his astonishment. This was the most he'd ever heard Fitch articulate to anyone about his personal opinions.

Shaw beamed at Viggo. "See? I told you so."

Bartley elbowed Fitch sharply in the ribs. "*Psst*," he hissed. "Who is this bloke?!"

"It's your favourite thrall."

Bartley stared.

Fitch made a face. "Viggo Stonewall? The Ironfist Brute?"

Bartley blinked. His eyes bulged and his mouth rounded on a gasp. He stared at Viggo, starstruck.

"Is it true you can bend steel with your bare hands, sir?!" he blurted.

Shaw snickered. Leon looked on disapprovingly. Rufus muttered something under his breath.

Viggo scratched his cheek awkwardly, not quite sure what to make of the constable's enraptured gaze. "Yes."

Bartley reached inside his jacket and jerkily removed a notebook and a magic quill. He shoved them in Viggo's face. "Could I please bother you for an autograph, sir?!"

"For the love of God, Bartley," Rufus groaned.

Bartley pretended not to hear the inspector. "It will be our family's pride, sir," he pleaded.

Viggo hesitated before reluctantly taking the notebook.

Leon's expression went from disapproving to plain disgusted.

"Mrs. Scarborough is already inside," Fitch reported to Evander while the Brute gingerly signed the paper. "There have been no disturbances since we started our watch yesterday."

CHAPTER 26

Philippa Scarborough's tall figure was silhouetted against the morning light streaming through the windows of Whitley's lab. She turned as they entered, her golden eyes taking in Viggo and Leon with a single, assessing glance from behind her wire-rimmed spectacles.

"Your Grace." She greeted Evander with a slight inclination of her head before addressing Viggo. "Mr. Stonewall. It's been a while since our last meeting."

"Indeed it has," Viggo said with the faintest of smiles and a nod. "Thank you for everything you did for Magnus."

Mrs. Scarborough smiled back. "I was just doing my job."

Evander introduced Leon.

The curse-breaker acknowledged the Frenchman's "Enchanté" with a polite nod before gesturing towards the bookcase that had triggered the shadow creatures' attack the day before.

"Shall we get to work? I've been examining the residual magic you two left behind and I believe I've identified the secondary ward protecting whatever lies behind this bookcase."

Surprise jolted Evander. "Secondary ward?" He exchanged a glance with an equally astonished Leon. "We believed this was a nested ward with a shadow trap."

"Indeed it is," Mrs. Scarborough confirmed. "From Inspector Grayson's report, Mr. Beaulieu's *Nullification Magic* removed those, but there remains a subtle layer of magic beneath—a secondary trigger ward that activates only when the outer protections are fully breached."

Viggo stared, puzzled. "*Nullification Magic?*"

Evander hesitated. "Leon possesses a rare type of magic that can undo almost all other magic and spells. It's what saved us from danger yesterday."

Viggo frowned at the Frenchman's mildly smug look.

Evander studied the bookcase thoughtfully. "Whitley must have been incredibly paranoid to install such a trap. It must hide something important."

"Can you disable the trigger ward?" Leon asked Mrs. Scarborough.

"Of course." She extracted a small vial of silvery liquid from one of the many pouches at her belt. "This is a neutralising agent I designed specifically to counteract trigger wards."

The curse-breaker approached the bookcase, her

golden eyes narrowed in concentration as she traced the edges with her hand. She paused after a moment, fingers hovering over a small, almost invisible rune carved into the bottom-right corner of the frame.

"There."

Evander squatted beside her and clenched his jaw as he stared at the magic symbol. "I completely missed that yesterday."

"You're not the only one, mon cher," Leon grunted.

Mrs. Scarborough applied a single drop of the silvery liquid to the rune. It sizzled briefly upon contact and emitted a faint purple glow before fading to nothing.

"The ward is neutralised." She straightened. "Now for the concealment charm itself."

She placed her palm flat against the centre of the bookcase and murmured a spell Evander didn't recognise, her pupils and fingertips glowing with the purple light of her magic. For a moment, nothing happened.

Shaw gasped when the bookcase vanished, revealing a dark opening in the wall behind it.

"Bloody hell!" Viggo mumbled.

"Where did the bookcase go?" Rufus asked, his eyes wide.

"It's still here, in a manner of speaking," Mrs. Scarborough explained. "It will return when summoned with the proper counter-charm."

Viggo stepped forward and peered into the darkness beyond the opening. "There's a passage."

Evander's pulse quickened as he joined him. He removed the folding cane strapped to his forearm and twisted the small crystal at the top. A soft white light emitted from it as the magic it contained activated: it illuminated a short, narrow, rough-hewn corridor that ended at a landing and a staircase that spiralled beneath the building.

He led the way inside, the crystal's light casting their elongated shadows on the bare stone walls. Viggo followed close behind with Leon and Rufus while Shaw and Mrs. Scarborough brought up the rear.

The air grew cooler as they descended the stone steps. It carried with it the faint scent of mould, old parchment, and something metallic Evander couldn't quite identify.

The staircase dropped some twenty feet before opening abruptly into a tenebrous, circular room. Evander's heart raced as he stopped in the middle of it and raised his cane. Shaw spotted a pair of magic lanterns on the walls and activated them.

The shadows retreated as light illuminated the thirty-foot-wide chamber.

"Mon dieu," Leon murmured.

Unlike the meticulously ordered laboratory they had just left, this space was chaotic. The walls were covered with diagrams and notes, the arcane symbols scrawled across them almost glowing in the gloom. The worktables were cluttered with more paperwork, instruments, and half-assembled devices, while the shelves on the walls were full of research journals and glass containers holding swirling, luminescent substances. A filing cabinet stood next to a bookcase crammed with arcane tomes.

"What in the name of all that's holy?" Rufus whispered, his usual brisk demeanour momentarily abandoned in the face of their discovery.

Shaw shivered. "This place gives me the willies."

Evander moved towards the closest table, his scalp prickling with dread. "It seems Whitley was working on something he didn't want the Institute to know about."

Leon picked a couple of research journals from a shelf while Viggo crossed the floor to a wall where a series of anatomical diagrams had been pinned. His expression darkened as he examined them.

"What is this?"

Evander joined him. He frowned as he studied the drawings.

There were a dozen of them, all depicting the human brain structure.

"It looks like he was studying neurology for some reason," he murmured, puzzled.

"Not just neurology." Leon approached, his expression grim. He indicated the journals he was holding. "These contain information about thralls specifically." His voice had grown tight with barely suppressed anger. "It seems someone, or rather a group of people, performed detailed examinations of their brain structure. Dozens of them, in fact. This wasn't Whitley's doing, Evander." A muscle jumped in the Frenchman's jawline as he glanced at the shelves. "Half these journals belong to Professor Chevalier. If I'm correct, this stems from his research when he was part of *Les Prophètes Illuminés.*"

Horror drenched Evander in a cold sweat. He glanced at Viggo.

The Brute had gone as still as stone.

"*Les Prophètes Illuminés?*" Rufus repeated.

Leon hesitated before explaining briefly about the disbanded research group Chevalier used to belong to. "Please keep what I've revealed to you in the strictest confidence," he finished stiffly. "If this secret gets out, it could damage diplomatic relations between our two countries."

Shaw and Mrs. Scarborough exchanged a troubled look.

Viggo spoke in the fraught silence.

"Does that mean they killed thralls so they could study their brains?" His voice was devoid of emotion.

Evander's throat tightened painfully at the silent rage radiating off him.

To Leon's credit, he did not look away from the Brute's hot gaze. "I do not know for certain. Vivisection is not legal in the Empire or the Continent. There is a strong possibility Chevalier and his colleagues studied the brains of thralls who died from natural causes."

Viggo didn't respond for a moment.

"I hope you're right," he finally ground out. "Because if I and other thralls find out they cut the skulls of living people, there will be a reckoning like none the world of magic has seen before!"

His threat hung heavily in the air, a stark reminder

of the divide that still existed between them. It took all of Evander's willpower not to reach out and comfort his lover.

"Your Grace." Mrs. Scarborough approached, her golden eyes narrowed behind her spectacles as she read the paperwork she'd picked from a table. "It wasn't just thralls." She showed them another set of diagrams. "They were studying the brains of mages as well. Specifically, those with rare or powerful abilities."

Evander's blood ran cold as he stared at the drawings. He met Leon's troubled stare.

"It seems Cecillia and Headmaster Rigley were wrong about Whitley's intentions, after all," Rufus said, scowling.

Evander wasn't so sure. Whitley's behaviour before his disappearance had not been that of a man hiding his unethical research, but rather someone who was being targeted.

"There's a good chance Whitley is innocent of any wrongdoing," he said thoughtfully. "I think he stumbled upon something he shouldn't have heard or seen."

"I agree, your Grace." Shaw hurried over from the filing cabinet, the drawer she'd been rifling through half open. "I found this at the bottom." She handed him a sheet of paper.

Evander took it off her, the others gathering around him.

It was a letter addressed to Whitley, from Chevalier.

Mon cher ami, I fear I have been blinded by academic curiosity. The implications of what our sponsor is suggesting go far beyond theoretical exploration, like you suspected. I already carry a wealth of guilt for the actions of my past, foolish self. I agree with you. We cannot, in good conscience, continue down this path. We should gather the evidence of this research to show to the authorities and put a stop to this madman's plans.

The letter was dated a month ago.

"Mon dieu," Leon murmured, his face pale. "Just what kind of trouble did they get themselves into?!"

Evander's heart slammed against his ribs as he reread the letter.

"Your Grace, could this be the announcement Whitley intended to make at the faculty dinner he failed to attend?" Shaw said sharply. "The one Cecillia mentioned?"

Evander clenched his jaw. "I believe you may be right. It would explain why he seemed scared out of his mind." He looked around the chamber. "And it would account for this room."

Rufus's eyes widened. He looked around. "This is where he was gathering his evidence!"

Evander nodded grimly. "And Chevalier's by the looks of it. It's clear Whitley didn't trust his colleagues, hence why he chose to hide it down here, far from prying eyes."

"Does that mean he suspected someone in the Institute of being a mole for this sponsor?" Viggo said. He frowned at their stares. "What?"

"By jove, he's right!" Rufus mumbled.

Evander silently cursed himself for not having arrived at the same conclusion sooner. "That would explain many things."

The implications of their findings hung heavy in the air between them.

Evander came to a decision. "Shaw, get a team from the AFD to examine this room and gather all the evidence here. We should take everything to Scotland Yard posthaste. But discreetly, mind. We don't want to alert whoever may be watching our movements."

Shaw nodded.

They were about to leave the chamber when Mrs. Scarborough paused, her head tilted to one side as if listening to something the others couldn't hear. She moved towards a section of wall that appeared unremarkable, one hand outstretched before her.

Evander stiffened, his foot on the bottom step. "What is it?"

"There's something else here," she murmured, her fingers tracing invisible patterns on the stone. "Another concealment charm."

They regrouped around her.

"Can you undo it?" Evander asked tensely.

Mrs. Scarborough frowned. "I can. But he'll do it faster." She looked pointedly at Leon.

Leon's face tightened. He nodded.

They moved back and gave the Frenchman room to work.

A wary expression clouded Viggo's face as Leon's magic charged the air with static. The charm shimmered into view.

"Fascinating," Mrs. Scarborough murmured, her eyes gleaming behind her glasses.

"It won't be if a bunch of shadow creatures come

out after he's finished," Shaw said tartly. She shrugged at Evander and Rufus's frowns. "What? It's the truth."

Evander's pulse quickened when Leon nullified the charm.

They waited expectantly.

Nothing happened.

The Frenchman furrowed his brow and ran his hands over the stonework. "There must be some kind of hidden mechanism we need to engage."

"Here, let me try something," Viggo said.

He waited until Leon moved away, drew his arm back, and punched the wall with his fist. Stone crumbled under his knuckles, revealing a small compartment hidden inside the wall.

Evander groaned while Leon drew a horrified breath.

"What if you destroyed what was inside there?!" the Frenchman barked, incensed.

"I'm sure there are some clever people in this city who could fix it," the Brute replied with no sign of compunction.

Something glinted inside the dark cavity.

Evander approached and moved the crystal on his cane close to the opening.

There was some kind of device inside the compartment.

"Be careful," Viggo warned as Evander reached for it.

His fingers closed on something cold and hard.

The metallic scent he'd detected when he was coming down the stairs filled his nostrils as he removed the object. It was a central glass cylinder connected to smaller vials through intricate copper tubing, all mounted on a brass base etched with runes he didn't recognise. It fit in the palm of his hand.

Though it bore no resemblance to the *Blood Siphon*, the device made the hairs rise on Evander's nape.

CHAPTER 27

IT WAS EARLY AFTERNOON WHEN THEY RETURNED TO
Scotland Yard.

Evander's mind was still reeling from their
discoveries at the Royal Institute as they navigated the
corridors of the Arcane Division. The device they'd
found hidden in Whitley's secret chamber was now
safely stowed in a warded container Shaw carried in
her tool bag. The forensic mage had gone ahead to
deliver the item to Elias McAndrew, the AFD's chief
artificer.

A message was waiting for him and Rufus when
they reached the reception.

Dr. Mortimer had sent word that he wished to see
them as soon as they returned.

Evander led their small procession of four through
the familiar maze of hallways, Viggo's shoulder
occasionally brushing against his where he walked
beside him.

"Should he really be tagging along?" Leon said where he trailed behind with Rufus.

The Frenchman had been unusually quiet since they'd departed the Institute. Evander suspected their findings had rattled him, especially since it appeared the French Ministry of Arcane Affairs may have committed inhuman crimes towards thralls in the name of scientific research.

"Winterbourne gave his permission," Evander shot over his shoulder.

He glanced at Viggo. The Brute's face was set in forbidding lines, his expression increasingly troubled since they'd left the Institute.

"Are you alright?" Evander asked quietly.

Viggo's dark eyes met his. "I can't stop thinking about those diagrams of thrall brains," he admitted in a low voice. "If this group—these *Prophètes Illuminés* Leon mentioned—were involved in such unethical experiments..." He lapsed into silence, a muscle jumping in his cheek.

"We don't know that for certain," Evander countered softly.

A ghost of a smile crossed Viggo's face. "Ever the optimist."

"Someone has to be," Evander replied with a sad smile.

The Arcane Forensics Division maintained their morgue and necropsy rooms on the third floor of the west wing. A distinctive chill permeated the corridor they entered, ice magic being in use to preserve the bodies being kept there.

The main examination room was located at the end of the long hallway. Dr. Ambrose Mortimer greeted them with his usual macabre cheerfulness when they entered.

"Ah, your Grace! Inspector Grayson." The tall, gaunt physical examiner offered them a ghastly smile from where he was cleaning his equipment at a metal sink. "And company, I see." He studied Viggo and Leon with undisguised curiosity.

"This is Viggo Stonewall of *Nightshade* and Leon Beaulieu, Special Arcane Investigator from Paris," Evander introduced briskly. "They're consulting on our case."

Viggo gave a stiff nod while Leon inclined his head politely.

"The famous Ironfist Brute and a French Arcane Investigator in my humble domain?" Mortimer's eyes glittered as he washed and dried his hands. "What an honour."

"Have you completed the necropsy on James Harker?" Evander prompted, directing his attention to the sheeted form on the table.

"Indeed, your Grace." Mortimer's expression sobered as he joined them. "I must say, the findings are most unusual."

He pulled back the sheet with practiced efficiency, revealing the body of a young man. James Harker appeared to be in his early twenties, with unkempt brown hair and the lean frame common among London's working class. His skin had taken on the waxy pallor of death.

"At first glance, death by drowning seemed the obvious conclusion," Mortimer began, gesturing to the body. "The usual signs were present—lungs filled with water, foam in the airways, and so forth. However, upon closer examination, I discovered something quite extraordinary."

The pathologist lifted one of Harker's eyelids, revealing an iris shot through with faint silvery lines that seemed to glow weakly in the lamplight.

"What in God's name?" Rufus murmured. He leaned closer, a handkerchief pressed to his mouth and nose.

"Precisely my reaction, Inspector." Mortimer moved to a nearby bench and retrieved a small glass vial containing a viscous silvery liquid. "I found traces of this substance throughout his body. It was particularly concentrated in his brain and nervous system."

Viggo stiffened. "What is that?!"

"I'm still trying to determine its nature and I will need to have Mr. Brown confirm it, but I suspect what we're looking at is the breakdown product of magic." Mortimer met Evander's gaze steadily. "Though it looks different from the black substance we found in Alastair Millbrook's body, the way it formed may follow the same scientific principles."

Shock reverberated through Evander. Rufus gasped.

Leon stepped forward, his expression strained. "May I?" He gestured to the vial.

Mortimer handed it to him.

The Frenchman held it up to the light, his grey eyes narrowed in concentration.

"I've seen mention of this before," Leon said after a

moment, his voice tight. "It was described in detail in the research archives of *Les Prophètes Illuminés.* They called it 'arcane residue.'"

Evander didn't like the sound of that one bit. "What's its significance?"

Leon met his gaze, his own deeply perturbed. "It's the physical remnants of magical energy that has passed through a vessel not designed to contain it."

A chill ran down Evander's spine. He glanced at the dead thrall on the table, his heart drumming a heavy beat against his ribs.

"Are you suggesting that someone attempted to channel magic through this man?!"

"That would be consistent with my findings," Mortimer observed thoughtfully. He moved to the next table, where he'd laid out Harker's internal organs. He gestured for them to look closer at the dead man's brain. "Note these lesions on the brain stem. It's as though magical energy literally burned pathways through his nervous system."

"Like lightning through a conductor that cannot support the current," Leon murmured.

Dread tightened Evander's chest. In what way any of this was connected to magical transference, he could not yet tell. But he couldn't help but feel the Frenchman was close to the truth.

Viggo's expression darkened. "So you're saying they're using thralls as magic conduits?" His words fell like stones in the silent room.

"It appears that way," Evander said grimly. "The question is, conduits for what purpose?"

"Not that it's any consolation, but this may go some way towards explaining why all those thralls went missing," Rufus contributed tensely.

Mortimer hesitated. "Though there are no marks on his body to suggest foul play, Mr. Harker may not have been in a fit state to save himself when he entered the water, hence the signs of drowning."

A fraught hush descended upon the room, the implications of the physical examiner's conclusion hanging heavy in the air.

The dread dulling Viggo's eyes echoed Evander's fears and made his insides twist all over again. Evander clenched his jaw.

How many more thralls would they pull out of the river before they stopped whoever was behind this?

"Dr. Mortimer, would you compile your findings in a full report for Commander Winterbourne?" he requested, keeping his tone level despite his churning stomach. "Include everything, no matter how impossible it might seem."

"Of course, your Grace," Mortimer replied with a slight bow. "I've already begun. It should be on his desk by this evening."

They had just left the morgue when they were met with a breathless alchemist.

"Your Grace! Thank heavens you're here!" She glanced nervously at Evander's companions. "Mr. Brown requests your urgent presence in our lab."

Evander exchanged a tense look with the others. They followed the alchemist swiftly to the AFD's Alchemical Analysts' lab.

Vincent Brown was bent over his workbench. The alchemist's expression brimmed with barely contained excitement when he looked up at their approach.

"Ah, your Grace." He beamed at the sight of Viggo. "Mr. Stonewall, a pleasure to see you again."

Viggo greeted the alchemist with a faint smile.

Evander briefly introduced Leon.

Brown stared curiously as he greeted the Frenchman.

"I've completed my analysis of those glass fragments Miss Shaw recovered from the Institute." The alchemist indicated what he'd been working on.

The tray on the bench contained the shards of glass Shaw had collected, now meticulously arranged to show their original form—a small, round bottle.

Evander's pulse accelerated. "What did you find?"

"It was a most fascinating concoction." Brown picked up a vial containing a pale purple liquid from a rack of tubes. "I can understand why you and Miss Shaw originally thought it might be *Noctis Bloom* from the colour, but it was far from it. The residue contained in these fragments is a highly sophisticated transfiguration potion."

"Transfiguration?" Rufus repeated with a frown.

"You mean like shape-shifting?" Leon said sharply.

Brown nodded. "Precisely. This particular formula is designed to alter the physical appearance of the imbiber—changing hair colour, facial features, even height to a limited degree."

Evander gave the alchemist a puzzled look. "Why not just use an Illusion Amulet?"

"This potion has a long half-life," Brown explained. "It offers more protection to someone who wishes to disguise themselves for an extended period of time. An amulet might fall off or get accidentally discarded."

Evander rubbed his jaw thoughtfully. "This vial was discovered the night James Thornfield went missing."

"Could he have used the potion to escape the people who were after him?" Rufus suggested.

Leon lowered his brows. "That would be a clever way to fool his pursuers. The first-year student I spoke to did mention seeing two women fleeing across the quadrangle that night."

"Which means he probably had someone helping him," Evander concluded in a hard voice.

There was a good chance James Thornfield had gone into hiding instead of being kidnapped by whoever had gone after Whitley and Chevalier. They had to find him before their enemy did.

They thanked Brown and departed the lab.

Evander shot a frown at Rufus. "It's about time we paid a visit to Lady Whitley."

The inspector nodded.

"I'm afraid I shall have to pass," Leon said, chagrined. "I have a report to write for my superiors in Paris."

"And I need to return to the guild and help set up the bait plan for those dark mages," Viggo admitted reluctantly.

Evander hesitated when they reached the reception. "Will I see you later?" he asked quietly.

Viggo's soft smile set his heart aflutter. "We're

laying the trap involving Solomon tonight. It will be late, but I'll make sure to come to you after."

CHAPTER 28

Rain drummed against the police carriage windows as Evander and Rufus made their way through Kensington's tree-lined streets. Evander gazed blindly at the elegant houses they passed, lost in contemplation.

"Do you believe Lady Whitley knows more than she's letting on?" Rufus asked, breaking the silence. "Shaw did interview her briefly the morning she came to report her husband's disappearance."

"That's what we're here to determine," Evander replied as the carriage slowed before a handsome brick residence set back from the road. "This visit is well overdue."

They alighted under the shelter of their umbrellas and made their way up the gravel path to the front door. The sombre-faced housekeeper who admitted them into the house led them to a well-appointed drawing room where Elizabeth Whitley awaited.

She was a slender woman in her mid-forties, her

intelligent face composed despite the strain evident in the shadows beneath her eyes. She wore a dark green dress that spoke of restrained elegance and wore her golden hair neatly coiled at the nape of her neck.

"Your Grace." She rose and greeted Evander with a formal curtsy. "Inspector Grayson." She addressed her housekeeper. "Betty, some tea, please."

"Yes, my Lady." The housekeeper left.

"Thank you for agreeing to see us on such short notice, Lady Whitley," Evander said as he and Rufus took the seats she offered.

"It is I who must thank you for coming in person." A trace of bitterness underscored her voice. "I would rather this than the incessant barrage of visitors from the Institute."

Evander exchanged a surprised glance with Rufus.

"You've had unwanted guests from the Institute?"

"Yes. Some of Walter's colleagues have been to the house." Lady Whitley's expression grew pinched. "Most came to enquire about my welfare, but a few persisted in suggesting Walter had simply gone on an unannounced research trip. As if he would ever behave so irresponsibly after twenty years of marriage."

Rufus removed a small notebook from his coat pocket. "When did you last see your husband, Mrs. Whitley?"

"Four days before I reported him missing."

The housekeeper returned with their drinks. Lady Whitley waited until she'd served them and left before continuing.

"Walter came home late the previous night. He was

in a state of considerable agitation. He spent the entire evening in his study with the door locked." Delicate lines marked Lady Whitley's brow. "I could hear him moving about and there was a distinct smell of burning paper."

Evander exchanged a significant glance with Rufus. "Did he explain what was troubling him?"

Lady Whitley's fingers whitened on her cup. "He told me his research had taken an unexpected turn and that certain parties might be interested in applying his findings in ways he could not condone."

Her words chilled Evander as much as they did Rufus.

Lady Whitley's testimony confirmed what Chevalier had written in his letter to Professor Whitley.

"Did he mention who these parties might be?" Evander pressed quietly.

"No." She hesitated. "But he did tell me that he and the French professor he was working with had made a disturbing discovery regarding their research sponsor."

"Did he name this sponsor?" Rufus asked tensely, his magic quill poised over his notebook.

Lady Whitley shook her head. "Walter was always discreet about such matters. But I gathered it was someone of considerable influence. Possibly someone outside the Institute."

Renwick's mysterious master immediately came to Evander's mind. Though there was no definite proof of any connection between the eponymous *I* and their current case, the probability was high that there was.

Evander leaned forward. "Mrs. Whitley, did your husband ever discuss his work with you?"

Her expression clouded over. "Not in detail. He had become increasingly secretive in recent weeks. When I asked him about it, he said it was safer for me not to know the particulars." Lady Whitley's composure briefly cracked, revealing the fear beneath. "The morning he left, he embraced me as though"—she stopped and swallowed—"as though he might never return."

Evander maintained a diplomatic silence while their host regained her poise.

"Is there any news of Walter?" Lady Whitley asked in a low voice, her eyes gleaming with hope.

"Not yet, but I believe we are getting close to finding out what happened to him," Evander replied. "Can we take a look at his study?"

Lady Whitley blinked. "Of course."

She led them through the house to Whitley's office. Unlike the messy rooms at the Institute and the chaotic chamber hidden under Whitley's lab, the study was tidy and well organised.

"The forensic mages Officer Shaw sent have already been over this room," Lady Whitley said uncertainly, hovering near the doorway.

"We know." Evander flashed her a reassuring smile. "Still, it doesn't hurt to take a second look."

He released a faint pulse of magic as he crossed the room and didn't pick up on anything unusual. He made his way to the fireplace while Rufus moved to examine Whitley's desk.

The grate was clean.

Evander frowned. "Did your servants clean this?"

"Yes." Lady Whitley clasped her hands tightly. "To be honest, he doesn't normally like anyone in here unless he's present on the premises. But I asked our servants to tidy things up the morning I last saw him. Should I not have?" Guilt darkened her eyes.

"There was no way you could have known what would come to pass," Evander said gently. He frowned at the fireplace. "Besides, if all that was left was ash, then it would not have been helpful to our investigation."

"Oh."

Evander looked over at Lady Whitley.

She had gone pale and was pressing a hand to her mouth.

Evander tensed. "What is it?"

"There was something that fell beneath the grate," she mumbled. "A scrap of paper. I completely forgot about it with everything that's happened!"

Evander rose stiffly, his pulse racing. "Do you still have it?"

"Yes," Lady Whitley nodded shakily. "I shall go and fetch it." She disappeared and returned a moment later with a small folded piece of paper that looked to have been torn out of a journal.

Rufus joined Evander as he took the paper and carefully unfolded it.

Though the outside was marked with smoke and stained with ash, the inside was relatively unscathed.

Written in a cramped hand was an address on Flower and Dean Street.

Evander lowered his brows. It was a lodging house in one of the poorest areas of Whitechapel.

"I'm so sorry," Lady Whitley said in a voice full of regret. "I wasn't sure whether my husband meant to discard it, so I kept it. I was going to ask Walter about it when I next saw him." She bit her lip. "Do you think it important?"

Evander folded the paper and tucked it inside his coat. "I'm not sure yet. But we will investigate it." He gave Lady Whitley a kind smile. "Thank you for your cooperation. We'll do everything in our power to find your husband."

Lady Whitley's expression grew mournful. "It's the least I can do. I pray Walter comes home safe and sound."

They left the professor's residence under a downpour and hurried over to the carriage.

"Stepney please," Evander instructed the constable in the box seat curtly.

Rufus gave him a surprised look as they climbed inside. "Where are we going?"

"To see Viggo," Evander replied grimly.

CHAPTER 29

VIGGO OBSERVED THE CRUMBLING TENEMENT FROM HIS position in the shadows of an abandoned tannery. The stench of chemicals and rotting hides lingered in the air around them.

Dusk was settling over Whitechapel, the fading light casting long shadows across cobblestones slick with the day's earlier rainfall. The glow of gas lamps flickered to life in windows, illuminating the squalor of the East End in a sickly yellow haze.

"Are you certain this is the correct address?" Rufus said uneasily.

"Yes." Viggo shot a look at the inspector and hid a dry smile at his obvious discomfort. "I know this place like the back of my own hand."

Evander stood still beside him, his ice-blue gaze focused on the lodging house's entrances.

No one had been more surprised than Viggo when the pair of them had walked into *Nightshade* that afternoon and requested to see him. He'd been in the middle of coordinating the team that would discreetly guard Solomon on tonight's mission.

Much to Finn and Solomon's amusement, Rufus had stood out like a sore thumb in the middle of the guild's main office while Evander explained the reason for their presence.

A figure appeared presently at the building's main entrance. Hawk waited until a cart trundled noisily by before casually crossing the road and strolling into an alley one building over from the tannery.

He joined them in the shadows a moment later.

"There's a room on the third floor, at the rear," he reported quietly. "Two women took lodgings there two nights ago. They've barely left since and they've paid extra for their meals to be delivered to their door. One appears younger, perhaps twenty or so, with auburn hair. Her companion is older, plainer, and carries herself like a servant. The landlady told me they paid for a month in advance with silver coins."

Evander exchanged a startled look with Rufus.

"The timing coincides with James Thornfield's disappearance."

"And silver coins aren't normally common in these parts," Viggo murmured. "Thanks, Hawk. You can return to the guild and continue with tonight's operation. We'll take it from here."

Hawk nodded and disappeared as silently as he'd appeared.

Viggo stretched out the kinks in his neck. He was more at ease here, in the familiar territory of the East End, than he'd been during their visit to the Royal

Institute. This was his domain, not the pristine streets of London's wealthier districts.

Though Evander's expression remained controlled, Viggo had learned to read the subtle signs of excitement in the set of his shoulders and the slight narrowing of his ice-blue eyes.

The mage could smell prey and he was keen for them to get on with their hunt.

"What's our approach?"

"Direct confrontation would be unwise," Viggo advised. "The building has multiple exits, including two through the back alley. If one of those women is indeed Thornfield and he panics, we could lose him in the maze of the rookery."

"We should contain the situation, then," Evander said with a frown. "Rufus and I can approach from the front, while you secure the rear exit. If Thornfield attempts to flee, you'll be waiting."

Viggo nodded. It was a solid plan and it played to their respective strengths. "There should be a window in their room that overlooks the back alley. If they try to escape that way, they'll need to drop nearly twenty feet. Not impossible, but difficult for someone unused to such manoeuvres."

"Very well," Evander said with a brisk nod. "Let's move quickly. The longer we linger around, the more attention we'll attract."

They separated, Viggo slipping through a narrow passage between buildings that led to the rear of the tenement. The alleyway behind was deserted save for a mangy dog nosing through a pile of discarded food scraps. Viggo positioned himself in a recessed doorway across from the building, his dark clothing and the deepening gloom of the rainy evening rendering him nearly invisible.

He frowned as he calculated the time it would take Evander and Rufus to climb to the third floor. The tenement was old, its stairs likely creaking with every step. If Thornfield was as nervous as a fugitive should be, he might hear them coming.

Viggo's instincts proved correct. Barely five minutes later, the window above him scraped open. A face peered out briefly—young, feminine, with auburn hair and a determined set to the jawline. The figure glanced down before withdrawing.

A rope fashioned from knotted bedsheets unfurled from the window a moment later. Viggo remained motionless and watched as a slender figure in a plain dress began a clumsy descent, followed by a second woman who moved with more confidence despite her older appearance.

He waited until they were both committed to their escape and halfway down the improvised rope before stepping into view.

"Going somewhere, ladies?" he called up to them.

The younger woman froze, head whipping towards Viggo with wide eyes. For a moment, no one moved.

Surprise jolted Viggo when she released the sheet and dropped the remaining eight feet to the ground, landing with surprising grace. She immediately pressed her hands against the cobblestones.

The ground rumbled beneath Viggo's feet.

The alley floor buckled, bricks and dirt erupting in a wave that rushed towards him. Viggo gasped and leapt sideways, narrowly avoiding the brunt of the attack. A jagged stone pillar shot up where he'd been standing a heartbeat earlier.

He scowled. It was earth magic, powerful and controlled.

"Mary, run!" the young woman shouted.

The maid had reached the ground. She shot a scared look at her companion.

"I'll be fine," the young woman reassured, her tone resolute despite the fear rendering her pale.

The older woman nodded jerkily and darted down the alley, heading east. Viggo caught a glimpse of Evander appearing at the far end to intercept her.

The young woman sent another wave of earth magic surging towards Viggo, cobblestones and soil twisting into crude projectiles. The Brute ducked and rolled. His immunity to magic only extended to direct attacks on his person.

Physical objects hurled by magical means could still harm him.

"We're not here to hurt you," Viggo called out as he jumped to his feet. He closed the distance between them with powerful strides. "Duke Ravenwood is investigating Professor Whitley's disappearance—"

The young woman could not hear him in her terror. "Stay back!" she yelled. Her hands twisted in a complex gesture.

The brick wall beside Viggo cracked. Chunks broke

free and slammed into his shoulder before he could move.

Viggo grunted from the impact but didn't slow. Another move from his opponent and the ground beneath his feet turned to quicksand. He cursed as he was quickly engulfed to his knees, the muck grabbing insidiously at his legs.

The young woman didn't wait to see if her trap would hold. She bolted, weaving agilely between the eruptions of earth she'd created.

Viggo wrenched himself free of the magical quicksand with a roar of effort and went after her. She was fast but hampered by the skirts of her dress. A momentary stumble gave Viggo the opportunity he needed. He launched himself forward in a diving tackle that sent them both crashing to the wet ground.

The young woman struggled violently beneath him, a stream of Latin incantations spilling from her lips as she tried to summon more earth magic. Viggo pinned her hands, disrupting the casting.

"Enough!" he growled. "If we meant you harm, you'd already be dead."

His captive stilled, chest heaving beneath the dress. Up close, Viggo could see subtle signs that challenged her feminine appearance—a strong jawline, hands slightly too large for a woman of her stature.

"Who are you?" she demanded, fear and defiance warring in her voice.

"Viggo Stonewall," he replied, cautiously releasing his grip but remaining ready to restrain her again if necessary. "I work with Duke Ravenwood. We're investigating Professor Whitley's disappearance."

Recognition flickered in her eyes. "The Ironfist Brute," she breathed. Her gaze darted to the ruined cobblestones her magic had torn up. "So it's true. You're immune to magic. That's how you withstood my attacks!"

"Most of them," Viggo grunted. He stood up and helped her to her feet before rotating his shoulder where the brick had struck. It would bruise, but nothing was broken. "Your earth magic is pretty impressive."

She swallowed.

Rufus appeared at the entrance to the alley, panting slightly from exertion. "Did you—ah, I see you have our quarry." The inspector eyed the devastated alleyway cautiously as he approached. "What happened?"

"She resisted," Viggo muttered.

The young woman's expression remained wary. "Where's Mary? What have you done with her?"

Evander's voice came from behind them. "Your maid is safe."

Viggo turned to see the mage approaching with the older woman, his hand resting lightly on her elbow. Unlike her companion, she showed no signs of having fought back.

"I've explained our purpose," Evander said. "She seems to think you should hear us out."

Mary nodded, her plain face etched with worry. "It's true, Master James. The Duke says they're trying to help find your professor."

The captive stiffened at the name.

Evander's gaze sharpened. "James Thornfield, I presume?" He studied the young woman's face with new intensity. "The transfiguration potion you used is quite remarkable. I'd wager it's your own creation."

For a moment, Thornfield seemed ready to deny it. His shoulders slumped in resignation.

"How did you know where we were?"

"A first-year student saw two women fleeing the Institute the night you disappeared. One of our forensic mages found the broken vial containing traces of the transfiguration potion in the quadrangle." Evander's mouth quirked in a slight smile. "You would have gotten away with it had it not been for the clue Lady Whitley gave us this afternoon. Why did Professor Whitley have a piece of paper containing the address to these lodgings in his possession?" He glanced at the building beside them.

Thornfield rubbed the back of his neck. "He'd anticipated that people working for his sponsor might come after us. I thought it far-fetched at the time but after the professor disappeared, I knew I could be next on the list. We'd agreed that if anything happened, we would meet here."

"Perhaps we should continue this conversation somewhere less exposed," Rufus suggested, glancing at the curious faces now peering from the windows above them.

Evander followed the inspector's gaze.

"Your room would suffice if you're willing to invite

us in properly this time," he told Thornfield with a frown.

Thornfield brushed dirt from his skirts. "Very well. But I warn you, if this is a trap—"

"It isn't," Viggo interrupted firmly. "Though I can't say the same for whatever you were running from."

The young man's face tightened. "Follow me. We'll use the back stairs."

CHAPTER 30

THE ROOM THORNFIELD AND MARY HAD RENTED WAS small and spartan, with peeling wallpaper and two narrow beds. A trunk in the corner appeared to contain their only possessions. Despite the squalid surroundings, someone had clearly made efforts towards cleanliness—the floor was swept, and the bedding, though worn, was neatly arranged.

Thornfield sat on the edge of one of the beds while Mary busied herself making tea on a small spirit stove. The student addressed Viggo.

"I apologise for attacking you." He glanced at Evander and Rufus. "When I heard footsteps on the stairs, I assumed the worst. There are only three rooms in use on this floor. The other lodgers aren't due back until late tonight and it is not yet meal time."

Evander could see the fear still gripping the young man from the way his hands trembled slightly.

"Who did you think we were?" he prompted.

Thornfield's expression darkened. "The same people who took Professor Whitley."

Rufus leaned forward. "Do you know their identity?"

Thornfield frowned and shook his head. "No. We were certain we were being watched the past few weeks, but we never actually saw anyone suspicious around us. There was just this…feeling of eyes observing us." He shivered and rubbed his arms briskly.

Evander exchanged a guarded glance with Viggo. The theory they'd discussed in bed that morning was starting to look more and more convincing.

"Viggo and I wonder whether the dark mages who were after you were using shadow magic to spy on you." He hesitated, conscious of Rufus's surprised stare. "We think that may be how they've been watching the thralls they kidnapped too."

"Why did you not tell me this earlier?" the inspector asked in a chagrined tone, his gaze swinging between Evander and Viggo.

"It was pure speculation on our behalf until now," Evander said apologetically. "And we only discussed it this morning."

Rufus's mildly flustered expression told Evander he'd guessed under exactly what circumstances they'd conversed about said theory.

Thornfield had gone pale. "Thralls have gone missing?!"

Evander nodded stiffly. "They're not the only ones. Did you know Professor Chevalier also vanished?"

"What?!" Thornfield gasped, horrified.

"A Special Arcane Investigator from Paris arrived in London yesterday," Evander explained. "Chevalier disappeared five days ago from the Paris Institute for the Arcane. No one has seen or heard from him since."

Thornfield's knuckles whitened in his lap. "My God!"

He startled when his maid gently took his fingers, unfurled his fist, and placed a steaming cup of tea in his hand.

"Thank you, Mary," Thornfield whispered shakily.

The old servant smiled softly, affection gleaming in her eyes.

"Mary was my nursemaid." Thornfield's face radiated gratitude as he gazed warmly at his servant. "She insisted on coming with me when she found out I intended to disappear for a while."

"I promised your mother on her deathbed that I would do everything to make sure you live a long and happy life, Master James," Mary murmured as she served Evander, Viggo, and Rufus tea in chipped cups.

Thornfield's throat worked convulsively. He took a sip of his tea.

"It's best you show them what you've been hiding, Master James," Mary encouraged gently.

Thornfield faltered before bobbing his head.

The student put down his cup, went over to the trunk, and withdrew something from it. Evander's pulse quickened at the sight of the leather-bound object in Thornfield's hands.

"Is that—?!"

Thornfield dipped his head, his features set in determined lines.

"This is Professor Whitley's research journal. He entrusted it to me the day before he disappeared." He crossed the floor and handed over the journal.

Evander carefully accepted it.

"The professor discovered something terrible," Thornfield said, his voice dropping.

It took all of Evander's willpower not to immediately open the worn leather volume in his hands.

"What did he discover?" he asked Thornfield instead.

Thornfield looked nervously at them before squaring his shoulders. "Have you heard of the Magical Conduit Theory?"

Evander shared a puzzled look glance with Viggo and Rufus before shaking his head at the student. "We're aware Whitley was researching magical transference."

"The Magical Conduit Theory is based on magical transference," Thornfield said grimly. "It's a concept Professor Whitley and Professor Chevalier were researching." Thornfield shot an awkward glance at Viggo. "It postulates that some thralls possess a unique neurological structure that allows them to temporarily hold magical energy."

Evander's blood ran cold at this, the anatomical diagrams from Whitley's hidden chamber swimming in front of his eyes.

Viggo straightened where he'd been leaning against the wall, his expression growing thunderous.

"Wait. You're saying whoever's targeting thralls is intending to use them as—as experimental subjects for magic?!"

"Probably," Thornfield said in a small voice. "Whitley and Chevalier believed thralls born with the distinctive biological property that makes them ideal conduits for magical storage cannot generate or wield magic themselves." He faltered. "But their bodies can be used as vessels to hold and transfer magical energy between sources."

Tension hummed through Evander. He narrowed his eyes.

"By 'sources,' you mean between mages?"

A muscle ticked in Thornfield's cheek. He nodded reluctantly.

"How are the dark mages selecting these thralls?" Viggo asked, his voice tight.

Evander was not fooled by his apparent self-possession. He could practically feel the anger and outrage bubbling beneath the Brute's skin.

"They will be targeting people with high intelligence and special talents," Thornfield admitted quietly. "Chevalier discovered that thralls who possess that particular biological ability are usually above average intelligence and gifted in ways that make them stand out from their peers."

Evander's breath locked momentarily in his throat as the pieces of the puzzle began to fall into place.

Horror drained some of the colour from Viggo's face.

"So those thralls are the kind of people who could end up working for the nobility?" the Brute said hoarsely.

Rufus sucked in air, realisation dawning on his face. "By the Gods!"

Thornfield fidgeted uncomfortably. "I suppose so. But that in itself is a double-edged sword."

"What do you mean?" Evander asked, his heart pounding.

Thornfield ran a hand through his hair. "Whitley told me Chevalier had a certain theory about the magicless who possessed those biological characteristics. Being regularly exposed to magic could actually refine their neural circuits and make them even more receptive to storing it inside their bodies."

Viggo scowled.

A thought came to Evander then. It pierced the storm roaring through his mind, so chilling he almost wished he'd never imagined it.

"Professor Harrington told us Whitley, and likely Chevalier, were researching rare magical abilities," he said, his mouth dry. "Of those, the powers of Archmages were of particular interest."

His words echoed in the hush that befell them.

Thornfield swallowed nervously at his unblinking stare.

"Yes, he was," the student finally confessed, his voice barely above a whisper.

A buzzing filled Evander's ears. The young man's

expression had given him the answer he was after. An answer he wished was not true, but knew in his bones was likely on the mark.

"Did they find a way to steal rare magic from mages and gift it to other mages?" he asked leadenly.

Horror widened Rufus's eyes. Viggo cursed viciously, causing Mary to startle.

Thornfield looked miserable in the face of their accusing looks.

"It was never their purpose to do something that horrific," he protested. "Their research was meant to be theoretical. Or so I was led to believe."

"It seems the people sponsoring them felt otherwise," Evander said bitterly.

Dread tightened his chest.

If "*I* " was indeed the one behind these crimes, then it seemed subjugating thralls was not his only mission. He intended to make himself and the ones faithful to him the most formidable mages in the Empire by stealing magic from others. Having living vessels that could store limitless magic meant they would never run out and would be in a position to access enormous power at will.

Evander clenched his jaw so hard he almost cracked a tooth.

And if he gets his hands on the powers of several Archmages, he will be invincible.

A sharp knock at the door made them all tense.

"It's probably just Mrs. Flack with dinner," Mary whispered, though she didn't sound convinced.

Viggo moved silently to one side of the door.

Evander's hand drifted to his hidden cane, magic surging in his veins. Rufus positioned himself defensively in front of Thornfield and his servant.

Evander signalled to Thornfield with a curt bob of his head.

The student swallowed. "Who's there?" he called, his voice rising to a feminine pitch once more.

"Comte Leon Beaulieu, Special Arcane Investigator from Paris," came the low reply. "Duke Ravenwood sent a message to Scotland Yard. I came as quickly as I could."

Evander released a pulse of magic. It was met with the familiar power of his former lover. He nodded to Viggo, his shoulders unknotting.

The Brute cautiously opened the door.

Leon stood in the dim hallway. He was immaculate despite the weather, his elegant clothing a stark contrast to the squalid surroundings.

"How did you know we were in this room?" Viggo asked the Frenchman suspiciously as he closed the door after him.

Leon lowered his brows. "You caused quite a fracas in the alleyway. It didn't take long to figure out where you'd gone." He assessed the cramped room and its occupations with a sweeping gaze. "What do we have here?"

Evander quickly explained their findings at Whitley's home and what had ensued. Surprise widened Leon's eyes as he listened.

"This is Monsieur Thornfield?" he asked, shocked.

"Yes."

"Remarkable," Leon murmured, studying the young man's disguise. "That transfiguration potion was worth every penny you paid for it."

"I made it myself," Thornfield muttered.

"Even more admirable, then," Leon concluded. His gaze settled on the journal in Evander's hands. "Is that—?"

"Professor Whitley's journal," Evander said grimly.

He summarised what Thornfield had told them.

Leon visibly stiffened. "The Magical Conduit Theory?"

CHAPTER 31

"You're familiar with it?" Thornfield asked, surprise evident in his voice.

"Unfortunately, yes." Leon's expression darkened. "It was one of the reasons *Les Prophètes Illuminés* was disbanded. Chevalier would have been privy to their findings."

"*Les Prophètes Illuminés?*" Thornfield repeated, confused.

Evander gave him a brief explanation before turning his attention to Leon. "What do you know about it?" he pressed. "Thornfield explained the theory but what about its application and practicalities? Are there any limitations to this science?"

Leon scowled. "The French Ministry deemed the research too dangerous to continue due to the ethical implications. I can only conclude they felt the knowledge could be put into practice by a group willing to go that far. As for its limitations, I suppose death would be the ultimate one."

Thornfield blanched.

Evander narrowed his eyes. "You mean the science is unstable?"

"In the hands of the foolhardy, yes." Leon scoffed. "One wrong move and you could kill both the giver and the recipient of magical energy."

"Somehow, I think our enemy anything but foolhardy," Viggo said sourly.

Evander was in agreement. Vanishing two eminent professors and over eighteen thralls was evidence that they were dealing with sophisticated criminals.

"The power to wage war. To subjugate thousands." Viggo's hands clenched into fists. "Is that what they're ultimately after?"

"I think it's more than that." Evander could not stop the dread creeping into his voice. "Acquiring the powers of Archmages would allow them to reshape society itself."

A brittle silence descended upon the room as the full implications of his words settled over them.

"There's something you need to see." Thornfield indicated the journal in Evander's hands with a jerk of his head. "A page at the back. It's some kind of map Professor Whitley drew before he disappeared."

Evander's pulse thundered in his veins as he carefully opened the journal and leafed through it. It wasn't hard to find what Thornfield had alluded to.

The page stood out like a sore thumb.

The others gathered around him as he pored over it.

It was a sketch of what appeared to be a large,

circular chamber with strange apparatus arranged around the perimeter.

Leon frowned. "That looks like some kind of lab."

"Professor Whitley believed the ones after us were building a facility to conduct their experiments—somewhere hidden, yet accessible," Thornfield said nervously. "I don't know how he came upon this schematic but this place could very well exist, here in London."

Viggo straightened. "Then that's where the missing thralls will be."

Evander's knuckles whitened on the journal. "And we'll hopefully find Whitley and maybe even Chevalier there too."

"We need to inform Commander Winterbourne about this immediately," Rufus advised in the fraught hush.

"I agree." Evander observed Thornfield carefully. "Do you have any idea who else within the Institute might be involved? It's clear someone on the inside is working for these dark mages. It's the only way to explain how Whitley got abducted and why we were attacked during our investigation."

"Professor Dearmont comes to mind," Rufus muttered morosely.

Thornfield hesitated. "Professor Whitley had suspicions, but nothing concrete. He never mentioned Professor Dearmont, but he did wonder if the one in league with his and Professor Chevalier's sponsor had a connection to the War of Subjugation. He thought whoever it was likely still clung to old resentments and ideologies that never truly died."

The student's words struck a cold chord in Evander's chest and caused Viggo's expression to harden.

"Mr. Thornfield, we need to get you somewhere safe," Evander said, breaking the tense silence. "Your knowledge makes you a valuable witness—and a target. The Met has several properties in and outside London where you can go into hiding."

"What about Mary?" Thornfield asked immediately. He reached for his servant's hand. "She's risked everything to help me. I do not wish to be separated from her."

"Of course," Evander assured him. "She will go with you."

Relief brightened Thornfield and Mary's expressions.

Viggo moved to the window and scanned the back alley with a faint frown. "We should leave soon. Word travels fast in these parts. Our earlier commotion may have drawn unwanted attention."

Evander nodded.

Thornfield and Mary hastily gathered their meagre belongings.

"We can use the servants' staircase at the side," Thornfield suggested as they got ready to move. "It's narrow and not often used."

"Perfect." Evander studied Viggo steadily. "Let's separate in case someone followed us here. You and Leon take Thornfield and Mary out via the servants' stairs. Rufus and I will leave out front. We'll meet up at Scotland Yard in one hour."

Viggo looked like he wanted to protest, but the logic of what Evander had proposed was too sound for him not to agree. Protecting Thornfield and the knowledge he carried was paramount.

Leon looked about as enthusiastic at the idea of accompanying Viggo as a fox being told he had to mark time with a hound during a hunt.

"Don't take unnecessary risks," Viggo said thinly as they prepared to leave. He held Evander's gaze for a moment longer than strictly necessary.

Evander's expression softened. "The same goes for you."

Viggo slipped into the corridor ahead of Thornfield. Mary followed, clutching a small bundle to her chest.

Leon paused on the threshold, his expression conflicted.

"Stay safe, mon cher," he said quietly. He turned and disappeared into the shadows after Mary.

Evander and Rufus waited five minutes before leaving the room.

Evander was aware of the weight of the journal tucked safely inside his coat as they descended the stairwell leading to the front entrance. They stepped out into a night shrouded with fog and a light drizzle under the watchful gaze of the landlady and took briskly to the narrow alleys and shadowed passages of the labyrinthine East End until they reached Cannon

Street. There, they hailed a hansom cab that took them straight to Scotland Yard.

A message from Headmaster Rigley was waiting for Evander in the Arcane Division reception. Surprise danced through him when he read it.

The Royal Institute had officially closed its doors to external visitors and sent all its students home. Not only that, the board had agreed to the Met's demands to investigate its faculty.

"That happened faster than I anticipated," Rufus observed with a frown.

"They must be running scared," Evander said grimly. "After all, they've already been accused of harbouring one dark mage." He met the inspector's wary gaze. "If word gets out there are more among their faculty, their reputation will never recover."

They found Viggo, Leon, and their charges already waiting in Winterbourne's office. Mary looked decidedly ill at ease to be in the presence of someone of the commander's import.

The relief on Winterbourne's face was evident when they entered the room.

"Thank goodness you're both safe." His gaze settled on Evander as he urged them to take a seat. "I understand we've had a breakthrough? Mr. Stonewall and Comte Beaulieu just arrived."

Evander glanced at Leon.

"Go ahead," the Frenchman said with a faint smile. "You're the lead on this case."

Evander nodded and provided a concise summary of their discoveries—Thornfield's identity, the Magical

Conduit Theory, and their suspicions about a hidden facility where the abducted thralls and professors were likely being held. He placed Whitley's journal on Winterbourne's desk and opened it to the page containing the crude map of the facility.

"We believe this could be the lab in question."

The commander's expression had darkened progressively throughout Evander's account.

"Do you know where this might be?"

Evander shook his head. "Not yet. But we're working on it. The cryptology expert looking at Professor Chevalier's journal might be able to come up with a clue from her findings."

Winterbourne glowered at the paper for a moment, as if willing it to reveal its secrets. He leaned back in his chair and pinched the bridge of his nose.

"This goes beyond a simple investigation. If word of this gets out, it could incite panic throughout the magical community, not to mention what it would do for relations with the thrall population." He looked squarely at Viggo. "Mr. Stonewall, I trust *Nightshade* will exercise discretion in this matter?"

"You have my word," Viggo replied in a hard voice. "Though I intend to increase security for thralls working in noble households. Discreetly, of course."

Winterbourne nodded. "Of course. And I'll arrange for Mr. Thornfield and his servant to be transferred to a safe house outside London tonight." He turned to Rufus. "Inspector, I want you to personally oversee their security detail and see that they settle in alright."

"Yes, sir," Rufus responded promptly.

"And the journal?" Leon asked. He glanced at the worn leather volume on Winterbourne's desk.

"It stays here," the commander declared. "Under lock and key in the AFD's secured evidence room. I'll have our cryptologist analyse those schematics and see if she can determine where this facility might be located." He lowered his brows. "Any news from Elias?"

Evander shook his head, chagrined. "Not yet, sir. He's still working on identifying the device we found."

Winterbourne pursed his lips. "Maybe we should ask the Institute if they can help. Don't they have a specialist in the field?"

"They do," Evander volunteered uneasily. "Professor Abbingdon Musgrave is an expert on magical artefacts and enhancement."

Winterbourne sighed at his expression. "Out with it, Ravenwood."

"I would rather not involve other members of the Institute in our investigation, sir," Evander confessed in a firm voice.

"You don't trust them," Winterbourne stated steadily.

Evander hesitated and glanced at Rufus and Viggo. "No. Not after what happened with Renwick."

Winterbourne sighed. "Fair enough."

The meeting concluded shortly afterwards. Evander drew Thornfield aside as Rufus headed off to organise a team of officers to escort the student and his servant to the safe house.

"I'll keep you informed of any developments in our

investigation," he promised quietly. "Particularly if we discover any trace of Professor Whitley."

Gratitude shone in Thornfield's eyes. "Thank you, your Grace. I pray you find him safe and sound. He's a good man who was trying to do the right thing."

Evander nodded.

Thornfield looked at Viggo. "I never thought I'd meet the Ironfist Brute. Or fight him, for that matter."

A wry smile touched Viggo's lips. "You landed a blow, which not many have."

Evander blinked. "He did?"

"Yes." Viggo grimaced and rotated his shoulder. "Whacked me right here with some bricks."

Thornfield's expression turned apologetic.

"Get some rest, Thornfield," Viggo grunted. "You've earned it."

They parted ways in the courtyard of Scotland Yard, Leon heading for his lodgings to compose another urgent report to his superiors in Paris while Viggo returned to *Nightshade* to participate in the trap his guild had set that night.

"I need to ensure everything goes according to plan," Viggo explained regretfully once they were alone.

"Of course," Evander murmured. He fought the urge to reach for Viggo's hand in the public courtyard. "Will I see you later?"

The Brute's eyes softened, his voice dropping to a low rumble that only Evander could hear. "Count on it."

It was well past midnight when Evander was roused

from a fitful sleep by the mattress dipping beside him. His magic flared instinctively before he recognised Viggo's familiar presence in the darkness.

"It's only me," the Brute whispered as he slipped beneath the covers.

Evander turned drowsily, his body instantly seeking Viggo's warmth. "What time is it?"

"Late. Or early, depending on how you look at it." Viggo's arms encircled him and drew him close against his chest. "Sorry to wake you."

"How did it go?" Evander mumbled.

"Without incident, something I'm grateful for despite Solomon's feelings on the matter." Viggo's lips brushed Evander's temple. "He paraded around half of Mayfair in Ginny's livery without attracting any unwanted attention. We'll try again tomorrow night."

"No shadow creatures?" Evander asked sleepily.

"None that we could detect." Viggo's hand traced a soothing pattern along Evander's spine.

Evander made a soft sound of acknowledgement.

"Go back to sleep." Viggo pressed a gentle kiss to Evander's mouth. "Tomorrow will be another long day, I wager."

Evander drifted back to sleep in his embrace, the Brute's heartbeat drumming steadily against his cheek.

CHAPTER 32

EVANDER WOKE TO AN EMPTY BED THE NEXT MORNING.

He swallowed a stab of disappointment when his hand found the cool sheets beside him. Viggo must have left hours ago. He rose, crossed to the window, and parted the heavy curtains.

London had vanished beneath a dense blanket of fog.

The weather matched his mood as he dressed and made his way downstairs.

Hargrove was waiting for him with coffee and a plate of eggs and toast in the breakfast room.

"You were sleeping soundly, my Lord, so I did not bring you your morning tea," the manservant informed him smoothly.

Evander took the seat Hargrove pulled out for him. "When did Viggo leave?"

"At dawn, my Lord. He asked me to tell you he had urgent business to attend to."

Evander nodded. "Any messages?"

"One just arrived, my Lord." Hargrove brought over the tray with the morning paper and post. "It's from Comte Beaulieu."

Evander put his napkin down, picked up the message, and unfolded the note.

The elegant handwriting it contained informed him that Leon intended to visit the Royal Institute early this morning to follow up on some observations he'd made in Whitley's laboratory and the hidden chamber beneath it. The note concluded with a promise to meet Evander at Scotland Yard afterwards.

A strange sense of foreboding lifted the hairs on the back of Evander's neck as he stared at Leon's missive. He wrinkled his brow. Though there were officers stationed at the Institute, he didn't like that Leon had gone there on his own.

I'm being overly paranoid.

Still, he pushed his chair back and rose to his feet.

"Please give my apologies to Cook, Jasper. I shall be skipping breakfast this morning."

Concern clouded Hargrove's face. "Is it that urgent, my Lord?"

"Yes."

The manservant pursed his lips. "Still, you must make sure to eat, my Lord. Or else you won't be able to keep up with Mr. Stonewall."

Evander looked at him blankly.

Hargrove sighed. "I mean in the sack, my Lord."

Evander's eyes shrank to slits.

"Mr. Hargrove!" Mrs. Sinclair choked from the doorway.

Hargrove looked at her with a pained expression. "It's uncanny how you always happen to be nearby whenever I say something salacious, Mrs. S."

Evander left them to their bickering and had a maid ask Graham to bring his carriage around.

The Metropolitan Police Headquarters loomed out of the swirling mist when they pulled up in front of it sometime later. The fog had made travel slow and it was already after nine. He hurried inside and nodded briskly to the officers who acknowledged him with respectful salutes as he made his way to the Arcane Division.

Sergeant Griffiths was manning the reception.

"Inspector Grayson and Miss Shaw are waiting for you in your office, your Grace," he informed Evander.

"Thank you."

Evander found Rufus and Shaw discussing the case when he entered his office.

Shaw stopped and brightened at his sight. "Ah, your Grace. I'm pleased to see you. I just received a report from our handwriting expert on those letters *Nightshade* brought around yesterday. He confirmed they were indeed forgeries."

Evander straightened, his pulse quickening. "We should let Viggo know."

Shaw grinned. "Already taken care of, sir. I just dispatched a messenger."

"I've updated Shaw about what happened yesterday," Rufus explained. He looked curiously past Evander. "Where's Leon?"

"He went to the Institute this morning," Evander replied. He hesitated a beat. "We should join him."

Rufus and Shaw's expressions grew instantly alert.

"Is something wrong?" Rufus asked guardedly.

"I hope not." Evander tried to keep his tone light. "Are our two guests safely lodged?" he asked as the inspector joined him, Shaw trailing in his footsteps.

"Yes. Sergeant Griffiths and his team are guarding the safe house."

Evander's gaze switched to Shaw as they headed into the corridor. "How did it go yesterday?"

"We've catalogued and moved all the contents of the chamber beneath Whitley's laboratory to the Met, your Grace," the forensic mage reported. She made a face. "I did come upon something strange I was going to ask you about."

Evander's scalp prickled. "Strange? Strange how?"

"Some kind of magical signature," Shaw explained with a vague wave of a hand. "I asked Mrs. Scarborough for some of that potion she'd made. You know, the neutralising agent? Apparently, it can detect traces of other types of magic, not just hidden wards and spells."

Evander stared at her as they reached the stairs. "That would never have crossed my mind. Well done for thinking outside the box, Shaw."

"Of course, your Grace." Shaw sniffed and rubbed her nose proudly with a knuckle. "I'm the best forensic mage the Met has, after all."

Rufus rolled his eyes. "How about you tell us what you found?"

Shaw's expression turned shrewd. "Remember the compartment where that device was hidden?"

Evander stiffened. "The one with the strange metallic scent?"

Shaw blinked, her smile fading. "You could smell it?!"

Tension hummed through Evander. "Yes." He frowned. "But it didn't feel like magic of any kind I've ever felt before, so I didn't think much of it. Whitley's lab and that room contained all kinds of chemicals, after all."

"Cor," Shaw mumbled, impressed. "So that pretty nose of yours isn't just for show, huh?"

"Shaw," Rufus warned with a scowl.

"Sorry, your Grace. As I was saying, there was a magical signature there. I think it'd leaked from that device. It was like nothing I've ever seen before." Shaw scratched her head. "It was almost as if someone had tried mixing several different types of magic together."

Evander rocked to halt on a step. Rufus went as still as stone beside him.

Shaw studied their stunned expressions warily. "What?" It didn't take long for her confusion to fade. She gasped and covered her mouth with her hand. "Bloody hell! This is about what that Thornfield lad told you two yesterday, isn't? The Magical Conduit Theory?!"

They hushed her and looked around cautiously.

Luckily, there wasn't anyone within earshot.

Evander decided not to point out to the forensic mage that Thornfield was likely the same age as her.

"We should go take another look at where you discovered that magical signature," he said grimly as they descended the stairs at a brisk pace.

"There's something else, your Grace," Shaw added as they hurried through the Arcane Division. "I decided to see if that magic was present anywhere else in the south wing. Guess what? I found a trace of it outside one of the lecture halls."

Evander traded a surprised look with Rufus.

"Well done, Shaw," he murmured.

They were closing in on their enemy. He was certain of it.

The trip to Bloomsbury seemed interminable, the carriage forced to proceed at little more than walking pace through the soupy fog. Evander's fingers drummed restlessly against his knee as he stared out at the silhouettes of buildings drifting past. The ghostly shape of the Institute finally materialised up ahead.

The courtyard was even more eerily silent than yesterday, the fog shrouding the grand buildings in an otherworldly pall that made them look as if they belonged to another realm.

To Evander's surprise, they met Constables Fitch and Bartley in the main foyer.

The pair slowed when they saw their group. Both men looked pale and tense.

Alarm knotted Evander's shoulders at the sight of the truncheons in their hands.

"How did you get here so quickly, your Grace?" Fitch asked stiffly before he could question them.

"What do you mean?"

"We just sent an officer to headquarters to fetch you," Fitch explained rapidly, his eyes dark with concern. "Something's happening in the south wing. The French Special Arcane Investigator was inspecting one of the lecture halls when we heard an explosion inside. We rushed over there but there was some kind of magic barrier blocking our way. We couldn't get inside."

"We could hear fighting going on," Bartley mumbled. "The whole place stank, your Grace. Like something rotten!"

"We were just looking for a member of the faculty to help us," Fitch said.

Fear squeezed Evander's heart. *Leon!*

"Fitch, Bartley, don't let anyone inside the building if they're not with the Met!" Evander barked as he started running, Rufus and Shaw in his footsteps.

The constables nodded briskly.

"Get ready!" Evander warned Rufus and Shaw in a hard voice as they pounded the quiet halls. "We're probably dealing with a dark mage and a powerful one at that."

They had just passed the junction leading to the south wing when a voice called out to them.

"Your Grace? Inspector?"

Evander stumbled to a stop, Rufus and Shaw skidding behind him with a curse.

Cecillia watched them with a puzzled expression as she approached from the west wing, the sergeant and constables assigned to her security following in her wake.

"Is everything alright?"

CHAPTER 33

A SURGE OF DARK MAGIC PRICKLED EVANDER'S SKIN AND sent the floor trembling beneath their feet before he could reply.

Cecillia lurched unsteadily.

"What on earth?!" she gasped.

Evander came to a decision. "Come with us!" he requested urgently to the professor. "There's a dark mage in the building. He's attacking Comte Beaulieu. I could do with your assistance!"

Horror widened Cecillia's eyes. It was followed swiftly by understanding.

"Of course!"

Evander's gaze switched to her detail. "I want you to guard the entrance to the south wing," he instructed swiftly. "Make sure no one goes in or out. You have my permission to use offensive magic if need be."

The officers bobbed their heads tensely. "Yes, your Grace."

Cecillia grabbed the skirts of her dress and followed Evander and his group.

"Is the headmaster in the building?" Evander asked.

"No," Cecillia replied with a shake of her head. "He was called to a meeting at the Ministry of Arcane Affairs. He asked me to cover for him, hence why I'm here."

Evander told her about Shaw finding a strange magical trace as they hurried towards the lecture halls, carefully omitting any mention of the secret chamber beneath Whitley's lab.

"You believe this is the work of whoever kidnapped Walter?" Cecillia asked, shooting an anxious look his way.

"We're about to find out," Evander said in a hard voice.

The air grew chilly when they approached the section of the south wing that contained the classrooms. By the time they reached the hall where muffled explosions originated, their breaths were misting in front of their faces.

The bitter taste of dark magic rolled across Evander's tongue as they stopped in front of the double doors, the stench so foul it made his stomach roil. Even though he couldn't see the barrier blocking them, he could sense it with his magic.

Power bubbled through his veins. He lifted a hand and sent a burst of fire magic into the invisible wall. The runes making up the barrier sizzled into life at the same time the flames of his magic cleared some of the noxious air.

His heart sank.

The spell was complex—not just a standard protection ward, but woven from dark magic and something he couldn't put a finger on. He clenched his jaw.

"Whoever created this is incredibly skilled," Cecillia said in a voice full of dread.

She jumped when a muted crash came from beyond the doors.

A shout reached them faintly.

Evander's chest tightened at the panic lacing Leon's voice.

"Stand back!" he commanded.

Evander waited until his companions had backpedalled several steps before placing his palm in front of the barrier and reaching for his magic.

Wind flowed through him, lightening his body and ruffling his hair. The air began to stir, the currents swirling faster and faster until they formed a concentrated vortex around him. Heat blossomed inside his chest with his next breath. The fire that raced along his veins warmed his blood and made the vortex shimmer and spark.

He channelled his elemental powers into the barrier with a roar.

The flame storm that erupted from his hand raced across the corrupt wall with a boom that shook the corridor and sent the others sliding backward.

Cecillia gasped at the sight where she leaned into the wind.

The barrier shuddered under the elemental assault. A crack appeared. Then another.

Evander lowered his brows. *Almost there!*

Movement caught his eyes. He cursed.

A vile darkness was seeping around the edges of the doors.

"What the devil?!" Rufus shouted.

"Those look like shadow creatures, your Grace!" Shaw warned.

Evander gritted his teeth. He didn't have time to take down the barrier *and* fight those abominations.

Cecillia appeared next to him, her face set in determined lines.

White magic sparked in her pupils and glittered in the bands of water swirling around her fingertips. They merged and solidified into a dazzling ice spear.

She widened her stance, drew back her arm, and stabbed it into the barrier.

The magic she unleashed washed warmly over Evander as he continued pouring his powers into the barrier.

It collapsed under their dual attack with a sound like shattering glass.

The shadow creatures surged towards them.

"Together!" Evander barked.

Cecillia swallowed and nodded.

The pair of them blasted the monsters with their magic while Rufus and Shaw opened the doors to the lecture hall.

Evander's heart stuttered at the scene that met their eyes.

Leon stood with his back to the rows of seats and desks rising around the classroom, his chest heaving and his elegant attire torn and bloodied where he stood inside a maelstrom of his elemental magic. He was facing off against three writhing masses of shadows coalescing and separating like living ink where they hovered in front of him, their wraithlike forms evading his *Nullification Magic* attacks.

But it was the figure beyond the shadows that froze Evander's blood.

A man in a hooded cloak stood next to the lectern with his arms outstretched. Dark magic wreathed his hands as he directed the shadow creatures to attack the Frenchman. Though his face was obscured, there was something familiar about his stance. Something Evander recognised vaguely from the past few days.

"Professor Musgrave?!" Cecillia gasped.

The figure's head whipped around, eyes narrowing behind his glasses and his expression that of a madman. A chill shot down Evander's spine at the sight of the shadows crowning his head and moving sinuously around his body under the cape he wore.

It reminded him of how Renwick had looked in the warehouse.

"Bollocks," Shaw mumbled. "He's a proper dark mage!"

"Evander!" Leon's shout ripped him from his unpleasant memories and snapped him back to the present. The Frenchman was barely holding the shadows at bay, a pale wall of wind and water magic flickering weakly between him and the creatures. He met Evander's gaze wildly, his eyes dark with dread. "I could do with a little assistance!"

"Try and hold off Musgrave!" Evander commanded Rufus and Shaw as he strode purposefully towards the Frenchman. "Cecillia, guard the door so he doesn't escape!"

Ice magic crystallised around him as the closest group of shadow creatures turned on him.

He hurled the barrage of glittering shards. The frozen missiles tore through the formless bodies. The monsters screeched, a sound that bypassed his ears and cut directly into his brain. They re-formed and bore down on him.

Heat flooded Evander's veins. A circular wall of flames whooshed into life around him.

The shadow creatures recoiled with sibilant hisses.

"These ones seem resistant to elemental magic somehow!" Leon shouted as Evander closed the distance to him, his face pale with exertion. "Even my *Nullification Magic* isn't able to clear them fully. We need to try something else!"

Evander extended the barrier of fire around the relieved Frenchman and observed the twisting shadows surrounding them. He suspected these apparitions were different from the shadow creatures they'd encountered previously by virtue of how they'd been created.

If standard elemental magic doesn't work against them, then that *might.*

He was distracted by the sound of Musgrave

cursing where Rufus and Shaw now flanked him, truncheons in hand.

"Leon, remember that thing we tried once, when we were still at the Institute?" Evander's frowning gaze shifted from the dark mage to his former lover.

Leon blinked. His eyes rounded. "You mean when we almost destroyed the classroom?!"

Evander nodded grimly.

Leon swallowed. "Alright, I'll give it a try. Just—be gentle, mon cher."

Evander put a hand on his back. "Remember to breathe." He focused a controlled flow of magic into the Frenchman's body.

Leon gasped and straightened. His eyes glowed and the air around him sparked with a dazzling light as Evander augmented the core where his powers dwelled. He clenched his jaw, raised his hands, and gathered his *Nullification Magic* around them like a silver shield.

The floor cracked beneath their feet, the marble slabs unable to withstand the sheer forces radiating from both of them.

Leon staggered a little.

Fear twisted Evander's stomach when blood trickled out of the Frenchman's left nostril. He began retracting his magic.

"Don't stop!" Leon scowled at Evander. "I can take it!"

Evander hesitated before nodding jerkily.

He lifted his other hand and sent fire magic pouring into Leon's *Nullification Magic*.

"Now!"

The concentrated energy wave they released boomed in a blinding flash that rippled outward on a formidable shockwave.

Windows shattered and chandeliers cracked. Chairs and desks exploded, filling the air with debris. Fracture lines snaked across the floor and up the walls. Plaster dust rained down from the ceiling.

The shadow creatures recoiled, their formless bodies contorting in agony before they dissipated to wispy tendrils that quickly faded in the sunlight streaming through the broken windows.

Musgrave stumbled back with a cry of horror as he was momentarily robbed of his magic by Leon's powers. His murderous gaze found Evander.

"You will pay for this, Archmage!" he hissed.

Evander didn't waste his breath responding. He advanced towards the professor where the latter stood trapped between Rufus and Shaw, anger tightening his face.

"Where are Whitley and Chevalier?" Evander growled. "And what have you done with the missing thralls?!"

A bark of laughter that did not belong to a sane man escaped Musgrave.

"You think you've won, don't you?!" he sneered. "You and your damn friends and even that *whore* Harrington?!"

Cecillia paled as the professor shot a glare at her.

Musgrave's eyes shrank to slits at Evander's approach.

"I shall have your powers!" His gaze shifted to Leon. "*All* your powers! I will turn the pair of you into drooling rats that can't even light a candle with your magic!" His mouth stretched in a deranged smile. "And my master shall reward me for my efforts, just like he promised he would! I shall have you lick his boots, Archmage. For you are nothing compared to his greatness!"

Ice filled Evander's veins. He closed the distance to Musgrave and grabbed him furiously by the collar of his robe.

"Who is your master?!" he snarled.

Musgrave's eyes gleamed with macabre glee. He reached inside his cloak, removed a round metallic device, and pressed the button atop it before Evander could react.

"This isn't over, Ravenwood!" he cackled.

"Evander!" Rufus yelled in horror.

Leon cursed and dashed towards him.

The only thing that protected Evander from the brunt of the dark magic explosion was the wall of ice his body instinctively erected in an act of self-preservation.

Even then, the blast sent him flying backward into Leon's arms and sent them both tumbling to the ground.

By the time the smoke cleared, Musgrave had vanished.

"You idiot!" Evander snapped.

Leon winced as a healer took care of the cut on his scalp. "That's the tenth time you've said that, mon cher duc."

The healer maintained a diplomatic silence.

They were in the Met's infirmary. The fog had begun to dissipate by the time they returned to Scotland Yard. Weak sunlight filtered through the windows of the ward and washed over Leon where he sat on the edge of a treatment bed. He'd stripped to his waist and was holding an ice pack of his own making to his nose.

Remorse filled Evander as he studied the cuts and bruises on his former lover's body. He hadn't wanted to leave Leon after they'd arrived back at Scotland Yard and had directed Rufus and Shaw to deliver an urgent report to Winterbourne about this morning's incident in his stead. Cecillia had stayed at the Institute to await

Rigley's return and inform him about what had happened.

Evander reminded himself he was still upset with the Frenchman.

"Yes, well, it bears repeating considering the thickness of your skull," he said nastily. "So what were you doing in that classroom?"

"I was examining the secret chamber beneath Whitley's laboratory to see if we'd missed any clues when I sensed dark magic close by. I followed it to that lecture hall."

Evander lowered his brows. "And you found Musgrave there?"

"Yes. He seemed surprised to see me."

Frustration churned Evander's stomach as he realised once again how close he'd come to losing Leon.

"What the devil did you think you were doing, going there on your own?!" he yelled, throwing his hands in the air.

Irritation tightened Leon's mouth. "You do realise I'm a Special Arcane Investigator too?"

"That's not the point," Evander ground out. "We're dealing with powerful forces. You've seen what they can do. Even Whitley and Chevalier were helpless against them. And you're my friend before you're a Special Arcane Investigator, dammit!"

Leon blinked, surprise replacing the anger on his face. A lopsided smile curved his mouth.

"Is that all I am to you now? A friend?"

The healer sucked in air and shot an avid glance at the pair of them.

Evander's eyes shrank to slits. "I was about to add 'close' to the word 'friend' but since you insist on being an ass, I shall relegate you to a mere acquaintance."

"Ouch," the healer muttered under his breath, wincing.

"Come now, surely you jest," Leon protested. A groan left him when the healer started working on his bruised ribs.

Guilt choked Evander's throat.

"Evander?" Leon murmured weakly.

Evander leaned forward anxiously. "Yes?"

"I shall feel much better if you nurse me back to health," the Frenchman declared shamelessly. "With your own hands, I mean." His eyes twinkled. "A guest room in your home would make the perfect location for my convalescence, I wager. Why, I can already feel my energy returning at the thought of your tender, loving care."

Evander made an incoherent sound.

The healer shook his head with a disgusted expression and muttered under his breath about idiots taking a mile when they were given an inch.

They were distracted by the sight of Rufus and Shaw entering the infirmary.

The forensic mage frowned as she approached with the inspector.

"Everything alright, your Grace? You look a bit flushed."

Evander noticed the way Rufus registered Leon's brazen grin and grasped the situation fairly quickly.

"It's nothing," Evander said darkly. "Does Winterbourne have a message for me?"

"Only that we should accelerate our investigation now that the enemy knows we are closing in on them," Rufus related in a hard voice.

"I'll organise a team to investigate Professor Musgrave's office at the Institute and his residence," Shaw said sharply.

"Good." Evander frowned and rubbed his chin. "I'll send a message to Viggo. Now that we know of Musgrave's involvement, it would benefit us if *Nightshade* looked into his connections. It might help us pinpoint the location of that secret facility."

The door to the infirmary opened. A constable poked his head in. Relief brightened his face at the sight of Evander.

"Your Grace, can you please make your way to the Artificers' Lab? Mr. McAndrew requests your presence."

Tension knotted Evander's shoulders. He exchanged a cautious look with Rufus and Shaw and led the way to the door.

"What about me?" Leon called out indignantly behind them.

"You stay here and reflect on your actions," Evander snapped over his shoulder.

"You tell him, your Grace," the healer murmured.

The smell of raw magic washed over Evander when he entered the Artificers' Lab ahead of Rufus and Shaw.

Unlike the alchemists' crowded workspace, this room was an ode to meticulous organisation, not an instrument or an artefact out of place.

Elias McAndrew sat at his work bench, his hands steepled under his chin and his normally cheerful face set in lines of concern as he stared at the warded box in front of him. It contained the brass and glass contraption they'd discovered.

A protective magic field shimmered around the entire thing.

"You wished to see us?" Evander asked without preamble.

McAndrew startled and looked at him distractedly. "Ah, your Grace. I didn't notice you there."

Evander could tell whatever the artificer had discovered about the device was troubling him. Rufus and Shaw traded a worried glance.

"What can you tell us about this artefact?" Evander prompted McAndrew quietly.

The artificer's face darkened. "I know this is going to be hard to believe, but I think this thing has a similar function to the *Blood Siphon*."

Dread brought a sour taste to Evander's mouth. Though he'd suspected the same, hearing McAndrew confirm it made his worst fears seem like an inevitable reality.

"Are you certain?"

"As certain as I can be, your Grace," McAndrew confirmed. "Whereas the *Blood Siphon* was created to absorb and stabilise the life force of thralls, this artefact was created to extract and condense magic itself, likely before transferring it to a thrall vessel for storage, according to Whitley's research."

Rufus drew a sharp breath. Shaw cursed quietly.

"I have examined some of the documents uncovered in the room where this device was found," McAndrew continued grimly. "It's safe to say that what we're looking at here is just a portable version."

Evander froze. "A portable version?" An image flashed before his eyes then. The enormous contraption Renwick had drawn his magic from in the warehouse where he and Viggo had confronted the dark mage was still etched sharply in his nightmares. "You mean, there's a larger version of this?!"

"Yes." A muscle jumped in McAndrew's cheek. "I heard about the map you found in that missing professor's journal and the hidden facility it portrays. I bet you it's there, your Grace." The artificer hesitated. "I made one more disturbing finding."

Evander's pulse quickened. He wasn't sure how things could get any worse than they were, but apparently they could.

"There was an unusual magical signature embedded in the device."

"I knew it!" Shaw hissed with a triumphant expression.

Rufus hushed her.

"It's like nothing I've ever encountered before." Dread pooled in McAndrew's eyes as he met Evander's gaze. "I believe it's a hybrid form of dark magic that incorporates elements of *Blood Magic* and shadow manipulation."

Ice filled Evander's veins. Rufus and Shaw paled.

A heavy silence fell over them as they all contemplated the dire implications of the artificer's findings. There was no longer any doubt in Evander's mind.

"*I*" was involved in this evil scheme.

A commotion in the corridor outside the lab had them looking towards the doorway. Rapid footsteps approached, their cadence familiar.

Evander straightened when Viggo entered the room at a brisk pace. He took one look at the Brute's expression and knew something terrible had happened.

"It's Solomon," Viggo said hoarsely. "Solomon has gone missing!"

CHAPTER 35

THE CARRIAGE RATTLED THROUGH LONDON'S STREETS AT breakneck speed on its way to Whitechapel, the horses' hooves striking sparks against the cobblestones. Evander studied Viggo's taut expression as he gripped his knees with white-knuckled intensity opposite him.

"Was Solomon on his own when he went missing?" the mage asked quietly, trying to keep calm in the face of his lover's fear. He wanted nothing more than to cross the carriage and take him in his arms, but they had company in the shape of Rufus and Shaw.

"Yes," Viggo replied, his voice unnaturally controlled. "He was running an errand for *Nightshade*. He wasn't due to go to Ginny's place until later this evening, so we didn't have anyone watching him." Frustration underscored the Brute's words.

Evander could feel the weight of his guilt behind them.

Rufus exchanged a worried glance with Shaw.

"Did anyone notice anything unusual before his disappearance?" the inspector inquired.

"Finn is still interviewing people, but so far no one's mentioned anything that sounds like the work of a dark mage or shadow creatures." Viggo clenched his jaw. "We found his pouch of anti-magic devices. There was blood on it."

Dread tightened Evander's chest. He knew how much Solomon meant to Viggo. He just prayed the thrall was still alive, wherever he was.

The carriage slowed and came to a halt near the junction where Commercial Road met Sidney Street. Viggo was the first to alight, his powerful frame tense with barely restrained emotion as he scanned the area. Evander adjusted his coat against the chill as he stepped out after him, Rufus and Shaw in his wake.

People on the street had slowed at the sight of the Met insignia on the side of the carriage. Murmurs broke out, along with wary stares. Recognition flared on the faces of a few when they saw Evander.

His reputation as a friend to thralls had grown since the Millbrook case.

Finn emerged from the shadows of a nearby alley, his normally mischievous face pale.

"We've kept the area clear," he informed them. "Nothing's been disturbed."

Evander acknowledged this with a curt nod. "Take us there."

Finn led them to a narrow side street that ran between two weathered brick buildings, one a butcher and the other a laundry house. The alley appeared unremarkable at first glance—just another gloomy East End passageway littered with debris and redolent with the mingled stench of refuse and damp.

Even from a distance, Evander smelled a lingering trace of dark magic and the strange metallic tang he'd detected in Whitley's hidden room. The smell he now knew to be a form of a magical hybrid derived from *Blood Magic*, dark, and shadow magic.

Solomon's pouch lay on the ground a little more than halfway along the passage. Inky lines scorched the brick wall beside it.

It was clear some kind of battle had taken place there.

Evander crouched beside the pouch, touched the bloodstain marking it, and rubbed his fingers. It wasn't quite dry yet. He frowned.

"It's been less than two hours since he went missing."

"He was supposed to meet an informant at lunchtime," Viggo confirmed stiffly. "The man dropped by the guild when Solomon failed to turn up."

"It looks like he put up quite a fight," Shaw observed, her sharp gaze taking in the damage to the wall. She removed a small vial from her forensic bag and dabbed the silvery liquid it contained on one of the scorch lines with a cotton stick.

There was a purple sizzle.

Shaw frowned at the colour of the dark red residue it left behind. "This is the same magic I found in the hidden room under Professor Whitley's lab and outside the lecture hall where Leon was attacked, your Grace."

Viggo stared at them. "Leon was attacked?"

"Yes." Evander stood up, tension humming through him.

He briefly explained what had happened that morning, their discovery concerning Musgrave, and the conclusion McAndrew had come to about the artefact they'd taken to the Met.

Concern clouded Viggo's eyes. He took a step towards Evander. "Are you hurt?!"

Evander's expression softened a little. "I'm fine. Leon was the one who got injured."

Rufus cleared his throat discreetly.

Evander and Viggo became conscious of Shaw's avid stare.

The Brute lowered his brows. "If that device we found is similar to the *Blood Siphon*—"

"Then the sooner we find that hidden lab, the better," Evander agreed with a brisk nod.

He walked to the centre of the alley and released a pulse of magic, seeking any residual trace of arcane energy that could give them a clue to Solomon's possible whereabouts or his attacker's identity. His scalp prickled when a faint but unmistakable sensation brushed against his awareness—a shadow of the foul power he'd felt coming from Musgrave in the lecture hall.

Evander followed it to a pile of rubbish. His eyes narrowed when he spotted something glinting on the ground, half concealed by a crate. He squatted and used a handkerchief to retrieve the object.

It was a silver ring engraved with a rune.

"What is that?" Viggo asked, looming over him.

A thrill shot through Evander as he examined the item.

"It's a seal to remove wards." He took a careful sniff of the ring. "Judging from the stink of dark magic coming of it, it must belong to whoever took Solomon." He twisted and looked at the scorch marks on the wall. "Shadow creatures would not have made those, so Solomon must have fought a dark mage directly." Evander met Viggo's gaze and saw the light of hope come to life deep in his dark eyes. "It looks like we were right about our theory. They must have been watching from the shadows all along."

Remorse tightened Viggo's face. "I should have kept some men on him."

"None of us could have anticipated this," Evander said firmly. He straightened and placed a hand on Viggo's arm. The tension thrumming through the Brute's powerful muscles made his heart ache. "This is the first time they've snatched a thrall in broad daylight, Viggo. Blaming ourselves for what happened is not going to help Solomon."

Finn's gaze darted nervously between them. "What do you mean, watching from the shadows?"

Evander explained the theory he and Viggo had come up with. A thought struck him then—a terrible, chilling possibility that made his breath catch.

"The shadow creatures," he said slowly, his mind racing. "What if they're not just weapons or guards? What if they're extensions of the dark mage controlling them? Eyes and ears that can move undetected through the city?"

Rufus sucked in air. Shaw frowned heavily.

Viggo's face darkened. "Like puppets operated from a distance."

"Precisely." Evander's heart drummed wildly against his ribs. "That would explain how they managed to track and capture specific thralls without being detected themselves. And maybe even how they kidnapped Whitley and Chevalier. For all we know, the creatures hidden within the shadows could observe their targets for days, learning their routines, and—"

"Waiting for the perfect moment to strike," Viggo finished in a voice raw with anger.

Shaw shuddered. "So they could be watching us right now?"

They scanned the shadows around them. The overcast day seemed more ominous all of a sudden, each patch of darkness in the alley potentially harbouring unseen enemies.

"Anyone else getting a sudden case of the willies?" Shaw mumbled.

"I suspect they've retreated for now," Evander said uneasily. "They have what they came for."

The stark reality of Solomon's fate hung heavily between them. If the pattern held true, he would be used as a vessel for stolen magic—a process that had already killed at least one man that they knew of.

Viggo gnashed his teeth. "We need to find that facility!"

"Scotland Yard." Evander met his eyes steadily.

"Let's reconvene there and pool everything we've learned." He touched the Brute's shoulder. "We'll investigate every avenue at our disposal to find Solomon, even if we have to turn the entire city upside down. You have my word."

A measure of relief lightened Viggo's expression.

The journey back to the Met's headquarters passed in tense silence. Evander could feel his lover's growing fear with every passing minute as daylight bled from the sky. He wasn't sure if it was the dismal weather or the impending nightfall that was making him experience a sense of deep foreboding.

Leon was waiting for them in Evander's office. To their surprise, he wasn't alone. Elias McAndrew stood beside him, deep in conversation with a slender woman with auburn hair whom Evander recognised as Vivian Richfield, the Met's cryptology expert.

They were bent over something on his desk, their expressions grim.

"Ah, your Grace," Richfield greeted Evander briskly when he entered his office with the others. "Perfect timing." Her gaze landed on Viggo.

Evander quickly made the introductions.

The cryptologist acknowledged Viggo with a frank stare. "The Ironfist Brute. It's an honour." To his surprise, she offered him her hand.

"I'm sorry about your friend," Leon told Viggo solemnly while he shook Richfield's hand.

Viggo accepted the commiseration with a stiff nod.

"Any clues from the scene?" Leon asked Evander.

"Yes." Evander showed them the ring they'd found.

Richfield and McAndrew examined it curiously.

"A runic seal," the artificer murmured thoughtfully as he held the ring up to the light. "How interesting. I wonder why a dark mage would feel the need to carry one of these around?"

Evander spotted the open volume on his desk. Hope quickened his pulse.

"You've found something in Chevalier's journal?" he asked Richfield.

CHAPTER 36

"INDEED I HAVE. WE WERE JUST DISCUSSING MY findings." The cryptologist gestured to the sheets of notepaper covered in complex calculations and translations spread around the leather-bound tome. "The professor encoded much of his work, particularly in the later sections. But once I identified the cipher—a rather clever adaptation of a Vigenère square using alchemical symbols—the text became quite clear."

"And?" Rufus prompted impatiently.

A hard smile curved Richfield's mouth. "There's a map hidden within the journal's endpapers. When exposed to the right magical frequency, it revealed architectural plans for an extensive underground facility."

She held up a sheet of translucent paper upon which she had traced the revealed design. It showed a series of interconnected chambers and passages arranged in a circular pattern around a large central space.

"When we overlay this with the sketch from Whitley's journal"—McAndrew carefully placed a second transparent sheet atop the first—"we get this."

Evander's breath caught. The combined images formed a complete blueprint of what appeared to be an elaborate subterranean complex, with annotations in both Whitley and Chevalier's handwriting.

"Cor blimey," Shaw mumbled. "That's a research facility? It's enormous!"

Viggo lowered his brows. "Does the journal indicate its location?"

"That's where things get interesting. I was just about to tell McAndrew and Comte Beaulieu what I discovered in the last hour." Richfield's eyes were bright with the thrill of discovery. "Chevalier's notes referenced a connection to 'the cradle of arcane learning' and 'foundations laid upon older foundations.'"

Coldness ignited in Evander's chest and spread through his body when he recognised the words.

"The Royal Institute for the Arcane," Leon mumbled hoarsely, the blood draining from his face. He met Evander's gaze dazedly. "It was built upon the ruins of a magical academy destroyed in the Great Fire."

A stunned silence fell over the room.

"So it's been right under our noses all this time?" Shaw said, aghast.

"The audacity is breathtaking," McAndrew admitted grudgingly. "It's the last place anyone would think to look. And I bet the ambient magic in that place helped mask their activities."

"The Institute covers a lot of ground," Rufus said uneasily. "Can we narrow down this facility's location in relation to the existing buildings?"

Richfield lowered her brows. "There were some strange numbers in Chevalier's journal I couldn't make heads or tail out of. Now that I think about it, they could be formulas for coordinates. I would need a blueprint of the Institute to verify them."

Leon narrowed his eyes. "The Institute and the academy that preceded it date back centuries. It's been expanded numerous times. There could be whole sections that aren't on any official plans."

"I know who might have a copy of the original blueprint," Evander said in a hard voice. The enormity of the truth that had been uncovered made his stomach roil.

Or rather, the elaborate ruse.

It was becoming clear that the sacred place of learning he had long looked up to masked many abhorrent secrets.

"Can you find Quentin Inkwell?" he asked Shaw. "I wager he has a map of the Institute."

The forensic mage nodded sharply and left the office. She returned minutes later with the Met's only Occult Researcher. Inkwell looked his normal flustered self as he entered the office, his eyes large and bemused behind his enchanted glasses.

"What is this about, your Grace?" he asked anxiously.

Evander spotted the rolled-up parchment under his arm. "Is that a map of the Royal Institute?"

"Yes. Miss Shaw said to bring it."

"Can we have it please?" Evander asked briskly.

Inkwell reluctantly handed him the map.

Evander spread it out on the desk.

"I need a protractor and a ruler," Richfield said.

Evander went round his desk, opened a drawer, and passed her the tools.

Richfield checked the coordinates in Chevalier's journal and made some complex calculations in her notebook.

Everyone held their breath when she began drawing lines on the blueprint.

"If I'm correct, these are the longitude and latitude. Which makes this final number depth." She stood back and narrowed her eyes. "Based on my calculations, the principal entrance to the facility lies thirty feet beneath the Institute's south wing."

A buzzing sounded in Evander's ears.

"Wait." Shaw's knuckles whitened on the edge of the desk. "Isn't that the lecture hall where we fought Musgrave?!" She shot a stunned look at Evander.

Leon straightened, his expression growing animated. "That's why Musgrave was there this morning. I must have caught him when he was exiting the facility!"

Viggo's face hardened. "We need to go there right now. While there is still a chance Solomon and the missing thralls are alive."

The Brute's words jolted Evander out of his daze. He gathered his composure with some difficulty and levelled a frown at his lover. "I understand your feelings on this, but we cannot just go in blindly. We'll be risking the lives of those who make up the rescue mission."

Viggo looked like he wanted to protest. He hesitated and clenched his jaw.

"What do you suggest?" he asked brusquely.

Evander studied the map intently, his mind racing. "We'll have to move quickly, but not recklessly. If Musgrave or his master catch wind of our plans, they could accelerate whatever they're doing—or worse, move the captives elsewhere."

"Or kill them," Viggo added darkly.

Evander nodded gravely.

"This facility was clearly designed with defensive measures in mind." He traced the concentric rings of the underground chambers. "And if they're using thralls as conduits for magical energy, disrupting the process could be catastrophic for the captives."

Viggo went as still as stone.

"Dammit. I didn't think of that," he confessed hoarsely.

Evander's chest tightened at his pale complexion. He wanted nothing more than to take the Brute's hand right now. His nails dug into his palms.

Winterbourne was right. There's a risk my judgment may be compromised because of our relationship. But why is it that I find myself not caring about any of that right now?!

"How do we get in?" Shaw asked, distracting him from his turbulent thoughts. "There's a chance Musgrave will have a brigade of shadow creatures watching that lecture hall."

"You could use the sewers," a voice suggested.

They looked around.

Inkwell swallowed nervously at their stares. He came over and pointed at a small notation in the corner of the map. "For example, this tunnel. It's at the correct depth and is connected to the old Roman sewers that run beneath that part of London." He traced several other notations with his finger. "These probably indicate passages that lead elsewhere in the city."

Richfield blinked. "He's right."

Evander's mouth went dry. "That makes sense considering the age of the Institute and the academy that preceded it." He met Viggo's gaze, his pulse racing. "This could work to our advantage. They wouldn't expect an attack from below."

"I know those sewers," the Brute said grimly. "*Nightshade* has used them before."

"Then we have our way in." Evander straightened, a plan forming in his mind. "We'll need a coordinated approach—one team to secure the Institute aboveground and prevent reinforcements from joining the fight, another to infiltrate the facility from below."

"I'll lead the underground team," Viggo declared adamantly.

"We'll assign Met mages to go with you along with a group of officers," Evander said firmly.

"I should join Viggo," Leon suggested. "My *Nullification Magic* could prove crucial if we encounter magical barriers or traps."

Surprise jolted Evander. Leon's proposal made tactical sense. He met Viggo's gaze.

"It's your call."

The Brute hesitated, a muscle twitching in his jawline.

"I would appreciate that," he told Leon gruffly.

"This operation requires significant personnel," Rufus pointed out with a frown.

"I'm sure Winterbourne will authorise a Met task force and a mage squad from the Arcane Division," Evander said briskly.

Shaw grimaced. "Technically speaking, he already gave you carte blanche to do whatever you want, your Grace."

"She's right," Rufus admitted grudgingly.

Evander came to a decision. "Very well." He turned to the inspector. "Have a team of twenty assembled and ready to move within the hour. Everyone should be briefed on what we know of these shadow creatures and how to combat them."

"And Musgrave?" Shaw asked tensely. "We haven't had time to send officers to his home yet."

"I suspect he's at the facility." Evander studied the map with a scowl. "That's probably where he disappeared off to this morning, when he detonated that device." He turned to McAndrew. "I know you're still working on it, but how soon can you and Mrs. Scarborough complete that anti-shadow magic device I tasked you with?"

The artificer scratched his head awkwardly. "I

didn't want to say anything yet, but we actually completed a working prototype last night."

Evander's stomach flip-flopped. "You did?!"

"Yes." Wariness clouded McAndrew's face at his expression. "Wait, your Grace. You're not thinking of taking it on this mission, are you?!"

"That's exactly what I'm proposing," Evander said grimly.

Horror widened McAndrew's eyes.

"Mrs. Scarborough's going to have my hide," he groaned. "She told me not to tell you for this very reason."

"Yes, well, the cat's out of the bag now," Evander muttered.

The mage caught Viggo's arm and drew him aside while the others dispersed to their assigned tasks and McAndrew left to give Mrs. Scarborough the unwelcome news.

"We'll find Solomon," he promised quietly.

Something raw and vulnerable flashed in Viggo's dark eyes—a glimpse of the fear beneath his anger. "He's like a brother to me, Evander. If they've hurt him—"

Evander wished sorely he could offer more comfort than words. "Solomon is strong and he's clever. If anyone can survive this, it's him."

Viggo nodded stiffly, his throat working as he swallowed.

CHAPTER 37

THE ROYAL INSTITUTE LOOMED LIKE A DARK SENTINEL at the end of the cul-de-sac as Evander headed briskly towards it with Shaw and a team of mages from the Arcane Division. This area of Bloomsbury was eerily quiet, the cordon they'd erected at the end of the street keeping much of the traffic out.

Sergeant Griffiths and his men were already at the gates.

"We've finished evacuating the properties within a five-hundred-foot radius of here, your Grace," the sergeant reported briskly.

"Good." Evander scanned the assembled men and women. "Remember, we're dealing with dark mages and shadow creatures. Do not hesitate to engage full offensive powers." He hesitated. "And fall back if you feel you're in mortal danger. That's a direct order. No one will think any less of you if you do. I would rather you walk out of here alive than die a foolish death."

The officers and mages nodded, their expressions resolute despite his warning.

A figure hurried towards them from the direction of the cordon. It was Rufus.

"Winterbourne has stationed officers at the other exits," he told them quietly.

Richfield and Inkwell had identified where the underground tunnels connected to the secret facility had openings in the city. If Musgrave or any of his associates attempted to flee, they would be intercepted.

The buildings of the Institute stood silent as they crossed the courtyard, windows dark and not a soul in sight thanks to the evacuation order Evander had convinced Headmaster Rigley to issue under the guise of structural concerns after the magical confrontation with Musgrave that morning.

His thoughts strayed briefly to Viggo. The Brute should be approaching the sewer entrance with Leon by now.

The hallways echoed with their footsteps as they navigated the main building, the department-issued light orbs floating above their heads casting their shadows ahead of them. Evander felt the stares of the portraits lining the walls as they made their way towards the south wing. He could not help but wonder how many of the famous mages gracing the hallowed halls of the Institute had known about the secrets lurking beneath their feet.

They slowed as they approached the lecture hall.

"Wait here," Evander ordered quietly.

Rufus and Shaw watched tensely as he raised a

shield of wind and water magic and moved cautiously towards the entrance.

Evander's hand found the small crystal pendant around his neck.

It was the amulet McAndrew and Mrs. Scarborough had created to help combat shadow creatures. Though the device would not block the monsters completely, it would disrupt them enough to provide some measure of protection. McAndrew had told him the object also possessed an inbuilt warning system to alert the user to the creatures' proximity. Thankfully, he and Mrs. Scarborough had prepared two prototypes in their general wisdom.

Evander had given the second one to Leon.

He stopped at the side of the open doors and cast a pulse of elemental magic into the lecture hall. It returned nothing.

He steeled himself and stepped inside, his eyes swiftly scanning the gloom.

The room still bore scars from their battle with the professor that morning—scorch marks on the floor, cracks in the walls, and broken windows hastily boarded up. The splintered furniture had been pushed to the sides.

He detected no signs of shadow creatures or dark mages in the uncanny stillness, the cold amulet against his chest confirming what his senses were telling him.

"It's safe," Evander called out to the hall.

He headed for the middle of the room while the rest of the team piled in behind him. It was where Leon had surprised Musgrave and the professor had subsequently pulled his vanishing act.

"Are you sure this is the right place?" Rufus asked tensely while their light orbs ascended higher into the air and illuminated the deserted lecture hall.

Evander nodded, his gaze fixed on the heavy wooden lectern. "The coordinates in Whitley and Chevalier's journals pointed to this position. The entrance must be here somewhere." He circled the structure before squatting to examine the floor.

Shaw crouched opposite him and studied the wooden base of the podium. Her eyes narrowed after a moment. "The wood grain doesn't match here." She indicated a barely discernible seam that ran along one side of the structure.

Evander's pulse quickened. He joined her and trailed his fingers over the smooth oak surface. "You're right."

They followed the near invisible line to the recess under the lectern.

A trace of magic prickled Evander's skin then. "There's something there."

He removed his foldable cane, engaged the magic in the crystal at the top, and moved the light closer.

Shaw spotted it first. "There, your Grace. Directly underneath!" She pointed excitedly.

Evander shifted the light closer.

There was an engraving in the wood on the underside of the lectern.

"That looks like the symbol on the ring you found in the alley," Shaw said excitedly.

Evander's heart slammed against his ribs as he withdrew the silver ring they had discovered close to where Solomon had disappeared. He'd been carrying it on his person ever since, suspecting it might prove useful. The ring felt unnaturally cold in his palm as he held it up to the light.

He and Shaw compared the rune inscribed in the metal to the engraving.

It was an identical match.

"This might be a key to the facility." Evander shot an uneasy glance at Shaw and the others. "It would be best if you moved back. This could trigger some kind of defensive measure once I activate it."

They retreated several paces, tension evident in the set of their shoulders. The four Met officers positioned by the doors shifted uneasily, knuckles whitening on their warded truncheons.

Evander focused his magic on the energy he'd detected within the lectern. It was a moment before the complex arcane symbols present beneath the layers of mundane wood became evident to his senses; they pulsed with a subdued power that made his scalp prickle. His heart quickened when the pattern became clear to him.

"It's a ward lock." He frowned. "Not unlike those used in the Ministry of Arcane Affairs for their most sensitive archives."

Rufus and Shaw exchanged a wary look.

"Go for it, your Grace," Shaw said in a hard voice.

Evander's shoulders knotted as he aligned the ring

and the engraving with deliberate care. Metal slotted smoothly into wood.

The silver band immediately grew warm in his fingers.

Arcane runes flared to life, the symbols glowing an eerie crimson before fading just as quickly.

The ground beneath them shuddered.

"Move!" Evander barked. He yanked the ring out of the engraving and pulled back just as the lectern began to sink.

Shaw gasped when a section of the floor disappeared beneath her.

"*Lyra!*" Rufus lunged to grab her.

Evander cursed and raised his hand. A powerful burst of wind magic surged from his fingertips and shot towards the plummeting forensic mage. The vortex wrapped around her, buffeting her body and halting her fall.

Shaw stared at the gaping void beneath her feet as Evander carefully floated her up to safety.

"Blimey, I thought I was a goner there," she mumbled.

Rufus and Griffiths took hold of her arms and steadied her as she stepped onto solid ground. They gathered cautiously around the previously concealed entrance.

A set of stone steps descended into darkness where the wooden platform and the section of floor had once been. Cool air wafted up from below. It carried the stench of damp stone and something else—something foul and ominous that set Evander's teeth on edge.

"By God, that's unholy," Rufus whispered, his face pale in the dim light.

Griffiths looked similarly troubled beside him.

Evander summoned a sphere of fire to illuminate the passage. It would serve not only to light the way but weaken whatever corrupt magic choked the passages beneath them. The orange flames cast elongated shadows across the stone walls as he took the first step down.

"Stay on your guard," he warned over his shoulder.

THE STAIRCASE DROPPED TEN FEET BEFORE TURNING AT A sharp angle, the steps worn smooth by countless passages over what must have been decades. The air grew increasingly stale and thick as they descended and the walls soon transformed from dressed stone to rough-hewn rock.

"Twenty feet down," Shaw murmured. "We're well below the Institute's foundations now."

The staircase ended abruptly at a narrow passageway lined with ensconced brackets for torches long since extinguished. Evander augmented the fireball and sent it ahead to illuminate their path.

"This architecture predates the Institute." Rufus frowned and ran his fingers along the ancient stonework. "These are Tudor-era construction techniques, possibly even earlier."

"It's probably part of the original arcane academy," Evander said tightly. "Shaw, do you have the map?"

"Hang on a minute, your Grace."

To everyone's consternation, the forensic mage reached discreetly inside her cleavage and slipped out the copy of the facility blueprint Richfield had made for them before they'd left Scotland Yard.

Shaw blinked innocently at their shocked stares. "What?"

"Was there nowhere else you could have kept that?" Rufus asked testily.

"I was afraid it would fall out of my coat," the forensic mage said with a dismissive shrug. "Besides, there's nowhere safer than my bosom. Ask the chap who tried to cop a feel the other day."

"Was that the man with the broken fingers you hauled into the Met?" Sergeant Griffiths grunted.

"Exactly," Shaw confirmed smugly.

Evander sighed and took the overly warm map off her before forging ahead.

The corridor branched several times, the vile power they'd sensed in the lecture hall intensifying as they progressed farther inside the complex. They finally reached a heavy iron door after what felt like an eternity navigating the subterranean maze.

Unlike the ancient stonework surrounding it, it was undeniably modern—crafted from burnished metal, it was inscribed with arcane symbols that glowed faintly in the presence of his flames.

"Is it another ward?" Rufus asked edgily.

Evander lowered his brows. "Yes."

He examined the intricate patterns etched into the metal before pressing the seal ring against the centre of the door, where the symbols converged. A series of mechanical clicks echoed around them as the complex locking mechanisms disengaged.

"Let's hope no one on the other side heard that," Shaw muttered.

They tensed when the door swung open on silent hinges.

A gloomy, empty corridor lay beyond.

"Engage your offensive magic," Evander quietly told the assembled officers and mages.

Runes and spells came to life behind him, the power crackling the air making the hairs on his nape stand on end.

Evander's heart raced as he stepped inside the enemy's lair, the others following silently in his wake. Rooms appeared on either side of the passageway, the shadows within them retreating as he cast light into the far corners. Some had sleeping cots and desks. One hosted a kitchen with a dining table. There was even a washing facility.

"Looks like people have been living down here, your Grace," Shaw whispered.

Evander clenched his jaw at the thought of all the evil that had played out in this place, deep beneath an Institute that was meant to guard against the very horrors it represented.

A low hum started vibrating through the floor as they advanced.

Evander stiffened and stopped when the amulet against his chest grew warm and began glowing with a pale light.

Rufus's wary gaze found the pendant. "Is that—?"

"Yes," Evander said in a hard voice. "There are shadow creatures close by."

A fraught hush fell around him.

Another door appeared up ahead. Unlike the first one, it wasn't warded.

Cold fingers danced down Evander's spine when he sensed the foul energy seeping around the hinges. He pressed his ear against the cold metal. No sound came from beyond it.

"Get ready," he warned.

He closed his fingers on the handle and swiftly pulled the door open.

The chamber beyond was vast, its ceiling lost in obscurity despite the illumination from Evander's flames. A burning chill raised goose bumps on his skin, the acrid taste and stench of corrupt magic so abominable it scorched his tongue and nasal passages and made his eyes water despite his defences.

Several officers and mages gagged and threw up. Griffiths pressed a hand to his mouth and nose, his face ashen.

Evander erected a protective barrier of wind and fire magic around them. It cleared the air and made it easier to breathe again.

"Your Grace!" Shaw barked.

There was movement above.

A shadow creature was dropping silently towards them, its maw opening to gargantuan proportion. Evander scowled when he spotted the writhing mass of monsters hiding near the ceiling behind it.

The shadow creature screeched and recoiled when

the power in the amulet reached it, the dark tendrils making up its form beginning to unravel.

It was all the time Evander needed to obliterate it with his fire magic.

The mages behind him cast a barrage of attacks at the remaining shadow creatures where they writhed and flickered in the air, temporarily weakened by the magic contained within the pendant around Evander's neck. His ice spears ripped the last monster to shreds that vanished with a fading shriek.

Ice chilled his veins when he finally got a look at the chamber the creatures had been guarding.

Row upon row of workbenches stretched before them beyond a shallow landing, each cluttered with arcane instruments, glass containers, and meticulously labelled specimens. The smell that had bothered Evander on the stairs was stronger here, rising even above the lingering dark magic. He now recognised it for what it was—antiseptic mingled with pure evil.

"What in God's name?" Rufus breathed.

Evander negotiated the short flight of steps and approached the nearest workstation. His stomach churned at what he found.

Anatomical diagrams had been pinned to a board, depicting the nervous system of what appeared to be a common house cat—except the annotations detailed how magical energy had been channelled through its body, with corresponding notes on the resulting physical changes.

"They were experimenting on animals," Shaw said, horror evident in her voice as she examined a series of glass jars containing preserved specimens sitting on a shelf.

Evander's nails dug into his palm. "These were probably precursor studies to test their theory."

Shaw met his gaze and swallowed. "You mean, before moving on to human subjects?"

Evander nodded, too incensed to answer.

The Met's officers and mages stared aghast at their frightening discovery. Evander could see anger replacing shock on many of their faces. Whatever their personal beliefs and opinions about magic users and thralls, they had all sworn to protect the people of this city.

They moved methodically through the chamber, uncovering the grotesque evidence of experiments spanning what must have been years of secret research. Some of the journals they found dated back more than a decade, suggesting the programme had begun long before Whitley and Chevalier had become involved.

"Evander," Rufus called urgently from the other side of the room. "You need to see this."

Evander hurried over to where the inspector stood before a glass-fronted cabinet that contained dozens upon dozens of vials. His eyes widened at the sight of the silvery liquid they contained.

"That's arcane residue!"

The vials bore markings indicating their contents: fire, water, wind, earth, light, shadow, and even a handful of esoteric magics Evander had only read about in ancient texts. His gaze landed on a shelf.

The sight of the labels made his heart thump violently inside his chest.

The vials were devoted entirely to different kinds of hybrid magic.

"What's all this, your Grace?" Griffiths asked in a guarded voice as he approached.

Evander briefed the sergeant about Ambrose Mortimer's autopsy findings.

Griffiths paled. Horror rounded the eyes of the officers and mages who'd followed him.

"You mean," one of them quavered, "all these vials represent failed experiments?"

Evander could see the sickening truth he'd already reached dawning on their faces.

"Probably." He studied the cabinet and its contents with a scowl. "And if that is the truth, then each of these vials likely represents a dead animal or person."

A sound from beyond the laboratory had them all freezing. The low, mechanical hum that had brought them there was growing louder, the buzzing punctuated by the gurgle of liquid flowing through pipes.

"Your Grace, there's another door!" Shaw hissed from the far end of the laboratory.

Evander and the others joined her swiftly.

A cold, blue light spilled under the door she had discovered, along with the smell of corrupt magic. Low voices came from beyond, their tone strangely rhythmical, as if they were chanting.

Tension knotted Evander's shoulders. He glanced at his companions and signalled with his hand.

"In five," he mouthed.

They nodded, determination filling their faces as they grasped their weapons and manifested their powers.

Evander gathered his magic protectively around him and was silently counting down when startled cries suddenly erupted on the other side of the door. An explosion boomed an instant later. The blue glow under the door shifted to crimson.

Fear choked his chest when he recognised Leon and Viggo's voices in the aftermath of the detonation.

He kicked the door open, heedless of losing the element of surprise. A revolting, metallic tang of dark magic mired with *Blood Magic* washed over him and caused him to gag. The amulet around his neck flared white.

Evander pressed a hand to his mouth and nose and froze, the sight before him making the air lock in his throat.

CHAPTER 39

THE STENCH OF THE SEWERS WAS ALMOST UNBEARABLE.

Viggo grimaced as he and Leon splashed through ankle-deep filth in their rubber waders and galoshes, the glow of their enchanted lanterns piercing the sulphurous gloom. They could not risk live fire down here, not with how flammable the noxious gases around them could turn out to be.

The damp air clung to the Brute's skin, carrying with it the putrid scent of decay and God only knew what else. Behind them trailed a contingent of Met officers and mages, their weapons and warded shields at the ready.

"I take it you've navigated these tunnels before?" Leon asked, his nose wrinkled in disgust as he held a handkerchief to his face. The prototype device McAndrew and Mrs. Scarborough had made swung lightly against his chest.

"More times than I care to remember," Viggo muttered. "Sometimes the only way to move undetected through London is beneath it."

Leon cast him a sidelong glance. "Somehow I find it difficult to imagine someone of your stature moving 'undetected' anywhere."

Viggo shot him a dark look. "You'd be surprised how invisible thralls can be in this city."

The Frenchman had the grace to look chastened.

"How much farther, sir?" one of the Met officers called out from behind, his voice echoing uncomfortably in the confined space.

"Another quarter mile," Viggo replied gruffly, ignoring the 'sir.' "The access point should be directly beneath the south wing of the Institute."

They had entered the labyrinthine network of tunnels through a maintenance entrance near Russell Square and were following the route Richfield and Inkwell had mapped out for them. Richfield's calculations had matched Viggo's knowledge of London's underground passages.

They reached a junction where four tunnels converged.

Viggo indicated the rightmost passage. "This way."

"You're certain this is the right direction?" Leon asked uncertainly as the Brute took the lead and headed into the tunnel.

"We'd make better speed if you stopped second-guessing me," Viggo muttered.

Leon sighed and seemed to immediately regret the act when he inhaled a particularly foul vapour that made him gag.

Viggo swallowed a grin.

The tunnel gradually narrowed as they continued through the warren of passages, forcing them to proceed in single file. The officer behind Leon muttered a string of colourful curses when a pair of rats slithered past his boot. They soon reached a brick archway that looked considerably newer than the surrounding stonework.

"Almost there," Viggo said. "This section was rebuilt after the Great Fire."

He finally halted beneath an iron grating set into the ceiling of the tunnel. Unlike the rusted fixtures they'd passed, this one gleamed dully in the lantern light, its bars untarnished by time or the corrosive effluvia of the sewers. It had been bolted shut with a padlock.

"This looks new," Leon observed.

Viggo frowned. "Yes."

He passed his lantern to Leon and reached up to test the grate. As expected, it was fixed solidly into the stone. Muscles bunched in his arms as he strained. He ripped out the grating with nary a grunt, revealing a dimly lit chamber of some kind. The padlock splashed into the sewers at his feet.

Leon's mouth flattened to a thin line. "I guess that's one way of opening it."

"It was the fastest method," Viggo said succinctly.

He grabbed the edges of the opening and hoisted himself up with ease, his powerful arms making light work of his weight. Once inside, he crouched and surveyed his surroundings.

The room was small and unadorned, its stone walls

bare save for a series of hooks. Stacked crates framed a closed door opposite him.

"All clear," he called down softly. "Come up one at a time."

Leon ascended first, the mage moving with the fluid grace Viggo had grudgingly come to admire over the past few days. The Frenchman's presence in the city might be a source of tension between them, but his physical capabilities were undeniable. The Met officers and mages followed, each one helped up by Viggo.

They quickly disposed of their waders and galoshes.

"Where are we?" whispered one of the mages, a thin woman with spectacles who specialised in defensive wards.

"Some kind of storage room." Viggo moved towards the door. "Stay alert. We don't know how many people might be down here."

He pressed his ear to the wooden surface and listened for any sound of movement beyond. None reached him. He tested the handle. It turned smoothly in his grasp.

"Ready?" Viggo asked, glancing back at Leon.

The Frenchman nodded, his hands already glowing with the pale light of his magic.

Viggo eased the door open and winced at the faint creak of its hinges. The corridor beyond was empty, the passage illuminated by enchanted sconces that cast a sickly glow across the stone floor. The air here carried a peculiar scent.

He couldn't sense magic the way mages could, but he'd been around it enough to recognise its effects. The atmosphere in this place was heavy, oppressive, as if the very air was saturated with malevolent intent.

From the way Leon's face tightened, he was right on the money.

"Which way?" the Frenchman asked.

Viggo consulted the map Richfield had given them. "Left. If the facility layout matches the professors' journals, there should be a junction ahead that leads to the holding cells."

They moved cautiously down the corridor.

It ended in a T-junction, just as the map had indicated. To the right, Viggo could see a series of doors interspersed along the passage, while the left branch continued unbroken into darkness.

Viggo indicated the right path with a jerk of his head. "The cells should be this way."

Leon frowned. "How can you be so sure?"

"Because that's where I'd put them," Viggo replied simply.

Leon studied him for a moment before nodding. "Lead on."

They proceeded down the right-hand corridor and passed several doors. A quick inspection revealed them to be storage areas and small laboratories. Viggo peered through an observation window in one and saw benches covered in arcane instruments and vessels containing mysterious substances. The sight made his stomach turn.

The faint sound of voices reached him after they'd advanced another thirty feet—a low murmur punctuated by an occasional thump and scrape.

Viggo stiffened and raised a hand, halting the group.

Leon moved to his side, his expression tense. "How many?" he whispered.

"At least two, possibly more."

The mage who had spoken earlier stepped forward. "Sir, I can create a sensory ward to mask our approach," she said in a low voice.

"Do it," Leon instructed.

She traced a complex pattern in the air, her fingers leaving faint trails of luminescence that quickly faded. A bubble of magic expanded around their group, distorting the air slightly before becoming invisible.

"We'll be harder to see or hear now," the mage explained. "But it won't last long—perhaps five minutes at most."

"It'll do," Viggo said in a hard voice. "Stay close."

They moved forward with renewed caution. The sounds grew clearer as they approached a section of the corridor that widened into a small antechamber.

Viggo's heart lurched. He stopped in his tracks, Leon freezing beside him.

Two men stood with their backs to them, deep in conversation while they moved an unconscious figure towards a doorway.

Viggo stilled at the sight of the slender, pale-faced blonde the men were handling with nonchalant care, heedless of the way they kept bumping her head on the floor. He was pretty certain he was looking at Katie Stoker.

Leon's eyes darkened.

Viggo could understand his fury. The blue robes the men wore were a symbol of the Institute he had once been a student of. The Brute was pretty certain they were not faculty members but dark mages who had acquired the attire to disguise themselves.

"—still unstable," one of the men was saying. He was tall, with stooped shoulders. "The transference rate is improving, but the mortality rate remains unacceptable."

"Musgrave doesn't care about that," the other replied dismissively. "He's more concerned with proof of concept than sustainability at this stage."

"Easy for him to say. He's not the one who has to dispose of the failures."

Viggo's vision narrowed at their casual discussion of human lives. He almost took a step forward in his rage, but Leon's hand on his arm restrained him.

"Wait," the Frenchman mouthed silently.

The two dark mages continued their conversation, oblivious to the intruders behind them.

"When is the next extraction scheduled?" the taller one asked.

"Tonight. Musgrave wants to attempt a second full elemental transfer using the thrall we captured today."

"You mean Lady Hartley's new servant?"

Ice flooded Viggo's veins. *Solomon!*

"Yes."

"Is he mad?!" the smaller man hissed. "We've yet to see a successful full transfer who survived the experiment. Sure, we've managed partial transfers, but you saw what happened with the last fellow he attempted to do a complete one on. He burned from the inside out! There was nothing left of him but a husk!" The dark mage gagged. "God, even thinking about how he smelled afterwards makes me want to vomit. I hope the thrall Musgrave is working on right now doesn't end up the same."

The taller mage frowned. "Pull yourself together, will you? Besides, that's not our concern. You heard what he said. His master wants results."

Viggo couldn't contain himself any longer. He shook off Leon's restraining hand and strode forward, his massive frame emerging from the ward's protective bubble.

CHAPTER 40

"Where is he?" he growled, his voice echoing in the confined space. "Where's Solomon and the other thralls you're keeping prisoner, you bastards?!"

The two mages dropped their charge clumsily and whirled around, shock evident on their faces. The shorter one recovered first. Dark magic flared in his hands as he prepared to unleash a spell.

Leon's *Nullification Magic* caused his powers to dissipate in the blink of an eye.

Viggo closed the distance to the mage in two powerful strides and drove his fist into his solar plexus. The man doubled over with a wheezing gasp. Viggo knocked him out with a sharp blow to the back of his head.

The taller mage backed away and fumbled for something in his robes.

A wall of water surged past Viggo before he could move. The Brute's pulse raced as Leon wrapped the man inside a bubble from which there would be no escape.

The device the dark mage had removed from his robes detonated in his hand, the sound of the explosion muffled by the water. He screamed and gurgled, the water around him rapidly turning red with his own blood. All that was left of his hand was a mangled mess where bone and gristle protruded.

Leon waited until he choked and lost consciousness before releasing his magic.

A few officers rapidly secured the fallen mages while Viggo checked on Stoker. He swallowed when he felt the strong pulse at her throat. Her breathing was slow and deep, indicating sedation rather than a state of near death.

"How is she?" Leon asked thinly, squatting beside him.

"Alive." Viggo gently pulled up the unconscious thrall's eyelid. Her blown pupil was all the confirmation he needed.

"They've drugged her," Leon stated in a hard voice.

"We should move her to one of the storage areas for the time being and have an officer and a mage guard her," Viggo suggested.

The mage who'd created the sensory ward volunteered. "I'll do it, sir," she said nervously. "My magic can help keep us hidden."

"Thank you," Leon said.

Viggo gave her a grateful nod. He rose and studied the metal door at the end of the antechamber. It was where the men had been heading. He shot a scowl at the unconscious mages.

"Check their pockets for a key or a seal ring."

To his chagrin, the officers found nothing.

Leon moved to the door and ran his hands lightly over the metal, his brow furrowed in concentration.

"It's warded," he confirmed grimly. "Multiple layers. It may take a little while to dismantle them safely without alerting anyone of our presence."

"We don't have time!" Viggo growled. "Just use your *Nullification Magic* to strip it bare. I'll take care of the rest."

A muscle jumped in Leon's jawline. He released a frustrated sigh and began undoing the wards.

"Don't blame me if a bunch of shadow creatures appear and eat your face."

"They won't," Viggo grunted. "That amulet around your neck hasn't glowed once in all the time we've been inside the facility."

Still, everyone held their breath when the Frenchman finished removing the magic wards on the door. To their palpable relief, no monsters appeared.

Viggo braced himself and drove his shoulder into the door with all the force he could muster. Metal caved under his blow. He moved back and repeated the movement with even more force. A tortured sound left the hinges. Viggo scowled, retreated a step, and kicked the door.

It went flying off the frame and clattered noisily inside a long corridor lined with cells.

The stench of fear and human waste washed over them.

"Solomon!" Viggo shouted, moving quickly down the line of cells. He peered desperately through the observation slits in each door. "Solomon, can you hear me?!"

A voice responded from one of the cells near the end. "Viggo? Is that you?!"

Relief made Viggo weak-kneed. He hurried to the door and found Solomon's tense face peering through the narrow opening. He had a few bruises and was favouring his right leg, but otherwise looked remarkably well considering the circumstances.

"Thank God," the Brute whispered shakily, his fingers finding Solomon's through the slit in the door.

"Took you long enough," Solomon said with a lopsided grin.

"Yes, well, Evander and I promised to turn this city upside down to find you," Viggo admitted with a weak smile. He studied the cell door. "Stand back."

He was about to kick it down when two officers rushed towards them, metal jingling in their hands.

"Sir, we found the keys!"

It took but a moment to open the cell door.

Viggo engulfed Solomon in a bear hug when he stepped out.

Leon began working on the next lock. The Met officers and mages joined him, splitting up to work on the remaining cells. The doors opened one by one, revealing thralls in various states of distress. Some could barely stand, while others seemed physically unharmed but mentally distant, their eyes dull and vacant.

Viggo counted twenty people in total. Eight of them wore clothes more befitting of nobles than thralls.

"Sir, some of these prisoners are mages," one of the Met's officers confirmed as he listened to a woman whisper something to him from parched lips.

Viggo searched the faces of the thralls. "Did you find Tom Simmons?" he asked Solomon.

"He's in the main chamber, along with the missing professors," Solomon replied darkly.

Viggo frowned. "Main chamber?"

Solomon's eyes grew haunted. "It's where they're conducting their experiments. It's a massive laboratory with these—tanks. There are people floating in them, kept alive somehow while they have their magic extracted." He shuddered. "I saw it when they brought me in. They were attempting to inject the magic they'd stolen into a thrall."

Viggo and Leon exchanged a grim look. The description matched what they had most feared.

"We need to hurry," Solomon urged. "When they took Simmons, I heard one of them say he was ready for the 'final stage.' I haven't seen him since."

Dread settled in Viggo's gut. The final stage was no doubt the full elemental transfer the two mages they'd knocked out had alluded to.

"Please, help them."

Viggo and Leon turned to the female mage they'd rescued. She was staring at them, her eyes wide and her hand clutching the arm of the officer who was helping her stay upright.

"I'm a scientist myself. What they're attempting to do isn't stable," she mumbled with a German accent. "Most of the thralls won't survive."

Viggo's throat tightened. "How many have died already?"

The woman exchanged a harrowed glance with one of the other prisoner mages. "Four that we know of since we were brought here a month ago. They—they screamed for hours before the end." Her face crumpled, a low sob escaping her.

Rage and horror warred within Viggo's chest.

Leon placed a hand on his shoulder. "Focus," the Frenchman said in a hard voice. "You can indulge your anger later."

Viggo took a shallow breath and nodded stiffly, not trusting himself to speak.

"Let's go," Solomon said in a resolute voice. "I'll show you where they are."

"You're in no condition to fight," Viggo protested.

Solomon lowered his brows. "You're not stopping me, Viggo."

Frustration burned through the Brute. "Alright," he reluctantly agreed. "Just make sure you stay behind me."

Leon studied the captives with a frown. "We should send these people back the way we came. A couple of the officers can guide them to the sewer entrance while the rest of us continue. The men Winterbourne has stationed there can take them to the Met's infirmary for care."

"Have them bring Katie too," Viggo said. "And they should take a pair of mages with them to be on the safe side."

Leon nodded.

The Frenchman assigned a small team to escort the freed thralls and mages to the room where they'd entered the secret facility while they continued on.

Solomon guided them swiftly down the left-hand branch beyond the T-junction. They navigated a maze of passages and passed several deserted rooms. He finally slowed at the entrance of a large antechamber.

Solomon stopped and frowned heavily at the metal doors ahead.

"The main lab is beyond those. It's vast and round—like a cathedral underground. There are tanks arranged around a central device, with walkways connecting them. The base of the chamber looked like some kind of cave, the bottom of which I couldn't make out." His voice faltered. "There were at least six mages working there when I was brought through, including the man in charge."

Leon's face tightened. He briefly described Musgrave.

Solomon nodded grimly. "That's him alright."

Viggo furrowed his brow. "Whitley and Chevalier are in those tanks too?"

"Yes." A muscle jumped in Solomon's cheek. "I spoke to several of the captive mages and thralls. They said the two professors were tortured for days to get information from them. This Musgrave guy then decided they weren't of any use to him and chose to use them as his lab rats instead. They were dragged out of their cells yesterday." He paused. "I think he's extracting their magic."

A fraught silence fell over the group, the implications of his words sending a chill through them all.

Viggo's thoughts strayed to Evander as he studied the metal doors.

He'll be closing in on this place soon, I'm sure of it.

"We end this now," the Brute said in a steely voice.

"Let me take the lead," Leon urged. "I can disrupt whatever arcane processes they have running in there."

Viggo started to object, then reconsidered. Regardless of his personal feelings about the Frenchman, it was a sound tactical decision.

"Very well," he agreed. "I'll be right next to you."

Leon smiled faintly. "I'm counting on you to have my back, Brute, just as you have his."

Admiration darted through Viggo then. He could vaguely understand why Evander had once loved this man. He turned to the remaining Met officers and mages.

"Are you ready?"

They nodded, determination evident in their faces despite the fear lingering in their eyes.

Leon positioned himself before the doors and gathered his powers around him like a cloak. He stiffened a little when the amulet around his neck began glowing.

"There are shadow creatures in there," the Frenchman stated grimly.

"Then we'll just have to deal with them," Viggo muttered.

Leon squinted at him. "I can see why he likes you."

Viggo blinked.

"On my mark," the Frenchman warned. He took a deep breath. "*Now!*"

Viggo thrust the doors open at the same time Leon unleashed a wall of magic.

The sight that greeted their eyes would haunt the Brute's nightmares for years to come.

THE CHAMBER WAS VAST, ITS CEILING AND THE bottomless pit beneath the series of metal walkways, stairs, and platforms that made up the lab shrouded in shadows despite the eerie blue glow emanating from the series of glass tanks arranged in a circle on individual platforms around a machine in the centre.

The air crackled with a corrupt magical energy that made Viggo's skin crawl and his hair stand on end.

There were people inside the tanks—mages and thralls suspended in a viscous fluid, naked and eyes closed in slumber. He recognised Whitley and Chevalier from their descriptions, as well as Simmons. An apparatus that pumped air in and out of their lungs covered their mouths and noses, while tubes and wires snaked out of their arms, legs, and heads, connecting them to the nightmarish device in the middle of the lab.

Viggo's head tilted as he stared at it, his mouth dry.

It was a towering construct of glass, brass, and

copper not dissimilar in appearance to the device they'd found under Whitley's laboratory. The main difference, bar its gargantuan size, was the dark crystal floating inside it. It was the size of a man's fist and pulsed with a malevolent force that looked to be powering the machinery, making it hum and throb like a living organ.

Viggo clenched his jaw. If he had to guess, he was looking at a core of *Midnight Obsidian*. It was the heart of the facility—an ode to magical perversion.

From the way Whitley and Chevalier twitched and winced sporadically inside their glass cages, the crystal was drawing magical essence from them.

A convulsion suddenly shook Simmons.

Viggo's eyes rounded in horror as silver lines began tracing patterns beneath his skin.

"They're injecting him with magic!" he growled.

Leon stayed his motion with a hand as he prepared to surge forward.

Five robed figures stood around the main machine on an elevated platform, their arms outstretched as they poured their corrupt magic into the device. Professor Musgrave orchestrated the proceedings at their centre, his face illuminated starkly by the glow of dark energy swirling around his hands.

They hadn't noticed them yet.

"I'm going to try and eliminate their magic," the Frenchman said in a strained voice. "Use these ice spears and hurl them at that machine." He manifested the weapons and gave them to Viggo. "I've made them strong enough to smash that glass. Aim for the crystal."

The cold burned Viggo's palms as he met the Frenchman's determined stare. He gripped the spears tightly and nodded.

Magic washed across his skin as Leon drew on his powers, the Frenchman's pupils flaring white.

One of the dark mages finally spotted them.

"We have intruders!" he yelled.

Startled shouts erupted from his companions as they whirled around and looked down upon them, their sinister ritual temporarily abandoned. The shadow creatures hidden in the murky gloom of the ceiling appeared as they called the monsters to them.

Musgrave turned, his expression shifting from shock to fury when he registered their presence. His gaze locked with Viggo's. A twisted smile spread across his features.

"Ah. The Duke's pet thrall."

"*Now!*" Leon barked.

Viggo drew his arms back and cast the spears with an explosive grunt. They flew straight and true one after the other, like deadly arrows.

Confusion clouded Musgrave's face when the shadow creatures and the corrupt power he and his companions wielded fizzled out under the tremendous wave of *Nullification Magic* Leon unleashed. Horror widened his eyes as he finally grasped their intent. His head snapped up, his frozen gaze following the ice spears' passage.

"No!" he roared. He reached out with his hand and guided a fading shadow creature into the path of the projectiles.

The first ice spear pierced the monster and smashed into the device, cracking the glass. The second ice spear struck the base of the first one like a hammer and drove it straight through the glass and into the dark crystal.

Musgrave cursed as the humming and throbbing stuttered. The liquid inside the machine began leaking around the edges of the fracture.

"Damn," Leon muttered, his tone full of admiration as he glanced at Viggo. "I couldn't have done that better if I'd tried!"

A high-pitched whine made them stiffen.

The dark crystal began pulsing with a crimson light that grew brighter and brighter until it practically seared their vision.

Viggo saw Musgrave dive to the ground through the dark spots swarming his eyes. He gasped when the device imploded with a mighty *whooph* that made his ears pop.

The negative pressure wave sucked him forward.

A cry of horror left Leon as it lifted him off his feet and pulled him inexorably towards the railing of the platform they stood on, his wind magic overwhelmed by the violent current.

"Leon!" Viggo yelled as he disappeared over it. He lunged forward, heedless of Solomon's shout.

The world tilted as he pitched over into a maw of darkness. His left hand closed on Leon's wrist at the same time his right hand found purchase on the edge of the platform base. For a moment, he thought they would be okay.

His fingers slipped.

Horror widened Leon's eyes below him as they plunged into the abyss.

A violent windstorm boomed around them, buffeting their bodies and freezing their fall.

"*Viggo! Leon!*" someone yelled.

Viggo's heart pounded violently in his ribs as he met Evander's frantic gaze across the cavernous chamber.

Darkness ignited the air around Musgrave, the effect of Leon's *Nullification Magic* abating. He manifested a veritable horde of shadow creatures and directed them to attack Evander.

EVANDER SCOWLED AND RAISED A WALL OF FIRE AROUND him and the officers and mages in his wake. The shadow creatures recoiled with high-pitched shrieks. They writhed and danced around them, their inky forms trembling under the effect of the flames and the amulet shining brightly against his chest.

His pulse thrummed as he carefully manoeuvred Viggo and Leon to the safety of the platform they'd fallen off. He focused on Musgrave next.

"You have nowhere to run, Professor," Evander said coldly. His gaze swept the machine with the dark crystal and the tanks where Musgrave's victims floated. His voice when he spoke again was lifeless, the fury making his body vibrate barely suppressed. "This facility is surrounded. We will not harm you if you surrender quietly."

Musgrave laughed, a mad sound. "Surrender?! Are you insane, Ice Mage?" He sneered. "Or shall I call you *Archmage?*" He glanced at the officers and mages slowly inching around the chamber to encircle them. A deranged smile stretched the professor's mouth. "We're in the midst of a delicate procedure, Duke Ravenwood. One that will revolutionise our very understanding of magic." He gestured to the tanks where Whitley and Chevalier hung suspended. "They had their chance to be part of something groundbreaking. They chose to be obstacles in my path instead." He straightened to his full height. "What you see here is merely the beginning."

"The beginning of what?!" Evander bit out, blood pounding in his skull. "Torture? Murder?!"

The violent magic churning inside his chest and beneath his skin itched for release. All it would take was lifting the lid a fraction and this entire laboratory would be reduced to rubble. He took a deep breath and fought for control.

"Progress." Musgrave's eyes shrank to slits. "The advancement of magical science beyond arbitrary limitations imposed by nature itself." His face hardened. "Surely you of all people can appreciate that. Your own magic is quite remarkable. Imagine if such a power could be replicated, distributed to those deemed worthy."

Evander gritted his teeth. "There's nothing worthy about what you're doing here!"

Musgrave sighed, as if disappointed by his lack of vision. "I expected more understanding from a member of the nobility." He shot a sadistic look at Leon. "And you, Mr. French Investigator. After all, it was your countrymen who pioneered much of this research." He smiled thinly as Leon paled. "Oh yes, *Les Prophètes Illuminés* laid the groundwork for this decades ago. We merely perfected their methods. If Chevalier hadn't discovered his morals, we would have made more headway by now."

Evander stepped forward, fury bubbling in his veins.

"You've broken every law of magical ethics, you damn fiend!" he snarled. "In the name of the Metropolitan Police and by the authority of the Crown, I am placing you under arrest!"

A laugh escaped Musgrave then—cold and devoid of humour. "I answer to a higher authority than your petty regulations, *Archmage*."

Evander narrowed his eyes. "Does the name of that higher authority begin with the letter 'I' by any chance?"

Musgrave lowered his brows. "I see you know of my master." He turned to his associates. "Kill them all, except for the Brute, the Duke, and the Frenchman. They will make interesting test subjects."

Musgrave's companions removed small black crystals from inside their robes.

Horror widened Evander's eyes when they swallowed them, Musgrave quickly following suit.

No!

He knew instinctively they'd just ingested a piece of *Midnight Obsidian.*

"Everyone, stay back!" Evander hollered.

His ears throbbed when the pressure inside the chamber dropped precipitously.

The coldness that descended upon the lab made frost form on his eyelashes and chilled him to his very bones. The air grew foul with a miasma of corrupt magic.

The dark mages' eyes glowed with an unholy light as they unleashed their powers. Hundreds of shadow creatures coalesced from the darkness and arrowed towards Evander and his companions with near-silent malevolence.

"PROTECT THE OFFICERS!" VIGGO SHOUTED TO LEON AS he charged towards Musgrave.

The shadow creatures their enemy had manifested descended upon them, maws gaping and insubstantial limbs reaching for the Met officers and mages. Leon's *Nullification Magic* flared brightly, his magic aided by the power in the amulet around his neck as he created an elemental barrier that the creatures could not penetrate.

The Arcane Division mages rallied behind his protection and launched counterattacks of their own; fire spells, ice and earth spears, and violent storms of wind rapidly swarmed the chamber.

Evander's magic and those of the mages at his side

made the air tremble as they defended themselves against the swarm of shadow creatures attacking them.

Viggo scowled and barrelled through the magical crossfire, relying on his immunity to direct magical attacks to close the distance to Musgrave. He could see Evander doing the same from the opposite side of the chamber, a barrier of wind and fire magic flickering around him. Their eyes met briefly through the shimmering wall.

Viggo smiled fiercely. Emotion tightened Evander's face.

A dark mage stepped into the Brute's path, hands glowing with a sickly energy. The spell struck Viggo's chest and dissipated harmlessly. The mage's eyes widened in surprise a second before Viggo's fist connected with his jaw, sending him crumpling onto the walkway.

"You can't stop this!" Musgrave barked. Sinister magic flared around him as he backed towards the central apparatus. "Even if you kill us all, the process is already underway." He gestured wildly to Simmons's tank, where the silvery traces beneath the thrall's skin had intensified despite the *Midnight Obsidian* crystal having imploded. "The transfer is nearly complete even though you broke the machine, you fool!"

Fear squeezed Viggo's heart when he saw the young man begin to convulse violently, his face contorting in agony despite his unconscious state.

"*No!*" he roared, the walkway rattling beneath his feet as he accelerated.

Evander got there before him, his ice-blue eyes glinting with cold determination.

CHAPTER 42

Elemental magic crackled along Evander's veins as he closed the distance to Musgrave, the power rushing through him a torrent that made the air shimmer around his body. He could feel the professor's corrupt magic pulsing outward in violent waves, the *Midnight Obsidian* he'd consumed amplifying his already formidable powers to nightmarish proportions.

"You think yourself so righteous, Duke Ravenwood!" Musgrave spat out, pressing his back against the ghastly device he and his lackeys had constructed. Shadows swirled and coalesced around him and the dark mages at his side. "What will your precious Queen say when she learns you've destroyed the greatest magical advancement of our age?!"

For one gut-wrenching second, Evander wondered if Musgrave knew his secret. He ground his teeth and squashed his trepidation.

"She'll thank me for ridding the Empire of a monster!" he growled.

He gathered his wind magic and propelled himself forward and upwards just as Musgrave commanded the shadows around him to attack. Dark tendrils lashed out, seeking to ensnare and strangle him. Evander sliced through them with blades of concentrated fire and ice, the corrupt magic howling as it disintegrated beneath his elemental assault and the power of the amulet swinging against his chest.

Viggo launched himself from the walkway below, his massive frame moving fluidly through the air. His hands closed on the railing and he swung his body smoothly up and over, the metal platform juddering under his feet as he landed on it with a thud.

Evander alighted beside him, his heart racing.

"We have to get Simmons out of that tank!" Viggo said.

He grabbed one of the dark mages lunging towards him by the collar and hurled him bodily into the mass of shadow creatures attacking the Met officers below them.

Musgrave's face contorted with rage. "You shall do no such thing! Do you have any idea what we've achieved here, you fool? The power we've harnessed will—!"

His words were cut short as Viggo charged into him with the force of a battering ram.

Musgrave went flying sideways and collided with the railing of the walkway with enough force to bend the metal. Something cracked audibly in his ribcage. Blood sprayed from his lips as he coughed, his face contorting with pain and fury.

"You filthy thrall!" he snarled, wiping crimson from his mouth. "How dare you lay hands on me!"

Magic throbbed around Evander as he blocked the path of the dark mages trying to come to Musgrave's assistance with an array of earth, ice, and fire arrows. Dread tightened his chest when he glimpsed Simmons's body convulsing inside the tank. Whatever magic they'd forcibly injected into him was continuing to spread. If Musgrave was right, they had precious little time to save him.

"Leon! We need you!" Evander barked across the chamber.

The Frenchman looked up from where he was deflecting shadow creatures with his *Nullification Magic*. "I'm a bit busy right now, mon cher!" he snapped.

Viggo fisted his hands, his brow furrowed in a heavy scowl. "Evander, what will happen if I crush that tank?"

Evander's mouth went dry. He clenched his jaw. "I'm not sure."

Determination brightened the Brute's face. "He's going to die anyway if we do nothing." He headed resolutely towards the walkway leading to Simmons's tank.

A metallic tang flooded Evander's nostrils. His head snapped around.

Musgrave's eyes flared with a corrupt, inky darkness.

Evander's pulse stuttered when he detected crimson

strands within the dark energy growing around the professor's fingers.

Is that Blood Magic?!

Musgrave raised his hands and released the torrent of vile magic directly at Viggo.

Evander cursed and barely managed to block it with a barrier of flames and ice.

Musgrave's companions rallied and launched their own attacks at the Brute.

Relief sang through Evander when the forces they'd unleashed dissipated harmlessly upon contact with Viggo's skin, his immunity to magic attacks rendering their assault utterly ineffective.

Fear flickered across Musgrave's face for the first time.

Evander seized the moment and channelled his elemental powers as he advanced towards the professor. Fire and ice gathered in his palms, the conflicting temperatures creating a crackling distortion in the air. He unleashed the combined attack not at Musgrave himself, but at the walkway beneath his feet.

Though he wanted nothing more than to question the professor about "*I*," he knew there would be no negotiating a surrender with the man. Musgrave was too far gone for that.

Musgrave moved as metal warped and twisted beneath him. It gave way before he could make his escape. He screamed as he lost his footing and plummeted towards the darkness below.

Evander cursed when his fall was arrested by a

swarm of shadow creatures. The professor's face was a mask of unhinged rage as he rose amidst them, his body wreathed in corrupt magic.

"Do you think I can be defeated so easily?" he snarled. "I have consumed the gift my master gave me! His power flows through me now!"

Horror twisted Evander's gut as shadows streaked with crimson extended from Musgrave's body and lashed out in all directions, striking Met officers and mages with devastating force. Two were thrown over railings, their cries echoing as they fell into the abyss.

Leon barely managed to snatch them with his wind magic, Griffiths and Shaw hanging on to him grimly where he leaned precariously over a railing.

Evander's heart pounded heavily as he clocked the expressions of the officers and mages scattered around the laboratory. Though many were still standing and fighting bravely, they swayed and trembled from exhaustion from fighting the dark mages and their shadow creatures.

I need to end this!

The elements responded eagerly to his wish as they bubbled and strained inside his chest, begging to be unleashed in their full, devastating glory. The lid he kept on his Archmage powers strained under the violent pressure.

Viggo had reached Simmons's tank and was taking it apart with his bare hands, metal crumpling as he dismantled it piece by piece.

Musgrave howled in outrage and sent shadowy tendrils converging on the Brute.

"Enough!" Evander snarled.

He released the restraints on his powers.

Magic surged through him with such force that it lifted him several inches off the ground. His skin glowed with an inner light, his eyes transforming into pools of pure elemental energy that shot out pale beams. The air around him began to swirl and crackle, the temperature fluctuating wildly as fire, ice, wind, and earth formed and reformed around his body.

The chamber trembled, dust falling from the ceiling and walls.

Musgrave's eyes rounded in terror at this display of raw power.

"What—what is this?!"

"This," Evander said, his voice echoing around the lab as it resonated with devastating elemental force, "is what a true Archmage can do."

He brought his hands together in a thunderous clap. The resulting shock wave exploded outward, tearing through the chamber with devastating precision. Shadow creatures were obliterated in its path, their corrupt essence purged by the purifying force of Evander's combined elemental magic.

Musgrave shrieked and attempted to shield himself as the monsters protecting him were ripped away like cobwebs in a gale. He fell into the abyss once more.

Shadows erupted yet again from his body, encasing him in a cocoon of darkness.

"My master will find another way!" he shrieked triumphantly as he began to escape in the inky folds. "Our work will continue!"

Evander's eyes narrowed to slits. "Not today," he growled.

He gathered the four elements in his hands, compressed them into a single, devastating spear of pure elemental energy, and hurled it directly at the dark cocoon swallowing Musgrave.

It shattered like glass.

The elemental spear drove straight through the professor's chest and emerged from his back in a spray of blood and corrupted magic.

He fell silently and was rapidly swallowed by the true darkness of the gulf.

The remaining shadow creatures throughout the chamber began to dissolve, their anchoring force severed with Musgrave's death. Deprived of their leader, the surviving dark mages were swiftly subdued by the Met officers and mages who surrounded them.

Evander released a shuddering breath and gradually reined in his Archmage powers. The intense glow faded from his skin as he landed lightly on the platform. He swayed a little and steadied himself against the railing.

A powerful arm wrapped around his waist and propped him up.

Evander blinked and stared at Viggo.

"Simmons?!" he mumbled.

"He's alive." Viggo turned, his eyes dark with relief.

Solomon and Leon were kneeling beside the unconscious thrall in front of the smashed-up tank. Simmons spluttered and coughed violently as they removed the breathing apparatus from his nose and mouth, some colour returning to his face. Leon covered him with his coat.

The silver lines marking the thrall's skin faded even as they watched.

Evander's gaze shifted to the other tanks. He straightened, drawing on his remaining strength.

"Time to take care of the rest."

Viggo nodded solemnly.

CHAPTER 43

Musgrave's townhouse in Bloomsbury sat nestled between other elegant residences on a tree-lined avenue not far from the Royal Institute. In the soft light of dawn, it appeared deceptively ordinary, its white stone facade and black iron railings indistinguishable from the surrounding properties.

Evander studied the building with a frown where he stood beside Rufus on the pavement, his breath misting in the chilly morning air. After last night's confrontation in the underground facility, he had expected to feel a sense of victory. Instead, a strange unease lingered at the back of his mind.

"Are we certain Musgrave lived alone?" he asked as they climbed the steps to the front door.

Rufus nodded. "According to the Institute's records. He never married and his housekeeper only came thrice weekly. His neighbours confirmed the same."

They were met by Shaw at the threshold, her normally cheerful demeanour subdued as she gestured them inside. The forensic mage had arrived with a team from the AFD at daybreak.

"You'll want to see this straight away, your Grace," she said quietly as she led them through an immaculate entrance hall.

The home was tastefully appointed with furniture that spoke of old money and conservative tastes, precisely what one would expect of a respected Institute professor. Evander could hear the sounds of the forensic team investigating the other floors of the property.

Shaw guided them to a study and headed for a door next to the fireplace. It looked oddly positioned and out of place with the decor, the wallpaper surrounding it darker than the rest of the walls. Evander noticed the bookcase beside it and the faint difference in the colour of the floorboards.

"Was this door hidden?" he asked with a frown.

"Yes. It was behind the bookcase."

Shaw twisted the knob, her expression strangely grim. Evander understood the reason for it when the door swung open, revealing a chamber that stood in stark contrast to the respectable veneer of the rest of the house.

Rufus cursed under his breath.

Where the home around them looked to be a model of Victorian propriety, this room was a veritable shrine to darkness. The walls were covered in notes and diagrams filled with ancient arcane symbols and anatomical structures, some drawn in what appeared disturbingly like dried blood. Display cases housed strange artefacts and animal specimens floating in jars, the glass glinting strangely in the dim illumination from the enchanted light in the ceiling. Books lined shelves that reached from floor to ceiling.

A quick perusal of the titles revealed many of the volumes to be about dark and esoteric magic.

"How long do you think this has been here?" Rufus asked as they trod the bare floorboards, his face tense.

"Decades, I wager." Evander's skin crawled at the lingering residue of dark magic that permeated the air. "This collection wasn't accumulated overnight."

A large oak desk stood at the centre of the hidden room, its surface crowded with notebooks, arcane instruments, and what appeared to be maps of London with certain areas marked in red ink. Shaw directed them to a leather-bound journal lying open.

"You should read this, your Grace," she said. "It details Professor Musgrave's interest in the War of Subjugation." She furrowed her brow. "Or rather, his admiration for those who led it."

Evander's eyes narrowed as he scanned the pages. Musgrave's handwriting was neat and precise, the words flowing across the paper in an elegant script that belied their disturbing content.

27th May, 1868 - Had I been born twenty years earlier, I might have stood alongside the Great Ones during the War. Their vision for a natural hierarchy with magic at its pinnacle was not wrong—merely premature. Society was not ready to embrace the truth of our superiority. My master understands this. The War was not lost, merely postponed. The seeds we plant now will bear fruit in time.

Rufus leaned over Evander's shoulder. "The 'Great Ones'? He's referring to the Archmages who led the subjugation, isn't he?"

"Yes," Evander replied tightly. He turned several pages forward, his pulse quickening as he found more recent entries.

15th January, 1870 - I received another letter from my master today. The preparations are progressing as planned. The fools at the Institute suspect nothing, least of all that their precious research funding comes from the coffers of people they consider their enemy. Whitley and Chevalier are making remarkable headway with their research, though they remain blind to its true purpose. When they discover the truth, I fear they will prove problematic.

Evander turned to Shaw, his heart thrumming a rapid beat. "Have you found any correspondence?"

The forensic mage nodded and crossed to a lacquered box on a side table. "Here, your Grace."

She handed him a stack of letters bound with black ribbon. The paper was expensive and heavy, the red ink script flowing and elegant. But it was the signature that caught Evander's attention. Each letter was signed simply with the letter "*I*."

"This is the same stationery and handwriting as the letter I received after Renwick's death," Evander said in a hard voice.

Rufus's brow furrowed. "So both Renwick and Musgrave had the same master, just as Musgrave revealed before his death."

"A hierarchy of evil," Evander stated darkly. He

examined one of the letters more closely, his scalp prickling at the cryptic instructions it contained.

The acquisition of the Crimson Codex remains our priority. Without it, our understanding of the transference process will remain incomplete. The subjects continue to expire too quickly, their vessels unable to sustain the power we inject them with. The modifications to the thrall conduits must be improved if they are to serve their purpose in the coming transformation.

"Do you know anything about this Crimson Codex, your Grace?" Shaw asked, peering at the letter.

"I've never heard of it." Evander frowned. "It sounds like it might be some kind of arcane text."

"We should take these back to headquarters," Rufus suggested. "Perhaps Inkwell could shed some light on the reference."

As Shaw and the forensic team began packing up journals, letters, and arcane items, Evander's gaze was drawn to a map of London pinned to the wall behind the desk. Unlike the others they'd found, this one had lines connecting various locations throughout the city, forming a complex pattern that seemed vaguely familiar.

He frowned and moved closer. A chill ran down his spine as recognition dawned.

"This isn't just a map," Evander murmured, his mouth dry. "It's a ritual diagram. If I'm reading this correctly, Musgrave was planning to use the entire city as a conduit for some kind of massive magical working."

Rufus glared at the map as if willing it to reveal its

secrets. "Could that be what the Crimson Codex is for?"

"I'm not sure." Evander carefully removed the faded paper from the wall. "Whatever it is, I suspect we've only scratched the surface of what 'I' has planned."

They returned to Scotland Yard ahead of the forensic team. Rufus went to report their findings to Winterbourne while Evander made his way briskly to the infirmary.

The large ward bustled with activity as healers moved between beds occupied by the thralls and mages they'd rescued from the underground facility. The room had been divided into sections, with screens providing privacy for those receiving treatment.

Evander found Viggo seated beside Solomon's bed, the Brute's massive frame dwarfing the chair beneath him. Solomon appeared to be sleeping peacefully, his chest rising and falling in a steady rhythm.

"How is he?" Evander asked quietly.

Viggo looked up, exhaustion etched into the lines of his face from lack of sleep. "Better. The healers fixed his leg and said he'll make a full recovery."

Relief washed through Evander.

Viggo had insisted on staying with Solomon after their rescue.

"I've spoken to a few of the thralls we found inside the facility," the Brute said quietly. "Our theory was correct. They were snatched by shadow creatures wielded remotely by Musgrave and his acolytes."

Evander studied the circles under his lover's eyes and wished he could erase them.

"How's Simmons?" he asked, taking the seat beside the Brute.

"He's stable, though he'll need specialist care." Viggo's expression darkened. "The healers aren't sure what to make of the magic Musgrave forced into him." His fingers found Evander's, the screen and their position protecting them from curious eyes.

Evander squeezed Viggo's hand, the Brute's warmth a much needed balm in the chaos of the past twenty-four hours.

"Finn sent word from *Nightshade* an hour ago," Viggo continued quietly. "Our agents have made progress tracking the *Noctis Bloom* suppliers. The shipments are coming through Liverpool, not the Thames as we first thought. They've identified several warehouses where it's being processed."

Excitement buzzed through Evander at the news. "Good. That's one thread we can pull on." He hesitated. "We found some disturbing evidence at Musgrave's home that points to what his master may be plotting."

Interest sparked in Viggo's tired eyes. "Tell me."

Evander had just finished recounting their discoveries when Leon appeared around the side of the screen.

CHAPTER 44

THE FRENCHMAN LOOKED EVEN WORSE THAN VIGGO, the dark circles beneath his eyes lending him a gaunt look and his normally immaculate appearance somewhat dishevelled.

Leon acknowledged Viggo with a curt nod. His gaze lingered on their clasped fingers before he addressed Evander.

"Whitley and Chevalier are awake. They're asking for us."

Viggo reluctantly let go of Evander's hand and rose to his feet. "I should go check on Katie and the others."

"I'll find you afterwards," Evander promised, trying to mask the sense of loss he felt at not being able to touch Viggo.

Leon watched the Brute leave with an impassive expression.

"You should be more careful, mon cher," he murmured as he led Evander across the ward.

Evander followed the Frenchman to a private room

at the end of the infirmary. Inside, Whitley and Chevalier reclined against pillows in adjacent beds. Both men were alarmingly pale, their faces haggard and their eyes sunken. Mrs. Scarborough stood between them. The curse-breaker was checking a complex arrangement of enchanted crystals that was monitoring their vital signs.

"Your Grace," she acknowledged Evander with a slight bow. She frowned at Whitley and Chevalier. "They insisted on speaking with you, though I advised them against any undue exertion."

"We've rested enough," Whitley said weakly. His voice was rough, as though he hadn't used it in some time. "There are things you need to know." His expression grew haunted as he met Evander's gaze squarely.

Mrs. Scarborough sensed the need for privacy and quietly left the room.

Evander approached Whitley's bedside. "We have a lot of questions for you." He looked over at Chevalier. "Both of you."

"We shall answer them to the best of our abilities, your Grace," Chevalier said solemnly, his French accent more pronounced in his feeble state.

Evander pulled up a chair between the beds. "How did you come to be involved in this research?"

The professors exchanged a weary glance.

"It began innocently enough," Whitley explained. "A generous research grant from a group of anonymous benefactors, channelled through the Institute. We were to study the neurological structure of thralls and how it differed from those with magical abilities."

"The aim was ostensibly to understand why some individuals are born with magic and others are not," Chevalier added. "A question that has puzzled arcane researchers for centuries."

"When did you realise the truth of what they wanted?" Leon asked from where he stood at the foot of Chevalier's bed.

The French professor's expression darkened. "When I recognised certain passages in Musgrave's notes from my...previous association. He had somehow acquired research from *Les Prophètes Illuminés*—research I had believed destroyed years ago."

"You confronted him?" Evander prompted.

Whitley nodded gravely. "We both did. We discovered he had been manipulating our findings and directing our research towards a specific goal without our knowledge. When we threatened to go to the authorities, he warned us that we would regret it." He paused and swallowed hard before glancing at Chevalier. "That was when Henri and I began gathering evidence to use against Musgrave. He invited us over to his home once, when Henri was visiting London. It was there that we came upon evidence of a secret facility beneath the Institute. We took precautionary measures to protect ourselves and were preparing to reveal our findings to the relevant authorities when Musgrave had us abducted and brought to that hellish place."

Evander digested this for a moment. "Did you learn

anything during your captivity that could help us find his associates?"

Whitley and Chevalier traded a wary glance.

"Only that his master was getting irritated at his lack of results," Whitley confessed.

A muscle jumped in Chevalier's jawline. "Musgrave didn't care about the failures. He spoke of dead thralls as 'acceptable losses' in pursuit of what he called 'the Great Transformation.' He and his master—this 'I' person—were convinced they could perfect the process with enough test subjects."

Evander drummed his fingers on his knee. "Did he ever mention something called a Crimson Codex?"

Both professors visibly stiffened.

"Yes," Whitley said. "He became quite agitated about it in the days before you rescued us. He received a message that led him to believe someone else was close to acquiring it."

"What's the Crimson Codex?" Leon asked with a puzzled frown.

Evander told him what they'd found at Musgrave's residence that morning.

"The Crimson Codex is an ancient text," Chevalier explained. "Musgrave and his master believe it contains the complete theoretical framework for magical transference and more. *Les Prophètes Illuminés* were also aware of its rumoured existence. They theorised that it was written by the very first Archmage, centuries ago."

Evander's scalp prickled. "Do you know where it might be found?"

Both professors shook their heads.

"From what we deduced, Musgrave's master has agents searching for it across Europe," Whitley said. "Musgrave mentioned something about a collection in Vienna, but nothing more specific than that."

Mrs. Scarborough stuck her head through the door. "Your Grace, I must insist these gentlemen get some rest. Their bodies are still recovering from significant trauma."

Evander rose to his feet, chagrined. "Of course." He gave the professors an apologetic look. "Thank you for your help."

"Not at all, your Grace," Whitley murmured.

"It is us who must thank you and your colleagues for getting us out of that place," Chevalier added gratefully.

A commotion outside had them all tensing.

"Lady Whitley, if you could please wait a—" someone said in a strained voice.

Lady Whitley barged inside the room, her chest heaving. Her clothes were in disarray and strands of hair had escaped her polished coiffure.

Her face crumpled at the sight of her husband. "Walter!" She covered her mouth with her hands, tears slipping down her pale cheeks.

Whitley's chin trembled, emotion painting red flags across his cheeks. "Elizabeth."

Lady Whitley ran across the room and launched herself into her husband's arms, her sobs muffled against his chest.

Evander and Leon left quietly.

The Frenchman stopped in the corridor outside

and ran a hand through his hair. "You realise what this means, don't you?" He studied Evander with a troubled expression. "If this Crimson Codex exists and if it does contain the knowledge they seek…"

"Then we need to get our hands on it first," Evander finished grimly.

"Your Grace," a voice called out behind them.

They turned to see Shaw approaching briskly.

"Commander Winterbourne requests our presence," the forensic mage informed them.

Evander and Leon exchanged a frown.

Winterbourne welcomed them with a distracted expression when they entered his office moments later. Rufus was already there.

The commander's desk was covered in the reports they'd compiled and there were several empty cups of coffee next to his hand. He ordered his secretary to bring them refreshments nonetheless before settling back down in his chair with a heavy sigh.

"Never in my career have I seen such an unholy mess," Winterbourne muttered. He pinched the bridge of his nose. "The Ministry of Arcane Affairs and the War Office are already up in arms about this. They are planning to petition Parliament for an emergency legislation that would allow them to regulate the affairs of the Royal Institute."

A chill danced through Evander at his words. "That's a preposterous idea! Rigley and the board will never stand for it."

"They may not have a say, Ravenwood," Winterbourne said thinly. He grimaced at Evander's frown. "Believe me, I wholeheartedly agree with you. Academia and government should never mix." He passed a report over to them. "I've just received confirmations from our counterparts in Paris, Berlin, and Vienna. The mages recovered from the facility have been identified as having gone missing from various academic institutions across the Continent over the past seven weeks."

Shaw and Rufus gathered around Evander and Leon.

Evander's heart sank as he read the paperwork. It appeared Musgrave and his master had decided abducting mages solely in England posed too high a risk of exposure.

"This suggests a coordinated effort spanning multiple countries," Leon said worriedly.

"Precisely." Winterbourne rose from his chair and moved to the window, his hands clasped behind his back. "Which is why I'm going to propose the formation of an international coalition to investigate these kinds of activities. One that cuts through red tape and allows officers of the law to cooperate and mobilise fluidly. The Empire cannot handle this threat and others like it alone."

A fraught silence descended upon the room.

"You believe your proposal will be well received, Commander?" Rufus asked dubiously.

"We have no choice in the matter, Grayson." Winterbourne turned back to face them, his brow furrowed. He glanced at Leon. "As it is, the French Ministry of Arcane Affairs floated the same idea a short while back. I don't believe we will have any trouble bringing the German and Austrian authorities around. Even the Russians have expressed interest."

"And the thralls who were abducted?" Evander asked stiffly. "What will become of them?"

"They will continue to receive the best care we can provide," Winterbourne assured him. "In fact, a group of your peers have insisted on helping too."

Evander gave him a puzzled look.

"Lady Hartley and Lord Fairfax paid me a visit this morning," Winterbourne explained. "Despite my reassurances, Lord Fairfax and his associates feel a certain responsibility for what happened to the thralls in their service. They will spare no expense to make sure they are looked after."

A warm feeling blossomed inside Evander's chest. He felt relieved at this news. It was something he'd been considering doing himself, albeit anonymously.

"It's the bloody Institute who should be sparing no expense," Shaw muttered.

Winterbourne's mouth twitched almost imperceptibly. "Indeed, Miss Shaw," he said drily. His expression grew serious once more. "What concerns me most is this Crimson Codex Grayson mentioned."

"I'm afraid Leon and I have some regrettable news about that," Evander said.

He updated Winterbourne, Rufus, and Shaw about Whitley and Chevalier's most recent revelations.

Winterbourne scowled. "So it's an arcane text this 'I' is after? And if he gets his hands on it, he may be in a position to complete whatever ghastly plans he has?"

"Yes," Evander said grimly. "By the sounds of it, we're now officially in a race against time to try and locate this book before he does."

Winterbourne sighed wearily and sat down again. "Alright. For now, our priority is to track down that arcane text. Inspector Grayson, I want you and Miss Shaw to continue investigating the evidence recovered from Musgrave's residence and the Institute. Comte Beaulieu, I understand your superiors are eager for your return to Paris?"

Leon nodded. "Yes, Commander. Though I've requested permission to remain in London a while longer to complete my reports for the Met and tie up any loose ends."

"You have my gratitude and that of Scotland Yard." Winterbourne finally turned to Evander. "Ravenwood, I'd like you to focus on finding the Crimson Codex and liaising with the international representatives who will be assisting us on this matter. As both a peer of the realm and one of the few people in England who understands the full scope of this threat, you're uniquely positioned to facilitate cooperation between our countries."

Evander nodded. "Of course, Commander."

The gravity of the role Winterbourne had entrusted him with was not lost on Evander. He swallowed a sigh at the thought of what the Queen would have to say about it when word reached her ears.

CHAPTER 45

RAINDROPS TAPPED A GENTLE RHYTHM AGAINST THE window of the private study adjacent to Evander's bedchamber, the dismal weather matching the turmoil of the past week and his mood.

He stood in front of the enchanted map of London above the marble fireplace, his gaze lost amidst the orange dots glowing warmly beneath the glass case while he sipped a glass of brandy.

Though his body ached with exhaustion from the events of the last two days, his mind refused to quiet. Solomon's abduction, the confrontation with Musgrave, the rescue of the missing thralls and professors, the reports to Winterbourne, and last but not least, the summons he had received that afternoon to appear before the Ministry of Arcane Affairs—all of it had left him drained to the marrow of his bones.

And yet, beneath it all, a fierce elation burned. They had succeeded against tremendous odds. He, Viggo, the Met, *Nightshade.* Even if the mysterious "I" remained at large, they had dismantled a significant portion of his operation in London and saved countless innocent lives in the process.

A gentle knock at the door pulled Evander from his thoughts.

"Your Grace?" Hargrove appeared, his eyes twinkling despite his neutral expression. "Mr. Stonewall has arrived."

Evander's heart leapt in his chest. "Show him in, please."

"Of course, my Lord." Hargrove hesitated. "Shall I have a light supper prepared?"

"Yes, that would be appreciated."

The manservant bowed and departed, leaving Evander to smooth down his waistcoat and run a hand through his hair. He'd returned home that morning to quickly shower and change out of his dirt-stained clothes. He was in dire need of a proper bath still.

Soft footfalls in the corridor announced Viggo's approach. It never ceased to amaze Evander how quiet his lover could be for a man his size.

The Brute entered the room and paused on the threshold, his massive frame filling the doorway. Although he too had changed, the shadows beneath his eyes betrayed his exhaustion.

Their gazes locked across the room, Viggo drinking in the sight of him like a parched man.

"You look terrible," he said, his lips quirking in a half smile.

Evander smiled back, his muscles finally loosening. "Your flattery never ceases to amaze me."

Viggo grinned. "It's the truth." He stepped inside and closed the door behind him. "Have you slept at all since yesterday?"

"Have you?" Evander said softly, walking over to him.

The Brute's smile faded as he accepted his embrace. "How could I? Every time I close my eyes, I see that laboratory and those poor souls trapped in those glass tanks." He sighed into Evander's hair, his arms tightening briefly on his back.

"How's Solomon?"

"Chomping at the bit to be discharged," Viggo drawled, exasperation underscoring his words. "If it wasn't for Ginny lambasting him, he would have sneaked out of the damn infirmary by now."

Evander chuckled. "I really need to thank her for everything she's done." He let go of Viggo and crossed the room to pour him a glass of brandy from a crystal decanter.

"To survival," Evander said quietly, raising his glass.

Viggo clinked his glass against Evander's, his eyes darkening. "To survival."

They drank in companionable silence, the tension of the past days slowly ebbing away. Evander found himself studying Viggo's face, tracing the lines of weariness around his eyes, the set of his jaw, the way the firelight played across his skin.

"What?" Viggo asked, catching his stare.

Heat rose to Evander's cheeks. "I was just thinking that despite everything, I'm glad we met."

Viggo's gaze softened. "Even with all the danger and mayhem it's entailed so far?"

"Even with that." Evander set his glass down on the mantelpiece and cupped Viggo's face with a hand. "It brought you into my life, after all. And had it not been for that fateful meeting, we might not have been able to save all those people."

The Brute's expression turned tender. He put his glass down and covered Evander's hand with his own before pressing a kiss to his palm that ignited his nerve endings.

"You know, for a man of your standing, you say the most remarkably sentimental things at times," he said gravely.

"Only to you," Evander murmured, aware he was baring his heart and not caring.

A banked heat ignited in Viggo's eyes at his vulnerable tone. He lowered his head and claimed Evander's mouth, his lips warm and insistent. The kiss began gently before deepening into something more urgent. Evander's arms wound around Viggo's neck, drawing him closer as the Brute's hands moved to his waist.

Both of them were breathing heavily when they finally broke apart.

A discreet cough made them jump.

Hargrove stood in the doorway with a serving cart and a salacious smile.

"My apologies," the man servant said in a syrupy voice. "I did not want to interrupt."

Evander sighed. "Jasper?"

"Yes, my Lord?"

"Get out."

"Yes, my Lord." Hargrove wheeled the cart inside the room before departing, still grinning.

Viggo's stomach grumbled loudly in the silence.

"Sorry," he said sheepishly.

Evander's expression softened. "Let's eat."

They spoke of trivial things while they partook of the food, both avoiding the grave matters that would have them busy again come morning.

Viggo sat back in his armchair after they finished their meal.

"That hit the spot," he groaned. "Your cook is the best."

Evander chuckled and took a sip of his wine.

Viggo watched him broodingly over his glass.

"What is it?" Evander said quizzically.

"I just realised I'm missing something."

Evander frowned. "You are?"

"Yes," Viggo said with a solemn nod. "My daily dose of the Duke."

Evander blinked. He flushed. "We just kissed. Rather spectacularly I must add, judging from Jasper's expression of delight."

Viggo arched an eyebrow. "That's not what I meant."

Lust started a siren song inside Evander, quickening his pulse and sending a shiver of anticipation dancing down his spine.

"You know, sometimes I think you're with me just for my body," he fake grumbled.

Viggo's mouth curved in a sensual smile that made his heart skip a beat, his expression telling him he wasn't buying his protest.

"It's a spectacular body, if I say so myself."

Heat pooled in Evander's groin as the Brute put down his wine glass, rose, and pulled him to his feet. The air sparked between them, so charged with sexual tension Evander found his breath catching.

Viggo rubbed the pad of his thumb over Evander's lips. "How about we take this to the bathroom?"

Evander swallowed and nodded.

Viggo took his hand and led him through the door at the back of the study that opened directly into his bedchamber, and from there to the luxurious bathroom beyond. He headed over to the shower and turned the array of taps. Hot water immediately burst from the multiple heads in the ceiling and walls.

Steam began to fill the room as he turned to Evander.

He closed the distance between them and began working on the buttons of Evander's waistcoat, his fingers moving with practiced dexterity.

Evander finally gave in to the passion singing in his blood, grasped Viggo's face, and yanked him down for a hungry kiss.

CHAPTER 46

VIGGO GROANED LUSTFULLY, HIS HANDS FINDING Evander's waist and pulling him close so their bodies moulded together. Evander shivered at the feel of Viggo's solid erection.

They discarded their clothes with increasing urgency as their desire mounted, the items forming a scattered trail on the bathroom floor.

Viggo cupped Evander's buttocks and hauled him up against his body as their tongues mated with passionate desperation. Evander wrapped his legs eagerly around the Brute's hips as he moved and stepped under the sprays of the shower.

The sight and feel of Viggo's bare skin, the feel of his thick cock pressing intimately against his own manhood, the musky scent of desire swirling around them. All of it filled Evander's chest to bursting.

He wrenched his mouth from Viggo's as the Brute gently let him down and stared into his eyes under the hot water cascading over them.

"I love you so damn much it hurts," Evander whispered.

Viggo's gaze darkened. He took Evander's mouth in a tender kiss that communicated his own feelings, to the point tears swelled in Evander's eyes.

Viggo pressed his lips against his lashes, licking and swallowing the salty drops.

"You don't know what you do to me, mage," he whispered, his own voice choked.

Evander laughed breathlessly. "I've not heard you call me that in ages." His breath hitched and his eyes rolled back in his head when Viggo moved his hands down his back and teased his entrance with his fingers.

The Brute's lips traced a burning path down his neck, pausing to lavish attention on the sensitive spot just below his ear.

"Viggo," Evander sighed, his fingers tangling in the Brute's wet hair. "Touch me, please."

Viggo complied with a soft curse, his large hand closing around Evander's eager erection. Evander rolled his hips and drove himself shamelessly through his lover's tight grip, seeking the pleasure only he could give him.

Viggo nipped his skin savagely before continuing his journey downward, exploring the pulse beating frantically at the base of Evander's throat before ravaging his chest with his lips and teeth and tongue. His touch ignited a fire within Evander that had him moaning incoherently, his body responding with an intensity that stole his breath.

Rivulets of water streamed down their bodies,

turning their skin slick and heightening every caress as Viggo continued stroking him briskly while he worked his way down his trembling frame.

Evander cried out when Viggo got down on his knees and took him inside his mouth. His body bowed and his hands fisted in the Brute's hair as the latter began working him with his lips and tongue. Evander blinked dazedly and met Viggo's hooded stare where he looked at him from under his lashes, his cheeks bulging and his mouth moving slickly on his shaft as he performed fellatio on him.

It didn't take long for him to come in the Brute's mouth, his cock pulsing and throbbing with exquisite delight as he emptied himself on Viggo's tongue.

Viggo released him and climbed to his feet, his expression feral.

"Turn around."

Evander complied, his body still shuddering from the aftershocks of his climax. He braced his forearms against the tile as Viggo's hands roamed his back, his touch reverent and possessive all at once. The Brute pressed ardent kisses along his spine, each one sending fresh ripples of pleasure through Evander's body.

Viggo lathered his hands with soap and used the foam to prepare Evander for his penetration, his thumb rubbing and circling his hole before he pushed inside.

Evander dropped his head forward on a groan and surrendered to the sensation that was Viggo working him loose. The Brute inserted two more fingers inside him, his breathing harsh and fast in Evander's ear as he thrust in and out and scissored him open. The hot water continued to pour over them, steam filling the bathroom and enclosing them in their own private world.

"I'm coming in," Viggo grunted, his voice almost pained as he removed his fingers.

He spread Evander open with his hands and pushed inside him with a savage sound of possession.

Evander gasped and shuddered at the exquisite fullness that was the Brute filling him up to the hilt. They remained still for a moment, Viggo's chest pressed against his back, their ragged breathing mingling with the sound of falling water.

Viggo nipped Evander's ear lovingly with his teeth as he waited for his lover's body to adjust to his girth. "I will never tire of this," he whispered. "Being inside you is the closest I can get to Heaven on this Earth."

Evander flushed, his heart so full he wished this moment would never end. But his body wanted more. Demanded it.

"Viggo?"

"Yes?" Viggo breathed against his skin.

"Make love to me. Please."

Viggo eagerly complied, pulling out and pushing back in with a sigh, his thrusts long and deep from the get-go. Evander pressed back against him, seeking even more, his body alive with sensation inside and out as water and steam enveloped them.

The world narrowed to the space between them, to the rhythm they created together, to the sounds they made as they lost themselves to the intoxicating heat and the unbearable friction of possession and being possessed.

When release finally came, it swept through Evander like a tidal wave, leaving him trembling and gasping Viggo's name. The Brute followed moments later, his powerful body shuddering violently as he found his own completion, his arm wrapped protectively around Evander's waist while he pumped his release inside him.

They remained entangled under the cascade of water for a long time, breathless and spent. Viggo pressed tender kisses to Evander's shoulder before carefully withdrawing.

They took their time washing and drying each other, their mouths meeting for languorous kisses.

Evander traced idle patterns on Viggo's chest as he lay in his lover's arms in bed a short while later.

"You know, you still haven't told me the story of how you got your tattoos," he murmured.

"I haven't?" Viggo asked, surprised.

Heat flooded Evander's cheeks. "The last time I asked, you got busy."

Viggo chuckled. "Ah. Yes, I remember that delightful incident."

Evander rolled his eyes and tried hard not to blush even more.

The incident in question had almost wrecked the desk in his office downstairs.

Viggo kissed the tip of his nose. "It's a boring story. Are you sure you want to hear it?"

Evander nodded.

"Alright." Viggo pulled Evander closer and tucked an arm behind his head, his gaze on the underside of the green canopy. "After my aunt Mary died, my uncle Jack encouraged me to become a sailor."

Evander's eyes rounded. He propped himself up on an elbow. "You? A sailor?!"

"Is that so hard to believe?" Viggo grunted.

"Kind of." Evander wrinkled his nose. "I bet you were devilishly handsome in a sailor's uniform."

Viggo burst out laughing. "Has anyone ever told you you're like a dog with a bone when it comes to what interests you, my Lord?"

Evander pinched his arm. "Behave. And continue with your story, please."

Viggo's chest rumbled with low laughter. "Jack counts many merchants among his friends, so getting me on their ships was never a problem."

He explained how he'd sailed across the world in the years that followed. Evander listened, enthralled, to the stories about his travels.

The Brute's captivating tales painted a colourful tapestry of rich and diverse cultures the mage had only ever read about in books. From Central and East Asia to Africa, the South Americas, and even the Pacific Ocean, Viggo had seen and done things Evander doubted he would ever get to do in his lifetime.

Viggo's tone grew more serious after a while.

"It was during my travels that I came to realise thralls could co-exist equally and peacefully with those who had magic in their blood," he said quietly. "That a lack of magical abilities was not and should never be a barrier to success and happiness." He tipped Evander's chin up with a knuckle and pressed a light kiss to his lips. "The Polynesian Islands were one such place I visited. It was where I got most of my tattoos."

Though Viggo didn't say it out loud, Evander could see it in his eyes and hear it in his voice.

The experiences and people the Brute had encountered had only fuelled his anger at the oppression and violence inflicted upon his kind in England. And it had evidently cemented his resolve to bring about change after what had happened to his own family, no matter the cost.

"I would love to visit those places with you one day." Evander pressed closer to Viggo. "I want to see the world with your eyes."

Viggo danced his fingers down his back in a soothing caress. "You already do. More than you can ever imagine." He kissed Evander's hair. "That's why I will follow you to the ends of this world and the next."

Evander smiled against his chest. "Promise?"

"I promise," Viggo whispered.

The rainfall tapping against the windows of the bedroom soon had them drifting off, the strong, steady beat of the Brute's heart the last thing Evander heard as he surrendered to his first restful sleep in days.

THE END

~

Dear Reader

Thank you for continuing Evander and Viggo's journey through the shadow-haunted streets of Victorian London in "Stolen Magic."

Writing this second instalment in "The Mage and His Brute" series has been both challenging and rewarding, allowing me to delve deeper into the complex world these characters inhabit. As Evander and Viggo's relationship blossoms amidst danger and intrigue, I found myself increasingly invested in their struggle against forces that would tear them apart.

Exploring the darker corners of magical London—from the hidden chambers beneath the Royal Institute to the murky sewers where secrets fester—has been a fascinating adventure. I've particularly enjoyed developing the mythology behind magical transference, elements of which will continue to shape this series as it unfolds.

If you've enjoyed this arcane tale of stolen power and enduring love, I would be incredibly grateful if you could leave a review. Your feedback not only helps other readers discover Evander and Viggo's world but also provides the encouragement that keeps me writing when the path grows dim.

The third book in the series is already taking shape and I promise that the revelations and confrontations to come will be worth the wait. Thank you for your continued support on this magical journey.

With deepest appreciation and gratitude,

Ava Marie Salinger.

BOOKS BY AVA MARIE SALINGER

FALLEN MESSENGERS

Fractured Souls - 1

Spellbound - 2

Edge Lines - 3

Oathbreaker - 4

Harbinger - 5

Crimson Skies - 6

Wicked - Fallen Messengers Short Story Collection

THE MAGE AND HIS BRUTE

Arcane Entanglement - 1

Stolen Magic - 2

CONTEMPORARY ROMANCE WRITTEN

AS A.M. SALINGER

NIGHTS

One Night - 1

The Escort - 2

Tokyo Heat - 3

Sweet Obsession - 4

Sweet Possession - 5

Twilight Falls

ABOUT THE AUTHOR

Ava Marie Salinger is the pen name of an Amazon bestselling urban fantasy author who has always wanted to write MM urban fantasy romance. When she's not dreaming up hotties to write about, you'll find Ava creating kickass music playlists to write to, spying on the wildlife in her garden, drooling over gadgets, and eating Chinese food. She also writes contemporary MM romance as A.M. Salinger.

Visit Shop AD Starrling and buy all of Ava's ebooks, paperbacks, hardbacks, and exclusive special edition print books direct.

Click the link below to discover where you can connect with Ava:
Linktr.ee